Summer
VOWS

ROCHELLE
ALERS

Summer
VOWS

HARLEQUIN®
entertain, enrich, inspire™

SUMMER VOWS

ISBN-13: 978-0-373-53477-7

Hideaway Wedding Series

Good-natured boasting raises its multimillion-dollar head at the Cole family compound during a New Year's Eve celebration. Family patriarch Martin Cole proposes each man in attendance place a one-million-dollar wager to the winner's alma mater as an endowment in their name. The terms: predicting who among Nicholas, Jason or Ana will marry before the next New Year's Eve.

Twins Jason and Ana Cole have given no indication they are even remotely thinking of tying the knot. Both claim they are too busy signing new talent to their record label. Former naval officer Nicholas Cole-Thomas has also been dragging his feet when it comes to the opposite sex. However, within the next six months Ana, Nicholas and Jason will encounter a very special person who will not only change them, but change their lives forever.

In *Summer Vows*, when CEO of Serenity Records Ana Cole signs a recording phenom to her label, she ignites a rivalry that targets her for death. Her safety and well-being are then entrusted to family friend, U.S. Marshal Jacob Jones, and Ana is forced to step away from the spotlight and her pampered lifestyle. She unwillingly follows Jacob to his vacation home in the Florida Keys until those responsible for the hit on her life are apprehended. Once Ana gets past Jacob's rigid rules, she finds herself surrendering to the glorious sunsets and the man willing to risk everything, including his heart, to keep her safe and make her his own.

Nicholas Cole-Thomas's entry into the world of horse breeding has caused quite a stir in Virginia's horse country. Not only is he quite the eligible bachelor, but there is also a lot of gossip about his prized Arabian breeding stock. In *Eternal Vows*, Nicholas meets Peyton Blackstone, the neighboring farm's veterinarian intern. He is instantly drawn to her intelligence, but recognizes the vulnerability she attempts to mask with indifference. Nicholas offers Peyton a position to work on his farm, and when they step in as best man and maid of honor at his sister's spur-of-the-moment wedding he tries to imagine how different his life would be with a wife of his own. Just when he opens his heart to love again, someone from Peyton's past resurfaces to shatter their newfound happiness, and now Nicholas must decide whether their love is worth fighting for.

Record executive Jason Cole will admit to anyone that he has a jealous mistress: music. As the artistic director for Serenity Records Jason is laidback, easygoing and a musical genius. His brief tenure running the company is over and he's heading to his recording studio in a small remote Oregon mountain town to indulge in his obsession. But all that changes in *Secret Vows*, when Jason hears restaurant waitress Greer Evans singing backup with a local band. As they become more than friends, he is unaware of the secret she jealously guards with her life. And when he finds himself falling in love with Greer, Jason is stunned to find she is the only one who stands between him and certain death, at the same time realizing love is the most desperate risk of all.

Don't forget to read, love and live romance.

Rochelle Alers

HIDEAWAY SERIES

Everett Kirkland - Teresa Maldanado* - Samuel Cole - Marguerite Diaz[11]

Martin Cole - Parris Simmons[1]

Oscar Spencer- Regina Cole - Aaron Spencer[5]

Claybonne   Eden

Tyler Cole - Dana Nichols[9]

Martin, II   Astra   Samuel, II

Arianna

Nancy Cole - Noah Thomas

Timothy Cole-Thomas - Nichola Bennett   Ynez   Grace   Malinda

Diego Cole-Thomas - Vivienne Neal[13]

Samuel

Celia Cole-Thomas - Gavin Faulkner[14]

Nicholas

Isabella

Matthew Sterling - Eve Blackwell - Alejandro Delgado[2]

Sara Sterling - Salem Lassiter[6]

Isaiah

Eve/Nora (twins)

Christopher Delgado - Emily Kirkland[7]

Alejandro   Esperanza   Mateo

Joshua Kirkland* - Vanessa Blanchard[8]

Michael Kirkland - Jolene Walker[3]

Teresa   Joshua-Michael   Merrick

Josephine Cole - Ivan Wilson

Gisela   Esther   Joseph   Felipe   Ashley

David Cole - Serena Morris[4]

Gabriel Cole - Summer Montgomery[10]

Immanuel   Anthony

Alexandra Cole - Merrick Grayslake[12]

Imani   Victoria   Cordero

Jason   Anna[15]
(twins)

LEGEND

* - Illegitimate Birth
1 - Hideaway
2 - Hidden Agenda
3 - Vows
4 - Harvest Moon
5 - Just Before Dawn
6 - Private Passions
7 - No Compromise
8 - Homecoming
9 - Renegade
10 - Best Kept Secrets
11 - Strangers In My Arms
12 - Secret Agenda
13 - Breakaway
14 - Summer Vows

Happy the husband of a good wife, twice-lengthened are his days; a worthy wife brings joy to her husband, peaceful and full is his life.

—*Sirach* 26:1, 2

Prologue

Martin Diaz Cole extended the lacquer and walnut burl finish humidor to his youngest brother, waiting for David to select a cigar. He repeated the gesture with his brother Joshua, and then his nephew Timothy before he selected his. It was hours from dawn and yet the other three men seemed reluctant to retire to the suites assigned them or to their respective homes.

It was a ritual that had been repeated for more years than Martin could remember. The entire Cole extended family came to West Palm Beach, Florida, on Christmas Eve for a reunion that usually culminated with a wedding before the end of the year. But unfortunately there had not been a wedding in several years—not since his nephew Diego married Vivienne Neal. His niece Celia didn't figure into the equation because she'd married her FBI special agent husband in Virginia and hadn't been able to repeat her vows for the entire family because a winter storm had blanketed North Carolina's Great Smoky Mountains with nearly two feet of snow. She'd also been in the second trimester of her pregnancy and had curtailed traveling until after the birth of her daughter.

Using a cutter, Martin snipped the end of the cigar, moistened, lit it and pulled in a mouthful of sweet, fragrant tobacco. It wasn't the quality of the finest Cuban cigar, but it came close.

David Cole blew out a perfect smoke ring. "Are you certain these aren't contraband, Martin?"

The first time Martin had smoked a Cuban cigar was when he'd visited his late mother's country of birth after graduating college, and he'd found himself enthralled with them. Over the years he'd smoked cigars from around the world, but none compared to a Cuban. "Bite your tongue, little brother. We both wish."

Squinting through a cloud of smoke, David Cole's jet-black eyes narrowed. "When am I going to stop being your little brother, Martin? I'm old as dirt, almost completely gray, *and* I'm a grandfather."

"And you still have two kids who should either become a priest or nun, because they're never going to get married," Joshua Kirkland teased.

David glared at his half brother, hoping to intimidate him, but knew there were few things or people who could intimidate or frighten the retired career army officer. "Don't act so smug, Josh. Serena and I had four children to your two, so there's no comparison."

A rare smile tilted the corners of Joshua's firm mouth. "My two kids have given me six grandchildren, and still counting, *hermano*. How many do you have?"

David took another puff of his cigar. Even after so many years the teasing had continued. As the youngest of five, he'd been the last to marry and father children. His wife had given him four children, the last two twins, and the taunts about his children being marriage-phobic subsided when his older son and daughter married. It was only his twins who appeared reluctant to settle down. He knew both were too involved in growing the record company he'd established years ago.

"Don't look so smug, Josh. I'm willing to bet when Jason and Ana marry they'll both have a whole bunch of children between them."

Timothy Cole-Thomas leaned forward, staring at his uncle. "Is there something you're not telling us, David?"

Dimples creased David's lean face when he smiled for the first time. He knew his twins better than anyone—and that included their mother. Both were comfortable divulging their closely guarded secrets about the business and their personal lives with him. Ana, as CEO of Serenity Records, had just signed a hot new recording artist that was rumored to become a crossover phenomenon. His daughter had confided to him that she now felt secure enough to shift her focus from business to her personal life. She'd recently closed on a condo and bought a new car—two things on her "to-do" list she'd neglected for years. For years she'd rented a studio apartment, while contracting with a car service to drive her around.

"Not really."

Martin ran a hand over his cropped silver hair. "I think David should put his money where his mouth is."

"Hear, hear!" chorused Joshua and Timothy.

Grinning, David shook his head. "You guys have got to be kidding."

"Do we look like we're kidding?" asked Joshua. "I agree with Martin. You should put up or shut up."

David squinted through a cloud of gray smoke as he met the gazes of his brothers and nephew. "Well, gentlemen, I'm willing to wager a million dollars that my son or daughter will marry before Nicholas. What's the matter? Is the wager a little too steep?" he asked when a groan and soft whistles echoed in the library.

"I don't mind donating the million if it's going to a worthy cause," Timothy said.

Joshua cleared his throat. "Who are we betting on?"

"It has to be Jason and Ana," Martin remarked.

"Don't forget Nicholas and Joe, Jr.," David reminded him.

Timothy Cole-Thomas crossed a leg over the opposite knee. "It can't be Joe, because his father's not here for the wager.

Martin nodded. "Timothy's right. It will just be the four of us. I'm willing to put up a million, but, David, you're going to have to ante up two mil because you have two kids to Timothy's one."

The seconds ticked as the three men stared at David. "No problem," he said after a pregnant pause. "I'll wager two million. Whoever wins will establish an endowment in his name at his alma mater. If none marry, then we'll set up a foundation in the family name: ColeDiz."

"What are the rules, Martin?" Joshua asked.

David frowned. "Why are you asking him? It's my kids you guys are betting on."

"Mine, too." Timothy reminded him. "It has to be either Martin or Joshua to determine the rules if this wager is going to be impartial."

"Timothy's right," Joshua concurred. "Let Martin establish the contest rules."

David's frown faded. "Okay."

Martin stood up and walked over to an antique desk and picked up a pad, then handed a sheet of paper to each of the assembled. "Write down the names in the order in which you believe Nicholas, Jason and Ana will marry. Also indicate the name of your alma mater.

Joshua Kirkland jotted down his wager. "David, if you're a little short on funds, I'll spot you a million," he teased.

"Yeah, right," David drawled. As Samuel Cole's son, purported to be the first black U.S. billionaire, money had never been a problem for anyone claiming Cole blood.

Martin completed his slip. "We'll put the slips in an envelope, seal it and everyone can put their initial across the flap. Next year this time we'll open them to find out the winner." Pushing off his chair, he stood up and stubbed out his cigar and placed the envelope in a wall safe behind a framed print of James Baldwin. "I don't know about the rest of you, but I'm exhausted. Happy New Year," he said, with a mock salute. "I'll see everyone at brunch."

One by one the men walked out of the library. David was the last one to leave. He wasn't as concerned with his children marrying because he and Serena had raised them to be free spirits. His eldest son and daughter had married and had given him grandchildren. That was enough for him.

Unlike his brothers, Martin and Joshua, David was not competitive. Never was and never would be. Martin had always been the consummate businessman and Joshua the military career officer. He'd had a brief stint as CEO of ColeDiz International, Ltd., but for him it had always been music. First it had been his band Night Mood and then his independent recording company Serenity Records. The label's focus had always been discovering new talent and it had continued until he retired and turned the day-to-day operation over to Jason and Ana.

The odds were in his favor, because he had two children with which to wager. And he predicted Ana would be the first to marry because he'd overheard her talking to her mother about her biological clock. At thirty-three she only had two more years before she would fall into the high-risk category. However, David wasn't as certain when it came to his son or nephew.

Nicholas owned and operated a horse farm in Virginia and the last he'd heard was that the former naval officer wasn't even remotely close to becoming involved with a woman. It was the same with Jason. His son hadn't been a relationship in years, and seemed quite content living the life of a bachelor.

Snuffing out his cigar, David pushed to his feet and left the library. He usually didn't make resolutions for the New Year, but this was one time he wanted to lord it over his brothers and nephew that there was nothing wrong with his unmarried twins. And if he did win the wager, then he would make certain to never let them forget it.

Chapter 1

Los Angeles, California

Camille Nelson felt a shiver of fear snake its way up her spine when a shadow fell across her desk. She was well aware of the company rule for not eating, reading anything not related to Slow Wyne Records, and other infractions like styling hair, repairing makeup or gum chewing while at her desk. Personal telephone calls were relegated to lunch hours, and only when not seated at the desk. She'd heard that an accounting clerk had been placed on probation for talking to her mother when she'd called to check on her sick preschooler during a staff meeting.

Her head popped up and she forced a smile when she saw her boss glaring down at her. "Good morning, Mr. Irvine."

A frown marred the forehead of the CEO of Slow Wyne Records when he saw the magazine spread out on his executive assistant's desk. Earlier that morning he'd read and reread every word of the *Rolling Stone* magazine article on

Justin Glover and he had to admit the reporter had hit the mark when he declared the young singing sensation was the second coming of the late King of Pop Michael Jackson.

"Put that away and come with me," he barked at Camille. "And bring your tools." Basil Irvine strode toward the carved double doors leading to his office, expecting her to follow him like an obedient child.

Camille gathered her steno pad and three pencils. Although her boss was only forty-three, he still hadn't come into the twenty-first century where executive assistants no longer took dictation, but transcribed their boss's notes from tape recorders. She didn't question her boss, because she needed the job. After a contentious and costly divorce Camille couldn't afford to do anything wherein she would lose her position at Slow Wyne Records. Even sleeping with Basil Irvine wasn't a guarantee that he wouldn't eventually give her a pink slip. She wasn't the first woman at the company to sleep with Basil, and she knew she wouldn't be the last.

She sat at the round table in an alcove of an office that was larger than her studio apartment, while Basil folded his stocky body down into a leather executive chair. Sunlight poured into the wall-to-wall, floor-to-ceiling windows behind him, reflecting off his shaved gold-brown freckled pate.

"I want you to send a letter to Ana Cole, CEO of Serenity Records. It's in Boca Raton, Florida." He waited for Camille to jot down her shorthand symbols. "Dear Ms. Cole. Everyone at Slow Wyne would like to congratulate Serenity Records for the successful launch of Justin Glover's first album. Mr. Glover's musical talent and success impacts the entire industry, and I'm certain it will usher in a new era with a fusion of musical genres." He paused, his gray eyes narrowing. "Use my usual closing." Unlocking a drawer, Basil handed her a flash drive when she approached his desk. "And Camille," he added when she turned to leave, "don't forget office rules apply to you, too."

Smiling, she nodded. "Yes, Mr. Irvine. It won't happen again."

Leaning back in his chair, Basil glared at her. "I know it won't—that is if you want to continue to work here."

Camille nodded as she walked out of the opulent office, softly closing the door behind her. What her boss didn't know was that she would've handed in her resignation a week after he'd hired her if she didn't need the money. Working for and sleeping with a record executive was a lot better than swinging around a pole in a gentlemen's club, where she'd had to put up with men pawing her just because they'd slipped her a few dollars. And when she'd finally made it to the champagne room where she had to give lap dances, she found herself more times than not holding her breath for fear she'd lose the contents of her stomach from their alcohol-soured breaths. Basil had become her temporary savior and her loyalty to him was limitless.

She didn't know about the other women who'd slept with Basil Irvine, but he'd disclosed things to her that she could use to bring down the man who ran his company like a maximum-security prison. He'd become the warden and his employees were the inmates.

She also knew his letter to Serenity Records was a ruse for a trap he had yet to spring. Basil's ego was as large as the Pacific Ocean and the one thing he refused to accept was failure. He'd failed to sign Justin to Slow Wyne, and had sworn he would make Serenity Records pay for what he deemed an act of betrayal. Basil had been the first to hear Justin's demo record, but after Slow Wyne offered the young twenty-year-old a deal that had him indebted to the company for the first two years of his contract, Justin's agent went to Serenity. Basil knew he needed to change the terms of the contract or he would lose Justin. Then it had become a bidding war with Serenity as the winner even though their last bid was lower than Slow Wyne's. Basil had sworn he would make the singer and Ana Cole pay for their deception.

Camille could care less about an East Coast–West Coast hip-hop rivalry reminiscent of the 1990s hostility between Death Row and Bad Boys Records. She was being paid a salary that exceeded her qualifications when she'd first come to work for the company. However, she'd made good use of the steady paycheck. She rented a small apartment in an up-and-coming neighborhood and had enrolled in a secretarial school where she'd taken the courses needed to become an efficient executive assistant.

She took care of Basil's needs in and out of the boardroom. In the throes of passion he'd admitted she was the best "lay" he'd ever had. Camille didn't mind the epithet, because she'd been called worse. She'd planned to use everything in her feminine arsenal to get whatever she needed from Basil before his reign of terror came to an abrupt end. And she knew it would end. She'd started hustling at an early age, and now at twenty-six she knew it was just a matter of time before her face and body would fail to attract men who were willing to trade money for sex.

Sitting at the desk outside her boss's office, she inserted the flash drive into a port and began transcribing the letter. After saving what she'd typed and printing it out, Camille returned the drive to a locked drawer in her desk. At the end of the workday she returned the flash drive to Basil, who locked it in his desk. There were documents on the drive that could incriminate the executives of Slow Wyne and could send them to jail for either life or for very lengthy sentences. She could care less about the inner workings of the record company. She was just an employee following orders.

Camille read and reread what she'd typed, tapped slightly on Basil's door and walked into his office when he told her to enter. She left the letter and envelope in his inbox and turned to leave.

"I'll see you later tonight." It wasn't a request, but a command.

She nodded, smiling. It was her birthday and Camille had hinted to Basil there was a bracelet in a Beverly Hills jewelry store she wanted. If he didn't get her the bracelet, then she was certain he would give her something comparable.

Boca Raton, Florida

Ana Cole sat across the table for two in her favorite Boca Raton restaurant, smiling at her cousin. She usually interacted with Tyler Cole twice a year—at Thanksgiving and the week between Christmas Eve and New Year's Day, but that was never enough for her. Of all of her many male cousins, Tyler was her favorite. He was like an older brother and father-figure rolled into one. And it wasn't that she wasn't able to talk to her father, but Tyler was usually more objective than David Cole—especially when it came to her relationships.

The first time she'd fallen in love and confessed to her father that her boyfriend had cheated on her, David Cole's response was that he would hunt him down and break his legs. Then it was her brother Gabriel who'd insinuated himself into her love life, monitoring and intimidating the men whose lifestyles were diametrically opposed to the way they were raised. Years later, after her first and only serious relationship ended, Ana lied to her father for the first time in her life. The man with whom she believed was her soul mate had also cheated on her. This time she confided in Tyler, who told her to regard every man who showed an interest in her as a potential husband. If she couldn't see herself spending the next fifty years with him, then she should not go beyond a third date. Ana had taken his advice and now at thirty-three she felt secure in her career *and* her personal life.

Her dimpled smile matched Tyler's. "How's the family?"

Picking up the napkin at his place setting, Tyler spread it over his lap. "They're wonderful. The boys are growing like weeds and Astra is the indisputable boss of the house."

Ana speared a forkful of the Cesar salad with grilled shrimp. "Don't you want another daughter, Tyler?"

Tyler's dark eyes met a pair in amber with gold glints. Ana reminded him of a delicate raven-haired doll. Her short hair was always coiffed, her olive-brown skin flawless and her delicate features, dimpled smile and petite figure had most men giving her a second glance.

"Are you certain you're not clairvoyant?"

Ana's fork paused in midair. "No. Am I missing something *primo*?"

"Dana's pregnant, and this time it's a girl."

A tiny shriek slipped past her lips and Ana glanced around the crowded restaurant to see if anyone had heard her. It appeared as if the other diners were too engrossed in their food or their dining companions. "That's incredible news! When is she due?"

"Mid-September."

She did the mental calculation. Her cousin's wife was five months pregnant, and this was her first time hearing about it. "Is Dana all right?" she asked.

Tyler expressive black eyebrows lifted a fraction. "She's good. We decided not to say anything until all tests indicated the baby is normal." He smiled. "I called my mom and dad earlier this morning to give them the good news."

Leaning back in her chair, Ana stared at Tyler. Like so many men in her family, he had begun graying in his thirties. The brilliant ob-gyn was now in his late forties and was to become a father for the fourth time. He'd named his first son after his father and the second one after his paternal grandfather, while he and Dana adopted their daughter after the infant's orphaned mother died in childbirth. Now Astra was about to become a big sister.

"I know you're here for a conference, but do you think you'll have time to go up to West Palm to see your folks?"

Tyler took a sip of sparkling water. "They're driving down tonight. I'm scheduled to chair one panel and sit on one, both on the same day. I'm not flying back to Mississippi until Friday. I told Dana I was going to stay an extra day to reconnect with my sister, but when I called Arianna her housekeeper said she, Silah and their kids had just left for Paris."

The Kadirs lived in Fort Lauderdale when their children were in school and in their fashion designer father's native Morocco during the summer months. The Kadir children spoke English, Spanish and French. Tyler shook his head. "My sisters are gypsies," he continued. "The only time I get to see Arianna is during Thanksgiving and the week of Christmas."

Reaching across the table, Ana placed her hand on Tyler's. "You're turning into your father, complaining that he doesn't see his children or grandchildren enough."

"Wait until you have children, Ana, and then you'll realize what it is to have your children spread out all over the world. My kids are still young, but I miss my sisters. Regina lives in Brazil, but she only comes to the States once or twice a year. Arianna divides her time between Florida and North Africa or Europe. At least your father has his children and grandchildren within a couple of hours of a car or plane ride." He reversed their hands. "Enough talk about the family. What about you? How are you doing?"

A smile parted Ana's lips. "Life is good for Serenity Records. Justin Glover—aka O'Quan Gee's debut album is number one on the Billboard chart."

Tyler angled his head and laughed, attractive lines fanning out around his large eyes. Anyone looking at him and Ana would've taken them for brother and sister. The first cousins had inherited their paternal grandmother's olive coloring, delicate features and dimpled smile.

"I wasn't talking about rappers and hip-hop artists, Ana. I'm talking about you. Are you seeing anyone?"

She averted her gaze. "Not right now." Her eyes met and fused with Tyler's. "To tell you the truth it has been a while since I've been involved with a man. I have male friends I can call if I don't want to go a social function by myself, but most times I attend the award ceremonies with Jason."

"You can't marry your brother, Ana."

She laughed quietly. "I know that, Tyler, but he's the only man, other than those in my family, that I can trust." Without warning, Ana sobered. "Can you answer one question for me?"

"What's that?"

"Why do men cheat?"

The seconds ticked as Tyler stared at something over Ana's shoulder. "I can't answer that because I've never cheated on Dana."

"How about your girlfriends before you married her?"

His gaze swung back to her. "I'd never cheated on them, either. Even if I'd wanted to I could never forget what *Abuela* went through with grandpa when she'd discovered he had fathered an illegitimate child."

"Uncle Josh is as much a part of our family as your dad or mine," Ana argued softly.

"I'm not saying he isn't, Ana. It shouldn't have taken more than thirty years for everyone to accept him as a Cole even though his last name was Kirkland."

She exhaled an audible sigh. "Our grandfather cheated on our grandmother, and I can't seem to find a man who doesn't think there's anything wrong with sleeping with more than one woman at the same time. It's the same with celebrities. They date one woman and father a child, then move on to the next without a pang of conscience that they've become a serial baby daddy."

"Therein is your problem. You have to stop dating guys in the business."

"I would if I happened to meet one who's not in the business. But, day in and day out it's songwriters, musicians, recording artists and producers. I'm ready to try one of those dating sites, but with my luck I'll end up with a psycho."

"Don't do that, Ana. I can always hook you up with one of my colleagues."

She shook her head. "And have him think I'm desperate. I don't have a problem attracting men, Tyler. It's just that I attract the wrong ones. Would you believe I was hit on by a twenty-year-old?"

Tyler swallowed a mouthful of savory crab cake. "Who's that?"

"Justin Glover aka O'Quan Gee aka OG."

"What's up with the stage names? Why doesn't he just go by Justin Glover?"

"He's a crossover artist. He'll record pop and R&B under Justin and rap and hip-hop as O'Quan Gee."

Tyler chuckled under his breath. "How does it feel to be a cougar?"

Ana rolled her eyes. "I don't think so, Tyler. There is nothing a twenty-year-old can do for me. I have enough trouble with immature thirtysomething baby boys. And for all his musical genius Justin may prove to be a problem."

"Why's that?"

"He's good and he knows it. But I'll let Jason handle the musical end of his career. I had enough issues trying to convince him to sign with Serenity instead of Slow Wyne. It ended in a bidding war where we signed him for less than what Slow Wyne would've offered, but our perks are more lucrative. We also included a morality clause at the insistence of our publicist: no drugs, DUIs or DWIs and he cannot become involved in any paternity suits for the term of his contract."

"How long is his contract?"

"Two years with an option to renew for an additional two. Slow Wyne wanted to tie him up for two years with a five year option. Negotiations became a little dicey when Basil Irvine went gangsta on me, but in the end he had to back down."

"What do you mean he went gangsta?"

Staring at the twitching muscle in her cousin's jaw, Ana chided herself for mentioning the telephone conversation between herself and the CEO of Slow Wyne. "He said I would pay for stealing Justin away from him."

"Pay how, Ana?"

She forced a brittle smile. "I don't know. He didn't go into detail."

"Aren't you concerned that he threatened you?" Tyler asked.

"Not really. He was just acting like a little boy who couldn't get his way. Basil Irvine doesn't have the best reputation when it comes to his artists. He will throw a few dollars at them—more money than they've ever seen to win them over. He also has a reputation for hosting elaborate parties for his artists complete with beautiful women, premium champagne and I suspect drugs, and in the end he'll own their souls. His performers make a lot of money, but unfortunately too many of them die before they're able to get what's coming to them. If they're not involved in some feud or have beef with another performer, then it's a drug overdose."

"I want you to be careful, because this clown sounds like he's going to be trouble," Tyler warned softly.

"If he wants trouble, then he'll get it," Ana countered. "As soon as he issued the threat I told him I was going to tape all of our conversations. I suppose it was enough for him to back off. He sent me a letter last month congratulating Serenity after Justin's album debuted at number one."

"What was your response?"

"I called and thanked him personally. He mentioned something about sharing drinks at the next Grammy awards, and

I told him I would make certain to set aside time to meet with him."

"So, you've kissed and made up?"

Ana's mouth twisted. "We're more like fremenies."

"Friend or enemy, you still should watch him."

Waving her hand in a dismissive gesture, Ana affected a bored expression. "I try not to give him a passing thought."

Tyler glanced at his watch, touched the napkin to the corners of his mouth and then placed it beside his plate. "I hate to eat and run, but I want to go back to my hotel and unwind before I go over my notes for tomorrow's presentation."

Ana realized her cousin must have gotten up early to fly in from Mississippi. She'd offered to have him stay in her condo, but Tyler said it was more convenient to check into the hotel where the conference was to take place. Reaching into her handbag, she took out her wallet and placed enough money on the table to cover their meal and a generous tip.

"Thanks for sharing lunch."

Tyler winked at her. "Thanks for inviting me and next time it's on me." Pushing back his chair, he stood up and came around the table to ease back Ana's chair. "Are you coming to Hillsboro for Thanksgiving?"

She looked at him. "Are you sure Dana's going to be up to hosting Thanksgiving so soon after giving birth?"

"We're having it catered."

She nodded. Although she wasn't married and had no children Ana always got together with her cousins and their families for Thanksgiving. Their parents had complained that Thanksgiving was a family holiday, but the younger generation stood firm when they'd decided to exercise a modicum of independence. The result was a livelier and unrestrained gathering with an ever-increasing number of children running around in abandon.

Arm in arm they left the restaurant and walked out into the brilliant late-spring Florida sunshine. Ana placed a pair of sunglasses on the bridge of her nose, Tyler following suit. "Where are you parked?"

He pointed to a late-model silver sedan. "I'm right here. Where are you parked?"

"I'm around on the other side."

"I'll walk you to your car."

"That's all right." Going on tiptoe, Ana pressed a kiss to Tyler's cheek. "If I don't see you before you go back to Mississippi I'll definitely see you for Thanksgiving."

Winding his arms around Ana's waist, Tyler pulled her close. Dipping his head, he whispered in her ear. "Stay out of trouble."

"What are you—" Her words stopped when a sharp sound pierced the humid air. Tyler's arms fell away as he crumbled to the ground in slow-motion like fluttering confetti. All warmth fled from her body, replaced by an icy-coldness that wouldn't permit Ana to move. It seemed like an eternity where it was only seconds before she was able to scream when she sank to the ground beside her cousin's body. The screams kept coming until people in the parking lot raced over to see what the commotion was about.

Her eyes wide with fear and panic, Ana screamed, "Help me!" She cradled Tyler to her bosom, her white blouse stained red with the warm blood seeping from his chest wound. His eyes were closed and his breathing shallow. The wait seemed interminable, but off in the distance she heard the sound of wailing sirens.

"Let me have a look at him."

She glanced up to find an elderly man kneeling beside her. Her brain refused to process what had just happened. How could someone shoot Tyler and she not see them? She hadn't noticed anyone close to them in the parking lot. Ana tightened her hold on her cousin's neck. "No."

"Please, miss. I'm a doctor."

"No!" She screamed again, this time when a pair of strong

hands pulled her up and held her fast. Ana fought like a cat, crying and clawing, but she wasn't able to free herself from the arms that held her like manacles.

Some of the fight went out of her, and she slumped against the wide chest of a man who towered above her by a full head. The wail of sirens came closer and closer and within minutes first responders and police officers filled the restaurant's parking lot. She was barely coherent when she gave an officer the account of what she *didn't* see.

Working quickly, the paramedics stabilized Tyler, placing him on a gurney as she stood numbly by. A crime-scene unit had arrived as Ana was helped into the rear of the ambulance. Reaching for Tyler's hand, she closed her eyes and prayed.

Ana sat in the family room at her parents' house, reacting like an automaton. She'd become a prisoner. Easygoing, laid-back David Claridge Cole had turned into a tyrant, taking the keys to her car and condo, while declaring he had no intention of burying any of his children and if he had to shackle her to keep her from leaving, then he would. Ana knew her father was incensed because she hadn't divulged the details of the negotiations to sign Justin Glover, and she'd argued because he was no longer involved with the day-to-day operation of the recording label she wasn't obligated to apprise him of the proceedings.

And the media had exacerbated the situation when headlines blared about the attempted murder of a member of one of Florida's most prominent families. An undisclosed source told a reporter at *The Miami Herald* about the alleged ongoing feud between Slow Wyne Records and Serenity Records, and that Dr. Tyler Cole unintentionally had become collateral damage. Ana prayed the source hadn't come from Serenity, because all the employees had signed a confidentiality agreement as a condition to employment. And if not them, the rumors had to come from someone in the Slow Wyne camp.

Reporters had also attempted to interview Jason, but his 'no comment' left them searching for other leads. Basil Irvine did agree to be interviewed, stating emphatically that there was no bad blood between his L.A.-based company and Serenity. He did admit he'd wanted to sign Justin Glover, but conceded when the singing phenom said the music produced by Serenity was better-suited for his singing style and vocal range. His Cheshire cat grin and velvety smooth voice had Ana screaming at the television that he was lying; she was incensed because she wasn't able to rebut his allegation.

It'd been three days since someone had gunned down Tyler and instead of fading, the image of her cradling him persisted. An unscheduled gathering of the family descended on West Palm Beach when the news hit that Tyler had become the victim of a possible sniper. Fortunately the bullet missed all major arteries; however, the wound was still serious enough for the attending physician to recommend he remain in the hospital for several days.

The police were able to find the spent round and a ballistics expert had identified it as military issue; surveillance feed from cameras outside the restaurant and several other buildings showed a figure in camouflage repelling down the side of an office building and speeding off on a motorcycle. The police were able to identify the make and model of the bike, but when the video was enhanced the Kawasaki was missing the license plate, leading them to believe either it was stolen or the plate was intentionally removed.

Ana had felt like a parrot, repeating the same thing over and over when interrogated by law enforcement officials. First it was the local police, then special agents from the FBI. The theory that the sniper was connected to the military was a cause for concern among family members. Particularly those who'd had military experience.

Pulling her knees to her chest, she rested her head on them

and closed her eyes. Why, she thought, did her parents insist on keeping their home so cool. "I'm freezing, Mom."

Serena Morris-Cole stared at her daughter. She was shaking and it wasn't from the air-cooled temperature but because she was still traumatized. "I'll adjust the air and bring you a cup of hot tea."

Ana's head popped up. Her registered-nurse mother had divided her time between sitting at Tyler's bedside and providing emotional support for Ana. "Thank you, Mom, but I can get my own tea." Serena gave Ana a look she recognized immediately: *do not argue with me.* "Okay," she conceded. It was as if all the fight had gone out of her when she'd never been one to back down from any confrontation.

David and Serena had raised their children to be free spirits in the tradition of 1970s hippies and Ana had become somewhat of a wild child. She was never one to turn down her brothers' challenges and she preferred hanging out with them rather her architecture-historian sister who was the consummate girly-girl. For Ana it was baseball instead of cheerleading, shooting pool instead of ballet lessons. She'd earned an undergraduate degree in business and finance before enrolling in law school, with a focus on business law.

She'd taken control of Serenity Records once her father retired, while her twin brother, Jason, had become the label's musical director and producer. She'd negotiated deals with artists who had served time for felonies, yet never at any time had she ever felt threatened or intimidated until now.

Ana didn't want to believe Basil's denial that there wasn't bad blood between them, despite his too-sweet letter congratulating Serenity on Justin's successful record launch. But the more she thought about it the more she felt it was retribution for signing up an artist the head of Slow Wyne coveted as if he were the Holy Grail.

A tentative smile parted her lips when Jason walked into the room. Ana patted the cushion beside her on the love seat.

"Hang out with me for a while." Fraternal twins, and older by fifteen minutes, Jason was her masculine counterpart. He was undeniably a Cole: tall, broad-shouldered, olive complexion, black curly hair, delicate features and dimples.

Extending his hand, Jason pulled her to stand. "Come with me."

Walking on bare feet, Ana had to practically run to keep up with his longer stride. "Where are we going?"

Jason flashed a wolfish grin. "To my place."

He was the only one of his parents' four children who still lived at home. He had his own apartment in the expansive house and had access to an in-home recording studio. Although he was provided ultimate privacy, Jason refused to sleep with a woman under his parents' roof. If his dates didn't have their own place, then he entertained them at hotels.

Jason had surprised everyone once he'd announced that he'd bought property in Oregon near the Cascades where he'd built a sprawling house he dubbed Serenity West. It was where he spent months writing and recording music, and he made it a point to spend at least half the year there.

Ana followed Jason into the living/dining area and sat with him on a sofa covered with Haitian cotton. The seating arrangement faced a wall of pocket doors that overlooked the patio and inground pool.

Shifting, he turned to face his sister. "They're making plans to send you away."

Ana's eyes widened until he could see the dark centers of the golden orbs. "Send me where?"

"Diego said he has a friend who is a U.S. Marshal. It appears the man has a house down in the Keys, and that he's taken an extended vacation leave, so Diego asked him to look after you."

"Look after me!" Ana's voice had gone up several octaves. "What the hell do they think I am? I'm not a three-year-old that has to be looked after."

Reaching out, Jason caught her shoulders and pressed his forehead to his twin's. "Calm down, Ana."

"Calm down! Would you be calm if someone decided to send you away against your will?"

His eyes, so much like Ana's, bore into hers. "I would if my life depended upon it."

There was something in her brother's voice and expression that made her pause. "What is it, Jay?" she asked, using her pet name for him.

Jason closed his eyes, a fringe of long, thick black lashes touching high cheekbones. "That bullet was meant for you."

She went still, nothing moving as Ana held her breath. "How do you know that?" she whispered once she exhaled.

He patted his chest over his heart. "I feel it here."

People had always asked them as twins if one felt when the other was in danger, and the answer was yes. And even before he'd gotten the phone call that Tyler was with Ana when he'd been shot, Jason had known something was wrong. He'd been in the studio editing a song when he'd suddenly felt as if someone or something had squeezed his heart, making breathing difficult. He'd called Ana's cell phone at the same time she was calling him, and he was at the hospital minutes before Tyler was wheeled into the E.R.

Ana's eyes filled with tears as she slumped against Jason, who was rubbing her back in a comforting gesture. She could admit unequivocally that she trusted her twin more than anyone. They shared a special bond that gave them the ability to complete one another's sentences and know when the other felt joy or sadness.

"You're saying I should go?"

"I'm saying you shouldn't fight Mom and Dad on this."

She eased back. "What about you, Jay? You're also Serenity Records."

He shook his head. "Not like you, Ana. You're front and center, while I work behind the scene. You negotiate the contracts and handle all the legal entanglements. I know that bullet was meant for you."

"I go away for a couple of weeks, then what? What if the police don't catch the person who shot Tyler?"

"The police have made this case a priority. They're going to find the shooter."

"What if they don't?" she asked again.

"Dad and Uncle Martin have contacted a P.I. firm who employ ex-military and law enforcement. They have their own methods of uncovering details the police may overlook."

Ana ran her fingers through her short hair. "What about Serenity?"

Jason gave her a long stare. "It's not going to implode because you're not there. I may not be familiar with all the legalese, but I do have an MBA. I believe that qualifies me to know a little about running a business."

Pinpoints of heat stung Ana's cheeks. "I didn't mean to imply it would fall apart without me, Jason."

He ruffled her hair as he'd done when she was a little girl. "Everything is going to be all right."

Ana sucked in a lungful of air, held it and then exhaled slowly. "It's not going to be all right until they catch the person who shot Tyler."

There was a light knock on the door and Jason and Ana turned to find Diego Cole-Thomas standing in the open doorway. Folding his arms over his chest, the head of ColeDiz International, Ltd. leaned against the frame. People who saw photographs of Samuel Cole usually did a double-take whenever they looked at Diego. He was his great-grandfather's clone. Not only did he look like the man who'd amassed a fortune growing tobacco, bananas and coffee, but his approach to business was similar.

"Did you tell her?" Diego asked.

Ana pushed off the sofa and approached her cousin. "Why are you talking about me as if I wasn't here, Diego? And yes,

Jason did tell me." She tilted her chin, staring up at Diego staring down at her. "Where exactly in the Keys am I going and who's going to babysit me?"

Diego flashed a rare smile, transforming his stoic expression. "His name is Jacob Jones, he lives on Long Key and he's not too pleased that he has to *babysit* you, but he's willing to do it as a favor to me. As soon as you pack enough to last you a couple of weeks I'll fly down with you. Jacob will meet us at the Marathon airport."

Ana's stomach did a flip-flop. "You want me to leave now?"

"Yes. That's what your folks want."

She wanted to ask him if what she wanted figured into the equation. Ana knew she definitely would've rejected anyone's suggestion she go into hiding if Jason hadn't voiced his fear that her life was in danger. "What time is liftoff?"

"Three."

Ana took a quick glance at her watch. It was eleven-thirty. She felt like crying, but refused to let her brother and cousin see her break down. She knew her family wanted her safe as much as she wanted to live. At thirty-three she had her whole life ahead of her. And like her sister Alexandra she wanted to fall in love, marry and have children. She wanted what most normal women wanted, but there was someone out there who'd decided they wanted her dead.

"Do I have time to see Tyler before I leave?"

Diego nodded. "I'll call the pilot and have him delay takeoff."

Ana knew they were flying down in the corporate jet, so she didn't have to concern herself with going through airport-security checkpoints. "I guess I better go and pack."

She walked past Diego and out of Jason's apartment and into the one that she'd occupied for years. The studio apartment rental and her condo had wonderful ocean views but lacked adequate closet space, so she'd stored most of her clothes in her parents' house. When she entered her bedroom Ana saw her mother sitting on a cushioned rocker. The strain of the past three days was etched around Serena's mouth.

Ana closed her eyes and when she reopened them she saw tears making their way slowly down her mother's face. "I don't want to go."

Serena stood up. "But you have to go, baby. And you have to stay away until we settle this."

She took a step, then another until she hugged her mother so tightly both struggled to breathe. "Will you help me pack, Mama?"

Serena nodded, unable to speak because of the constriction in her throat. It had been years since her wild child had called her Mama. Reaching into a pocket of her slacks, she took out a tissue and blotted her face. She kissed Ana's cheek. "We're going to get through this. It's not the first time we've had a family crisis and it probably won't be the last. Your father, uncles and the other men in this family will make certain nothing will happen to you. They always protect their own."

Ana held her mother as if she were her a lifeline. She didn't know why, but she felt as if she was going into exile without a hint of when she would return. Diego had mentioned she should pack enough for a couple of weeks, yet something told her it would be longer. She was leaving everything that was familiar to live with a stranger who'd assured Diego that he would protect her. She had to believe him or whoever wanted her dead would determine her destiny.

No permita que nadie le defina ni determine su destino. It was as if Marguerite-Joséfina Isabel Diaz-Cole was in the room whispering in her ear. Her grandmother had always cautioned her not to let anyone define her or to determine her destiny. Ana's grandmother had been born during a time when women had little or no rights, and even less when it came to selecting a husband. Cuban-born M.J. had defied her father, married an American and left the country of her birth to become the matriarch of a dynasty. Ana kissed her mother again.

"I'm ready, Mom." And she was ready to do whatever she needed to do so she could live her life without having to look over her shoulder.

Chapter 2

Los Angeles

Basil Irvine pounded a fist into his open palm when he really felt like punching the wall. Perhaps the pain would help him forget the debacle that resulted in Tyler Cole being shot instead of Ana.

Turning a menacing glare on his brother, he narrowed his eyes. "That's what I get for sending a boy to do a man's job."

A feral grin spread over Webb Irvine's scarred face. "Do you want to hear I told you so?"

Basil's gray eyes glittered like chipped ice. "If it will make you feel better, then say it."

Like quicksilver the smile faded and Webb peered down at the toes of his spit-shined shoes. "I'm not going to say it because it's not going to change anything. I told you that I'd take care of the bitch, but you wanted to do it your way."

"That's because I didn't want you involved. You just got out of jail—"

Webb waved a hand as if swatting away an annoying insect. "Don't worry about me going back to jail. That's not going to happen."

"I still don't want you involved in this."

Basil stared at his younger brother. They looked nothing alike, but blood ran deep between them. He'd stomped a man to death for stealing from him, and it was Webb who'd confessed to the crime. Webb, only fifteen at the time, was tried as an adult, and pled guilty to involuntary manslaughter; he spent three years in a juvenile facility before being transferred to minimum-security prison for the next ten years. Webb earned a high school diploma and, once paroled, he'd enrolled in college and had graduated with a degree in computer science.

"I won't be involved," Webb said softly. "I know someone who would be perfect for this project."

Basil sat down on a leather love seat, knees spread apart. Webb was the epitome of a successful businessman with his conservative haircut, tailored suit, custom-made shirt, silk tie and imported footwear. He'd repaid his brother ten-fold when he'd given him enough money to start up his own security company that created and sold state-of-the art surveillance equipment.

"Let me think about it. My man said he's going to wait a while before he begins hunting again."

The dark brown eyes in an equally dark face flattened. "Do you have an idea who told that reporter that you had threatened Ana Cole?"

Basil shook his head. He knew who it was, but he couldn't tell Webb.

Webb pulled his lower lip between his teeth. "What if it was someone from Slow Wyne?"

"I doubt that."

"Are you sure, brother?"

Running a hand over his shaved head, Basil chuckled under his breath. "I'm willing to bet our mama's life on it."

"Intimidation doesn't work on everyone."

Leaning lower, Basil rested his elbows on his knees. "There's only one person who knows what went down when I was trying to get Justin Glover to sign with Slow Wyne, and that is Omar Thornton."

"Watch him, Basil."

"Omar is trustworthy."

"I can find out how trustworthy he is if you let me bug his house."

Basil sat up straight. "What the hell are you saying, Webb?"

"Send him away on a business trip for a few days and my people will bug his house and phones. After a while you'll discover how trustworthy he is."

"You're paranoid."

"I am careful and thorough, Basil. I'm just trying to protect your reputation. I didn't do a bid for you to screw up because you're pissed off at a little girl who managed to get the best of you."

"She is not a little girl," Basil said between clenched teeth. "She's a shark masquerading as a piranha."

Throwing back his head, Webb laughed loudly. He sobered when he saw Basil's expression. "Do you want Justin Glover?"

"What the hell kind of question is that? Of course I want him."

"I can get him for you, big brother."

The buzz of the intercom preempted Basil's reply. "Excuse me, but I have to get that." He stood up, walked over to his desk and punched a button on the telephone console. "Yes, Camille."

"Mr. Edwards's secretary just called to say he's on his way."

"Thanks." When he turned around Basil realized he was alone. Webb had left. He didn't want his brother to do anything that could send him back to jail. The person he'd hired to kill Ana Cole had shot the wrong Cole. However, the hired gun vowed Ana Cole was as good as dead.

Jacob Jones maneuvered up to curbside at the Marathon airport, showed his shield and photo ID to the man who came over to the driver's side window. The officer's eyes shifted from the official photograph to the man with a baseball cap pulled low over his forehead. He took a step closer, glancing into the open window to see the holstered automatic weapon where his right hand rested on his thigh.

"I'm on the job," Jacob explained. "My party is on the ground and should be here in a few minutes," he said to the police officer. What he wanted to tell the man was that he wasn't officially on the job, but what he had agreed to do was akin to witness protection. The difference was Ana Cole wasn't a witness to a crime, but the intended target of a sniper with possible ties to the military.

"No problem, Marshal Jones. You have a good afternoon."

Jacob smiled and nodded. "Thanks."

When he'd gotten up earlier that morning he never would've expected a call from Diego Cole-Thomas asking whether he'd be willing to protect his cousin. It was the second day of a well-deserved eight-week vacation and Jacob planned to do nothing more than sleep late, fish, cook his catch and view several new movies in his extensive DVD collection.

Diego had also filled him in on the details of the shooting that had put Dr. Tyler Cole in the hospital with a chest wound. He wanted to refuse his friend's request, but couldn't because he was godfather to Diego's son.

He also wasn't looking forward to sharing his home with any woman. Whenever a woman crossed his threshold their stay was usually limited to a few days. One had been fortunate to stay for an extended two weeks, but anything beyond that had him formulating excuses to prepare them for their departure.

The week before he'd received an official memo mandating he take a vacation. Jacob couldn't remember the last time he'd actually taken time off just to kick back and relax. He'd bought the house in Long Key as a retreat, a sort of safe haven where he could go and forget about the prisoners housed in the Miami federal detention centers. He'd been promoted from the field to a desk position and it wasn't until he walked out of his office and drove south to the Keys had he realized how much he did need a vacation.

He spied Diego coming out of the terminal, his driver and bodyguard pushing a cart with designer luggage. His gaze shifted to the woman holding Diego's hand, recognizing her immediately. The first time he saw Ana was at Diego and Vivienne Neal's wedding, and then again at the baptism celebration for their son. It was apparent she and the man who'd come with her to the celebration following the baptism hadn't been seeing eye-to-eye because Ana had refused to talk to or even look at him.

There was something about the expression on the petite dark-haired woman's face that communicated to Jacob that she hadn't come willingly. Well, he thought, as he got out of his vehicle, the feeling was definitely mutual. He wanted to dictate where and how he wanted to spend the next two months of his life without having to consider another person. But, he'd promised his friend he would look after his cousin, and for Jacob, if he gave his word then he always followed through.

Adjusting the hem of the Hawaiian-print shirt to conceal the firearm, he walked over to Diego, who'd released Ana's hand. They shook hands and pounded each other's backs in a rough hug. He hadn't seen the CEO of ColeDiz in more than three months, and the first thing he noticed was he'd claimed a bit more gray hair.

"How's it going, buddy?"

"It's all good," Diego answered.

"How's the family?"

"They're good. Vivienne's been asking about you."

"I'd planned to take a few days off and come up to see you guys, but that was before you called me."

Diego put his arm around Ana's waist. "Ana, do you remember Jacob? He came to my wedding and the baptism."

She stared at the tall man in the gaudy shirt and tattered Miami Dolphins cap. Her gaze went from his face down to his jeans and worn sandals before reversing to linger on his face. He wasn't what she would consider handsome; nonetheless he was attractive in a masculine sort of way despite his tacky shirt and ragged hat. His dark eyes in a face the color of golden-brown autumn leaves were mesmerizing.

"Yes, I do remember him."

What she meant was she'd remembered him from the baptism, but not the wedding. Then he'd worn a tailored suit and shoes. But that was all she'd recalled because the man who'd come with her to the soiree that followed the sacrament at the church had made it his intent to put pressure on her to take their friendship to the next level. What he hadn't realized was that there was no next level, but that hadn't stopped him from reacting like a spoiled child when she'd told him it was to become their last date.

Jacob extended his hand, palm up. "And I remember you." He wasn't disappointed when she placed her tiny hand on his, he giving her fingers a gentle squeeze before he released them. He nodded to the taciturn driver/bodyguard who'd removed his sunglasses and wiped his face and sable-brown shaved head with a snow-white handkerchief. Despite the heat Henri wore a black suit, tie and white shirt. He hadn't removed his jacket, and Jacob knew the man always carried a concealed handgun whenever he traveled with Diego.

"Hello, Henri."

"Mr. Jones."

Pressing a button on the fob to the Jeep, the hatch lifted as Henri carried Ana's bags to the SUV, then returned to assist her up onto the passenger seat. "I'll take good care of her," Jacob promised Diego.

"I know you will." He leaned closer. "She's not too happy about this."

"She'll get over it."

Diego's eyebrows lifted as he stared at his cousin sitting in the vehicle. She was so still she could've been made of stone. "I'll call you with updates."

"I hope it won't take too long to catch the bastard. By the way, how's Tyler?"

"He'll be released tomorrow. He's going to stay in West Palm until he's cleared to fly. His wife and children are here, so there's no need for him to worry about rushing back to Mississippi."

Jacob rested a hand on Diego's shoulder. "I know you have your people on this, but tell them to concentrate on rogue professional snipers, former-military or even SWAT."

"We're going to find him, Jacob, and hopefully there'll be something left to prosecute." Diego saw Henri tap the face of his watch out of the corner of his eye. "I have to leave because we've been cleared for takeoff. I'll call you later on in the week to check on Ana."

Jacob smiled. "Have a safe flight." He knew as soon as the wheels were up that within minutes the Gulfstream Aerospace Corporation G550 would prepare to touchdown in West Palm Beach.

Turning on his heels, he walked to the Jeep and slid in behind the wheel next to Ana. The hauntingly sensual, subtle scent of perfume filled the interior of the vehicle. Sitting less than a foot away from her made him aware of things he hadn't noticed or had forgotten the last time they'd met.

He'd thought she was taller, her body fuller. And he'd remembered her hair was longer than it was now. However, the pixie hairstyle was perfect for her face, showing off her exquisite bone structure. "Do you have a cell phone on you?"

Ana turned to look at Jacob, her gaze fixed on the shape of his mouth. She hadn't wanted to admit it to herself, but he had the sexiest mouth of any man she'd ever seen. The top lip was firm, the lower fuller, sensual. "Yes. Why?"

He held out his right hand. "Please give it to me."

"Why?" she asked again.

"I'll tell you after you give it to me."

Reaching into her leather handbag, she took out the Black-Berry, placing it on his outstretched palm. "Now tell me."

"You are not to use your cell as long as you're here. If you need to make a call, then you can use the one in my house or my cell. Are you carrying any credit cards?"

Ana blinked as if she couldn't believe what she was hearing. There was no doubt Jacob wanted her to turn her credit cards over to him. "Yes. I suppose you want those, too."

"I do."

She gave him the case with her cards. "What if I need to buy something?"

A hint of a smile tilted the corners of Jacob's mouth. "I don't know what that could be, because it appears as if you brought your entire wardrobe." The back of the truck was filled with at least half a dozen bags. Her eyes narrowed, reminding him of a cat's.

"I wasn't talking about clothes, Mr. Jones." She'd spat out his name.

"It's either Jake or Jacob. The choice is yours."

"You didn't answer my question, Jacob. What if I need to buy something?" Ana asked again.

"I'll buy it for you." He held up a hand when she opened her mouth. "Your father can reimburse me when this is over."

"And I hope that's real soon," she said under her breath, "and I will reimburse you, not my father. He stopped paying my bills years ago." She'd come into her trust at twenty-five and therefore had become independently wealthy.

Jacob saw the stubborn set of her delicate jaw. "This isn't a walk in the park for me, either. When I put in for vacation I didn't expect to share it with someone who didn't want to share it with me."

Shifting on the leather seat, Ana gave him a lengthy stare. "I'm sorry if the attempt on my life threw a monkey wrench into your plans. And tell your girlfriend that I'll give her a gift card so she can buy something real nice to compensate for me taking up her boyfriend's time."

Throwing back his head, Jacob laughed loudly, the sound reverberating inside the SUV. "Do you really believe that all you have to do is write a check and make it okay? Money isn't the cure-all for everything in one's life," he added.

"Are you telling me your girlfriend would refuse a no-strings-attached gift?"

"I'm certain she would *if* I had a girlfriend. I happen not to like women who are fixated on money, because as a government worker I'll never make the Forbes list of the wealthiest people in America."

Punching the Start Engine button, Jacob signaled and then smoothly maneuvered away from the curb. Reaching for the sunglasses on the console, he placed them on the bridge of his nose as he followed the signs for the airport exit.

"You didn't answer my question, Jacob," Ana said when he headed north.

"What's that?"

"Why did you take my phone and credit cards?"

"The plan is for you to disappear."

Her eyes were wide behind the lenses of her oversize sunglasses. "Like in the Witness Protection Program?"

Jacob nodded. "Exactly. And you're not to use the internet. Without your cell and credit cards it will make it difficult for someone to track your whereabouts. It will be the same with your car parked in the reserved spot at your condo. Even if someone decided to fit it with a tracking device they'll be disappointed because it won't be moved for weeks."

"I live in a gated community."

"That may be a slight deterrent, but it's still penetrable. What makes you think your condo's security can't be compromised?"

She exhaled a soft breath. "I didn't think of that." A comfortable silence ensued, Ana staring through the windshield at the Atlantic Ocean on the right of the highway and the Gulf on the left. "And you think I'll be safe here in the Keys?"

Jacob took a quick glance at the woman who unknowingly had set into motion a private war that was certain to end in casualties, while he'd pledged Diego that his cousin would not become one of the victims. "You'll be safe with *me*."

"You sound very confident, Jacob."

He smiled, exhibiting a mouth filled with straight white teeth. "I am not a neophyte when it comes to protecting witnesses."

"I'm not a witness, because I didn't see who shot Tyler," Ana argued in a quiet voice. "One minute I was standing talking to him, and then the next second he was on the ground bleeding from a chest wound."

"Tyler's lucky that bullet didn't hit an artery otherwise his wife would've found herself a widow and her children fatherless."

Ana closed her eyes as if to shut out the scene that continued to haunt her. "His wife is five months pregnant with their fourth child."

Jacob didn't tell Ana that the shooter had probably worked

alone, but if he'd had a spotter, then she wouldn't be sitting next to him. He wasn't certain whether something had
spooked the sniper or he felt he had to get off the shot or lose
his target, but destiny had determined that his target would
get a reprieve.

"My dad hired some people to try to find whoever shot
Tyler. Do you think they'll catch who's behind it?"

"I'd like to believe they'll find him."

It was the first time Jacob heard a modicum of fear in
Ana's voice. He didn't want to believe that she didn't know
that the Coles would spend every dollar of their vast wealth
to keep her safe. He'd agreed to look after her because of his
close bond with Diego. It wouldn't be the first time he would
step in to help the Coles. At Diego's request he'd helped Vivienne Neal uncover who had been responsible for her husband's hit-and-run. His involvement in solving the conspiracy
that led to the death of the U.S. representative was instru-
mental when he was recommended for a promotion as an assistant director of the Miami-based federal detention center.

Diego married Vivienne and they had asked him to become godfather to their son whom they named Samuel Jacob
Cole-Thomas. Although they lived in the same state, he didn't
get to see his friends as much as he would've liked. Oversight of staff to supervise the U.S. Marshal Service at four
Miami federal detention centers left him little time to social-
ize. It was only when the mandate came down that he had to
take at least two months of his accrued vacation leave or he
would lose it had he become aware that his career had taken
over his life.

Jacob couldn't remember the last time he'd had a normal
relationship with a woman, at least one that lasted more than
a few months, because they were no longer a priority whenever he was directed to search for a fugitive or assigned to
witness protection. At first he'd come to regret sitting behind
a desk, because he'd missed the adrenalin rush of being in

the field, but after a while he'd come to appreciate a measure of normalcy when he wasn't on the job 24/7, or on an assignment that took him away from home for weeks, or on occasion months.

Ana had asked if she was safe with him and he hadn't lied to her when he said yes. No one he worked with knew he had a house in the Keys. Some of them had been to the renovated apartment he rented near downtown Miami whenever they got together to view a game, but on a whole most of his coworkers knew him to be a very private person. Even when some of the single guys got together socially they never saw him with the same woman more than twice.

Jacob didn't know why he wasn't able to form a lasting relationship with a woman because it hadn't been that way with his parents. Theirs had been a fairy-tale love affair when at the age of seventeen his father had spied the woman he would eventually marry. The pretty girl had been a cheerleader for the opposing football team. He took her to his prom and he was her date for hers, sparking a lot of controversy that she was dating the running back from their rival team.

"What made you decide to live in Long Key rather than Key West?"

Ana's query pulled Jacob from his musings. "Key West is too crowded and touristy. Long Key is more for those looking for laid-back solitude." He gave her a quick glance. "Have you ever been to the Keys?"

Ana gave Jacob a spontaneous smile for the first time. "When I was sixteen I'd decided to leave home. Destination: Key West. I'd accelerated in high school, graduating a year ahead of my peers and I was ambivalent about going to college. I'd read about Ernest Hemingway living in Key West, and I was always drawn to the bohemian lifestyle."

"How were you planning to support yourself?"

"I'd closed out my bank account, and I figured if I lived

frugally then it would've lasted me until I took control of my trust."

"How long was that going to take?"

Ana turned her head to stare out the side window. "Nine years."

"At sixteen you'd saved enough money to last you for nine years?"

A smile softened her mouth. "At sixteen I'd believed I could live on five thousand dollars for nine years. What did I know about money? All I knew was when I asked for it to buy something, I got it. I loaded up my car and took off in the middle of the night. I got as far as Miami before the police pulled me over."

"Were you speeding?"

"No. They told me the car had been reported stolen."

"Should I assume the car was in your father's name?" Jacob asked as he struggled not to laugh.

"It was. The police held me until Daddy arrived. What he didn't say frightened me more than if he'd gone off on me. He refused to talk to me, then loaded my bags in his car and arranged to have my car driven back to Boca Raton. I didn't get to see that car again until it was time for me to go to college. Having my dad, whom I adore, not talk to me for weeks cured me of wanting to live in Key West."

"What made you decide to strike out on your own?"

"It had to be impulsivity or a temporary lapse of common sense. When Daddy finally did talk to me he said that if I'd wanted to go off and see the world, then he would've hired a chaperone to accompany me wherever I wanted to go. The fact that I didn't trust him enough to tell him of my plan hurt him more than I could've imagined. He reminded me of that when the rumor about bad blood between Serenity and Slow Wyne was made public."

"You didn't tell him about what went down between you and Basil Irvine?"

"No."

"Why not?"

"Because if my father hadn't thought I was capable enough to run the company, then he wouldn't have relinquished control once he decided to retire. Would you have asked my brother that question if he were CEO?"

A frown settled into Jacob's features. "It's not about gender, Ana."

"Then what is it about?" she asked, her voice rising in annoyance.

There was only the sound of the slip-slap of rubber on the roadway as he drove onto the Long Key Channel. "It's about trust and respect," Jacob said softly. "It couldn't have been easy for your dad to start up a new record label when he had to compete with legendary giants like Atlantic, Capitol, Sony, Epic and RCA. Nowadays you have to go head-to-head with Virgin, Interscope, Slow Wyne and Island Records Def Jam and Roc-A-Fella. The genre and players may have changed, but the business is still the same."

"How do you know so much about record companies?" There was no mistaking the awe in her tone.

"I read a lot," Jacob said glibly. "I need you to answer one question for me."

"What's that?"

"Are you feuding with Basil Irvine?"

"No. Basil has been in business long enough to know he can't win every negotiation. Justin Glover isn't the first artist he's failed to sign to his label and I'm certain he won't be the last. I've lost count of the number of performers we've lost to other labels for one reason or another. I just suck it up and move on."

"Maybe that's because you're a gracious loser. I don't like to keep bringing up gender, but you have to remember you're a woman, so someone with an ego like Irvine's isn't going to accept defeat as graciously from a woman as he would from a man."

Ana knew Jacob was right about her gender when it came to Basil, but she wasn't about to admit that openly. Basil had earned a reputation as an astute and aggressive businessman, and despite his reputation as a misogynist women still fell over themselves to be seen with him.

Jacob turned off onto Royce Creek Drive, driving a short distance before pulling into the driveway of a two-story house. Maneuvering under a carport, he lowered the windows, and then cut off the engine. He rested a hand on Ana's shoulder. "Don't move. I'll be right back."

Unbuckling her seat belt, she shifted on the seat in an attempt to take in her surroundings. One side of Jacob's house overlooked a canal with direct access to the Atlantic Ocean. Ana smiled when she thought of waking up to water views. Her favorite pastime was sitting on her condo's balcony at sunset drinking a chai latte. It was as if all the stress of the day faded as the sun sank lower in the horizon before disappearing and leaving the darkening sky with splashes of red and orange.

She didn't have to wait long. Jacob returned, sans the hat he should've discarded a long time ago. To say he wasn't into fashion was an understatement. She did recall him wearing a suit to the baptism, but that was expected because it was held in a church. What she couldn't remember was him being at Diego's wedding.

Ana stared, her eyes becoming wider behind her glasses as Jacob came closer. Without the hat she was able see all of his face. Her gaze lingered on the elegant ridge of his cheekbones before moving down to his sensual, masculine mouth. She found her protector to be genuinely handsome, and she could not imagine why he didn't have a wife or a girlfriend. The only alternative was that he wasn't into women. That would have been devastating because he was the epitome of masculinity. His cropped black hair, tall, broad-shouldered physique, lithe stride and soothing, modulated deep voice should have drawn women to him like moths to a flame.

Jacob opened the passenger-side door and extended his arms. Placing her hands on his shoulders, Ana found herself cradled to his hard chest before he slowly lowered her feet to the ground. "You can go in now and look around while I bring in your bags."

She walked in through the side door, finding herself in a space that doubled as a pantry, laundry room and a place where Jacob had stored tool boxes, fishing rods and other boating equipment. A trio of bright orange life vests hung from hooks on the wall along with two racing bikes suspended from a rack. She then entered an all-white state-of-the-art kitchen. Beyond the kitchen was a living/dining room with a vaulted ceiling. A curving black wrought-iron staircase led to a loft. All of the floors on the first level were gleaming black slate, a shocking contrast to the lighter colored furnishings.

The house was airy, filled with an abundance of light, and spotless, and Ana wondered perhaps if Jacob employed a cleaning service. Ceiling fans in the living and dining rooms turned on at the lowest speed, dispelled the build-up of heat. She heard barking and went to investigate. She'd grown up with a menagerie of pets, but the condo where she now lived did not allow pets of any kind.

Making her way to the back of the house, she stared through French doors at a magnificent German shepherd locked in a large crate under a black-and-white-striped awning. She'd just unlocked the doors and opened them when Jacob's command stopped her.

"Don't go near him!"

She turned, seeing the frown between his eyes. "Why not?"

"He'll hurt you."

Ana froze. "What do you mean he'll hurt me?"

"If he doesn't know you, he'll attack."

She blinked once. "Why would you want to keep a dog like that around?"

Jacob shifted her bags under his arms. "He doesn't belong to me. I'm watching him for a friend who went on a fishing trip."

"Is that why you keep him locked up?"

"I only put him in the crate because you're here."

"You can't keep him caged just because I'm here, Jacob. That's cruel."

"After he gets used to your scent you'll be all right."

"How long will that take?" she asked.

"It shouldn't take more than a couple of days."

"That's two days too long."

Jacob's frown deepened. "What do you want me to do? Open the cage and when he goes for your throat shoot him?"

Ana felt her temper rising and counted slowly to herself. She didn't want to say something that she would later come to regret. "No. I don't want you to shoot him."

"If that's the case, then please let me handle this situation *my* way. As a matter of fact every decision I'll make for as long as you'll reside here will be to protect you. If you decide to challenge me, then I'll call Diego and have him take you to Brazil."

The seconds ticked as she stared at him. "Why are you mentioning Brazil?" she asked, whispering.

"That's where you were headed if I hadn't offered to let you stay with me. What's the matter?" Jacob taunted. "Cat got your tongue?"

Clenching her teeth, seething with anger, Ana stiffened as if she'd been struck across the face. It had been less than an hour since the jet had touched down in the Keys and she knew it wasn't going to be easy sharing a roof with Jacob.

And she had no idea that her family had considered sending her to stay with her cousin Regina Cole-Spencer.

Ana had been to Salvador da Bahia for Carnivale. Regina and her husband, pediatric-microbiologist Aaron Spencer, lived on a coffee plantation in the middle of what looked like a jungle. After partying nonstop for days, she'd return to their beautiful estate, collapsing in exhaustion until it was time to return to the States. She didn't think she would survive living in Bahia for an extended visit. Although she spoke fluent Spanish, there was a lot of Portuguese that she did not understand.

"Can you please show me to my room?" She wasn't going to give Jacob the satisfaction of acknowledging that he'd won.

"I take it you're staying and you're also willing to follow my orders?"

She lifted her chin and met his eyes with a smile that did not quite reach hers. "Yes, it does."

Jacob chuckled under his breath. "I thought you'd see it my way." He headed toward the staircase, leaving her to follow. "I fired the maid and that means you'll have to make your bed, do your own laundry and pick up after yourself."

Ana stared at the bright green leaves on his black-and-yellow shirt. "I don't know how to do laundry."

He stopped on the landing, staring at her in shock. "Who does your laundry?"

"I send it out. I call concierge and arrange for it to be picked up."

Jacob shook his head as if he couldn't believe what he was hearing. "Can you at least clean?"

She gave him a look of unadulterated innocence. "No."

"I suppose you have a cleaning service?" She nodded. "What do you know how to do?"

Her expression brightened. "I can cook. Very well," Ana added when he gave her a skeptical look. "My parents were both raised with household help who cleaned and did laundry. However, both know how to cook. My mother's skills are exceptional and she taught all her children to cook so they wouldn't have to rely on someone to feed them."

"Okay," he drawled after a pause. "Let's make a deal."

"What kind of deal?" she asked.

"I'll clean and do laundry while you cook."

"Who cleans now?"

He smiled. "I do. I don't like strangers in my home. Come, Princess. Let's get you settled. And because it's the first night at the Jones motel I'll do the cooking."

Ana followed Jacob into a large sun-filled room with white furniture. The pristine color was offset by pillows, seat cushions and the bed dressing in tropical colors of peach, orange and kiwi-green. She knew instinctually that a woman had decorated Jacob's house, because it claimed a soft touch and everything was chosen with a discerning eye for the climate and locale.

"Do I have time to take a shower and change into something cooler?" She had to get out of the jeans and T-shirt she'd hastily thrown on when Diego told her she was leaving Boca Raton.

"Sure," Jacob replied. "The bathroom is the door on the right. The walk-in closet is to the left. I'll bring your other bags up and leave them outside the door."

"What's for dinner?" she asked when he turned to leave.

"It's a surprise," he answered.

And you're quite the surprise, Ana mused. She didn't know what to expect when told she would have a U.S. Marshal protecting her, but she hadn't expected someone whose moods ran hot and cold as if flipping a switch. He laughed, frowned, joked and then had become deadly serious when he talked about shooting the dog.

He'd barked commands like a drill sergeant, expecting her follow them without question. Well, she would do his bidding and when the time came for her to return to Boca Raton she would do so without a backward glance.

"How do you know if I don't have food allergies?"

"Diego told me you didn't have any. I know everything about you, Ana Juanita Cole, so let's try and cooperate with each other, and I'll try and make your stay a pleasant one because that's what I promised your cousin. I'll see you later."

Ana stared at the spot where Jacob had been after he'd left the bedroom, softly closing the door behind him. She smiled. He'd said cooperate and she would, because she would make certain to limit their direct contact to meals. Not only had she packed enough clothes to last a month. She had also packed a number of books from her to-be-read list. When Jason had given her a tablet for Christmas he'd downloaded it with all of her favorite titles, and she was figuratively in hog heaven. However, she only used the electronic device when on vacation. Reclining on the beach under an umbrella, reading and sipping a potent concoction had become her guilty pleasure.

Living with Jacob until the person who'd attempted to kill her was apprehended was not what she deemed a vacation. Instead of bringing the tablet, Ana had decided holding a book would send a signal to Jacob that she didn't want to be bothered or disturbed.

What she didn't want to believe was that her life was now on hold because some maniac had taken out a hit on her. She'd stopped at the hospital to see Tyler, and Ana couldn't believe that he could joke that the Coles were tough men and it would take more than a high-powered bullet to take them out. He'd laughed when she'd wanted to cry.

In two weeks she was to go on vacation with several of her college friends. They'd arranged to charter a sloop, using it as their hotel, and sail down to Puerto Rico for ten days of complete hedonism. However, they would have to go without her while she was on what amounted to house arrest in the Florida Keys.

Chapter 3

Jacob carried the last two bags up the staircase, leaving them outside the door as promised. He hadn't lied to Ana when he said he knew about her. Diego had given him particulars on her, while confirming assertions that she was more than formidable as the head of the record company. Many of the clients preferred dealing with Jason because of his low-key, relaxed demeanor, whereas Ana's in-your-face approach was a lot more intimidating. His friend had also confided that he'd asked Ana to come to work for the family-owned import/export, real estate conglomerate, but she'd declined, saying she preferred the ongoing excitement and changes within the music industry.

And Jacob wasn't fooled by her willingness to follow his demands. Ana was used to giving orders, not taking them, and that meant he couldn't afford to let down his guard when interacting with her. Fortunately there was enough room in the two-story house where they wouldn't have to bump into each other at every turn. Ana would have the run of the entire second floor because he planned to sleep in the alcove off the family room at the rear of the house. The small but cozy space also contained a half bath that was just a little more than a water closet. There was just enough space for a shower and commode. Once Jacob had decided to utilize the alcove, he'd purchased a queen-size storage bed with drawer space for linens and several changes of clothes.

He wasn't too concerned about break-ins because the property was monitored by surveillance cameras. And like Ana, he hoped the shooter would be caught sooner rather than later. The longer the perpetrator was on the loose the lower the odds of capturing him.

Returning to the kitchen, Jacob stored his holstered handgun in a drawer under the island countertop, then opened the refrigerator and removed a labeled package of fish filets he'd taken out of the freezer before leaving for the airport. After he'd closed up his Miami apartment he'd driven to a local supermarket to buy enough food to stock the pantry and refrigerator for at least two weeks. He'd planned to alternate cooking for himself and dining in some of his favorite restaurants in the Keys. That was before he'd gotten the call from Diego.

Jacob still had to decide how much he wanted to expose Ana to the public because he wanted her to keep a low profile. Confining her to the house was certain to push both of them over the edge. And if they did go out, then a hat and sunglasses for her would be the norm rather than the exception.

A smile parted his lips when he recalled her saying she'd planned to run away from home to live in Key West. He didn't live in Key West, but it was close enough for him to drive her there to show her some of the historic cottages and restored century-old Conch houses. With the influx of tourists mingling with the locals they were certain to blend in enough to enjoy the nightlife.

Over the next forty minutes he busied himself uncovering

the deck furniture, hosing down the deck, and then opened several umbrellas, positioning one near the table and the other two behind cushioned recliners. Jacob tried, but he was unsuccessful in erasing the image of Ana's eyes whenever she gave him a direct stare. There was something about her eyes that reflected a boldness and wisdom that made him believe she was much older than thirty-three. Perhaps, he mused, it was the role she'd taken on as CEO of a very successful recording label. If she had been any woman other than David Cole's daughter she never would've been able to achieve the business success Ana had accomplished since she'd assumed control of Serenity Records. Jacob smiled. Her father had taught her well. He checked on the large dog in the crate that lifted his head from between his paws with his approach.

Bending slightly, he said, "Don't worry, boy. I hope to have you out of there sometime tomorrow."

Jacob had removed the fish from the packaging and had placed them in a bowl of cold water when the soft chiming of the telephone garnered his attention. He punched the speaker feature on the wall phone before the third ring.

"Hello."

"Jacob. It's your mother."

"How are you, Mrs. Deavers?"

There was a slight pause before Gloria Deavers's soft voice came through the speaker. "Why are you so formal?"

Resting a hip against the countertop, Jacob crossed his arms over his chest and stared up at the skylight in the kitchen. "You are Mrs. Deavers, aren't you?"

"I've been married to Henry for almost fifteen years, and yet you still haven't let me forget it."

"Mom, I know you didn't call me to talk about *your* husband."

"You're right. I called because when I contacted your office they told me you were on vacation leave. Are you all right?"

The lines of tension in Jacob's face softened. "I'm fine. It was mandated that if I didn't take at least half of my accrued vacation, then I would lose it."

"How much time is that?"

"Eight weeks."

There was another pause from Gloria. "When was the last time you took a vacation?"

Jacob shook his head although his mother couldn't see him. "I can't remember. It has to be more than five or six years." He'd accrued not only vacation leave, but also compensatory time.

"Maybe I'll take a few days off and come down to see you."

Now it was Jacob's turn to find himself at a loss for words. "When do you want to come?"

"It probably won't be until mid-July. That is if you don't have anything planned for that time," Gloria said quickly.

He quickly calculated. It was now the second week in June and he'd hoped it wouldn't take six weeks to catch the man who'd attempted to kill Ana. "That sounds good, Mom. However, if my plans change, then I'll call you."

"I know you don't like me asking, but I'm going to do it anyway. Are you seeing anyone?"

"No, Mom."

"Why not?"

"Because I don't have the time. At least not right now," he added truthfully. Even if he wanted to he couldn't see anyone—not with Ana living with him.

"When are you going to have time, son? Thirty is in the rearview mirror and you're fast approaching forty and you're still single. I would like to have a couple of grandkids before I die."

Exhaling an audible sigh, Jacob closed his eyes. Every

time he had a conversation with his mother invariably the topic of his single status would come up. He wanted to tell her he had yet to celebrate his thirty-sixth birthday, but then she would come back with "I happen to know the year, day and hour you were born."

"You'll be the first to know when I find the woman I want to spend the rest of my life with."

"Jacob?"

"What is it, Mom?"

"Nelson was picked up by the police yesterday."

"Picked up or arrested?"

"He was arrested."

"What did he do this time?" His stepbrother couldn't stay out of trouble if someone paid him a million dollars.

"They claim he and some other boys stole a car and then robbed a convenience store. A cashier was shot—"

"Stop right there, Mom," Jacob interrupted. "I'm not getting involved with this. Nelson Deavers is trouble and the sooner you and Henry accept that fact the better you'll sleep at night. The last time I intervened and got the police to drop the charges Nelson promised me he wouldn't get into trouble again. Stealing cars and shooting people are not misdemeanors and that means he's going to prison. Tell Henry I'm sorry, but his boy is on his own." He saw movement out the side of his eye and picked up the telephone receiver when Ana walked into the kitchen. "Mom, can I call you back later?"

"Of course you can. Please don't forget to call me."

His eyes met those of the petite woman in a tank top, shorts and flip-flops before glancing at the swell of breasts in the revealing top. Jacob didn't want to believe that an oversize T-shirt and jeans had concealed a lush, tiny, curvy, compact body. Even Ana's legs and feet were perfect.

"I won't." Jacob hung up, unaware that he'd been staring. Ana's hand went to her head as she attempted to fluff up the short, wet hair clinging to her scalp. "I'm sorry to intrude."

"It's all right. I was going to hang up anyway." Even if Ana hadn't come into the kitchen Jacob had planned to end the conversation he had with his mother. It hurt Jacob that she only called when she needed his help with her stepsons. "Did you need something?"

She nodded. "I don't have enough hangers."

He forced himself not to look at the outfit that showed a little too much skin while hoping Ana wasn't going to make it a habit of prancing around in next to nothing because it was going to make it hard for him to remember why she was living with him.

"How many do you need?"

"I'm not certain, but it has to be at least another twenty."

"What?"

A slight smile touched the corners of Ana's mouth when she saw his shocked expression. "I'll take ten, but that would mean doubling up some of my things."

"I have a few. But if you need more then you'll have to wait until tomorrow when I go out."

Ana lifted her shoulders. "I suppose I'll have to wait to hang up what's leftover."

"Why did you bring so many clothes?"

She took several steps, bringing them closer. "I didn't know whether you'd have a washing machine—"

"It wouldn't have mattered if I did or didn't, because you claim you don't know how to use it." Jacob saw a wave of color darken her face. "If you want I can show you how to use the washer and dryer." When Ana stared at him, he thought of the saying that if looks could kill then he definitely would've stopped breathing. "Suit yourself," he mumbled under his breath, "if you don't want to grow up."

"I'm definitely grown, Jacob. I can't get any more grown, just older," she retorted.

"Grown women I know do laundry, shop for groceries, cook and clean up after themselves."

Ana didn't intend to get into a verbal confrontation with Jacob over a lifestyle that had served her well with a minimum of angst. She knew who and what she was—privileged—and she wasn't about to apologize to anyone about it, and especially not to him.

"Can you please tell me or show me where the hangers are?"

"You'll find more in the bedroom across from the bathroom."

Ana flashed a dimpled smile. "Thanks." Spinning on her toes, she turned and walked out of the kitchen.

Jacob felt as if he'd been punched hard in the solar plexus when he gaped numbly at the firm roundness of her bottom in the revealing shorts. There was hardly enough fabric to conceal her buttocks.

"Ana."

She stopped but didn't turn around. "Yes?"

He opened his mouth, but the words wouldn't come out. Jacob wanted to tell his houseguest that what she considered something cooler was downright indecent. And it wasn't that he was a prude—far from it—but seeing her dress like that made him aware of how long it'd been since he'd slept with a woman.

"Would you be opposed to dining outdoors?" he said instead.

Ana peered at him over her shoulder, smiling. "Of course not, Jacob. In fact I was going to suggest it. As soon as I finish hanging up my clothes I'll be down to help you put dinner together."

"Make certain you put on sunscreen before we go outside. You've exposed a lot of skin," he explained when she gave him a questioning look, "and the UV index is quite high today."

A frown marred her smooth forehead. "I didn't bring any. Do you happen to have some?"

Jacob's smile was triumphant. "No, I don't." It faded as quickly as it'd appeared. "Did you bring a cover-up with you?"

Ana chewed her lip. "No. In fact I didn't bring a swimsuit. But you may be able to help me out."

"How's that?" Jacob asked.

"If you're willing to give up your rather garish shirt it could double as a cover-up."

He glanced down at his shirt. "My shirt may be a little colorful, but it's hardly garish."

Ana bit back a smile. "Surely you jest. It's loud and gaudy."

His eyebrows lifted a fraction. "It's garish, gaudy and loud, yet you want to wear it?"

She extended her hand. "I'll take it now if you don't mind."

"You want me to take it off now?"

"Why not? It's only going to take me a few minutes to hang up the rest of my clothes before I come back and set the table. You do use the table on the deck, don't you?"

"Of course I do," Jacob countered. "I'm not into lap trays." Ana reached out to unbutton his shirt, but he caught her wrist, holding it in a firm but gentle grip. "I'll give you another shirt and I'll make certain it's somewhat less loud."

Coward! Jacob silently berated himself. Why couldn't he just tell her that seeing her dressed that way made him uncomfortable? In fact he was quite turned on by her curves. First the call from his mother had disturbed him, and now it was seeing a woman with whom he would spend days or perhaps even weeks with who thought nothing of dressing provocatively that had him on edge.

"I'm not going to strip for you, Ana. Go upstairs and hang up your clothes. And when you come down I'll have something for you to put on."

Ana wrested her wrist from his loose grip with a minimum of effort. "Don't ever do that again."

Jacob's expression became a mask of stone. "Do what?"

Going on tiptoe, she thrust her face close enough for him to feel her moist breath on his jaw. "Talk to me as if I were either a child or an idiot."

Seeing her close-up, inhaling the subtle scent of her perfume made him aware of things that he hadn't noticed before. Her eyes weren't dark, but a clear brown with glints of gold. The color amber came to mind. She was short, much shorter than she appeared because of her slimness, and her damp hair was coal-black, the perfect contrast to her olive complexion. Not only was she beautiful, she was exotic.

It was Jacob's turn to swallow the acerbic words poised on the tip of his tongue. Diego had cautioned him that Ana was going to be defiant and challenging. She'd chosen a career dominated by men and she'd somehow learned to navigate the testosterone-filled waters with relative ease. That is until now. She'd run into a juggernaut when dealing with Basil Irvine, because apparently the man had not taken kindly to a woman besting him.

"I am not one of your employees or a performer in the Serenity Records stable, so however you interpret what I say to you is a personal problem, Ana. I'm also not accustomed to dealing with spoiled brats who expect people to genuflect before them. I am giving up the next two months of my life, where I'd planned to sleep as late as I want, fish, sail down to the islands and if I feel the need for female companionship, then I'd find a woman to spend some quality time with who won't bitch and moan because things aren't going her way.

"I promised Diego that I would look after you, and I always keep my promises. Not to do so would make me less than honorable. And that's not going to happen because you decide to throw a hissy fit. Now, please finish putting your clothes away, and when you come back I'll have something for you to put on that will give you some protection from the sun." He paused, watching the expressions on Ana's face change from anger to shock. "Does this meet with your approval, Princess?"

Ana engaged in what could only be interpreted as a staredown when she glared at Jacob. Not only was he arrogant, but also insufferable, and she wondered how long she would be able to live with him before calling her father and telling him she was willing to go to Brazil. It wasn't as if she didn't have other options, because she did. There was her cousin's horse farm in the western part of Virginia. Security on the farm was so tight, no one entered or left without being monitored.

If not Nicholas, then she could stay with another cousin in a remote region of North Carolina. Celia and her husband, FBI special agent Gavin Faulkner lived in a mountain retreat near the Tennessee border. In fact she had family members all over the country where she could stay in relative anonymity. Her brother Gabriel lived on Cape Cod with his ex-DEA agent wife, her sister's husband was a training specialist for the CIA, and there were enough former military intelligence relatives to set up their own agency. But her father and cousin had decided U.S. Marshal Jacob Jones would be the better candidate to protect her in the States because he wasn't family.

She continued to glare at Jacob. "I'm immune to bullying," she whispered, then turned on her heels and walked out of the kitchen, feeling the heat from his gaze on her back. If her host was looking for a fight, then she was going to disappoint him and not give in to his goading. If Ana had learned anything in life, it was how to deal with men with enormous egos coupled with an overabundance of arrogance.

First and foremost there had been her grandfather. Samuel Claridge Cole put the *a* in arrogance. Purportedly the first black billionaire—his actual wealth a closely guarded family secret—he used intelligence and intimidation to build his empire. His drive for success was passed along to his offspring who refused to accept defeat. And for Ana it was the same. She wasn't *that bitch, skirt* or any other derogative term attributed to women in positions of power, but someone ready and willing to conduct business in the most professional way possible.

She didn't entertain gossip, read the tabloids or grant interviews. What she did do was attend most music industry award shows with her brother, while wearing haute couture and mouthing the appropriate phrases. Once she'd assumed control of Serenity Records her love life and her personal life were kept out of the spotlight, leading entertainment journalists to create whatever spin needed to sell magazines or increase TV ratings.

If Jacob thought he was going to browbeat her or break her will, then he was in for a shocker. After all, she was a Cole woman and they ruled while their men served.

Ana found the hangers in the master bedroom's walk-in closet. Heavy mahogany furniture, furnishings and accent pillows in dramatic colors of chocolate, sand-beige and seafoam-green pulled it all together. She found the space as masculine as its occupant.

A wide smile crinkled the skin around her eyes. She'd misjudged Jacob. He had a good sense for fashion. She counted at least half a dozen beautifully tailored suits in different colors. Racks held shoes ranging from slip-ons to wing tips. Shirts with monogrammed cuffs, slacks and jackets were hung neatly on racks along with a collection of ties. When, she mused, did he have the time to wear the tailored clothing and where? It was apparent her protector wasn't what he presented to her.

He claimed he knew everything about her when she knew nothing about him other than his name, occupation and marital status. "Okay, Mr. Jones," she whispered as she gathered the remaining hangers, "now it's time for me to find out what you're all about."

Ana returned to the bedroom she would occupy during her stay in Long Key, hung up the remaining garments tossed on the bed and then retraced her steps along a catwalk to the staircase leading to the first floor.

She had to admit to herself that she liked the layout of the house. Unlike many homes built in the state it contained two levels. Her parents' home was constructed in three one-story sections. They occupied one section, which included a guest wing. Four bedroom suites, one for each of their children, took up another section, and the third contained a state-of-the-art recording studio and what had been Serenity's corporate office before David moved it to a Boca Raton downtown office building.

Although she knew Jason was more than capable of running the company, Ana wanted to be there just to feel the pulsing energy from prerecorded music playing softly throughout the offices. It hadn't mattered whether it was soft jazz, R&B, blues, pop, country, classical, hip hop or occasionally gospel, Serenity was always about music.

Her thoughts returned to her host and protector. Jacob had admitted he cleaned his own house and she had discerned at least one thing about him: he was a neat-freak. The floors were spotless; there was no dust on any flat surface and even her adjoining spa-inspired bathroom was impeccable. It was no wonder he didn't have a wife or girlfriend. He was more than capable of taking care of his own needs. And she didn't want to believe he could be so vulgar to mention that if he needed a woman to take care of his physical needs, then he'd just go out and find one to spend some quality time with. She would never go out and pick up a man if she felt the need for sexual release. because engaging in risky behavior was against her principles. It didn't mean she didn't have urges, but that was only when she was sexually active. But lately she'd undergone a sexual drought, because she loathed hooking up with a man just for sex. The women she'd planned to accompany on their vacation to Puerto Rico had made a pact that they would sleep with at least one man before returning to the mainland. She'd been the only one who hadn't agreed. They hadn't begrudged her for not going along with their scheme, and that's why she'd remained friends with them for so long. The motto between the five women was: judge not. They were very supportive of one another, and whenever one had a crisis they came together as one to provide emotional support.

Well, right about now Ana needed their support more than at any time in her life. Just seeing their faces or hearing their voices was like a soothing sedative. She'd promised Jacob she would help prepare dinner, but first things first. She had to call one of her girlfriends and let her know she would not be accompanying them to Puerto Rico.

Jacob was at the cooking island, chopping onions and red and green bell peppers. Several cloves of garlic were next to the colorful, finely minced veggies. His head popped up when she walked into the kitchen. Ana noticed that he'd exchanged his Hawaiian shirt for a white tee. Her jaw dropped, and mouth gaping she stared mutely at the breadth of his broad shoulders and muscular upper body. She was transfixed, watching the flex of muscle in his bulging biceps as he deftly diced strips of peppers.

Smiling, Jacob gestured to his colorful shirt hanging on the back of a high stool. "You can either use the loud and garish shirt, or there's a tee on the seat of the stool."

Ana forced her feet to move as she walked woodenly to pick up the T-shirt and pulled it on. The sleeves came past her elbows and the hem inches above her knees. "It's just a trifle bit large."

Jacob went back to cutting the garlic into minute pieces. "It's enough to protect your skin."

"It's the perfect nightshirt."

"I have more if you need nightshirts."

Ana walked over and stood next to him. He'd exchanged his jeans for a pair of khaki walking shorts. "No, thanks. I have my own." She stared at his large hands with long, slender fingers, noticing his nails were groomed. One of her pet peeves was men who either bit their nails or didn't file them. Jacob's were smooth and square-cut. "I'd like to use your phone to call someone."

He stopped chopping, placing the sharp knife on the butcher block countertop. "Whoever you talk to, please do not divulge where you are."

Resisting the urge to salute him, Ana wrinkled her nose instead. "I think I know the drill."

"My number will not be displayed on their caller ID, so they won't be able to call you back," he called out as she walked to the wall phone.

"That's okay," she said over her shoulder. Resting a hip against the countertop, she removed the phone from its cradle and punched in the number of her friend who operated her business out of her home and was available 24/7.

Ana counted off the rings before she heard the familiar greeting. "Good afternoon. You have reached Creative Editorial Services. This is Samantha."

"Sam, Ana."

"Ana! Where the hell are you? And why haven't you been answering your cell? You know I've been worried sick when I saw the news about someone shooting your cousin."

She couldn't help smiling. She'd met Samantha Mickelson when both were in the same college freshman English class. The fast-talking former book editor was open, friendly, spontaneous and her best friend. Ana had graduated and enrolled in law school while Samantha moved to New York City with the dream of becoming an editor. She'd managed to secure a position with a major publisher, working her way up from editorial assistant to an associate editor.

She discovered a brilliant mystery writer when she picked up his unsolicited manuscript from a slush pile and the rest was history. Their relationship went from editor and writer to husband and wife. Unfortunately for Sam her husband took his overnight success a step further when he literally became a literary rock star. Paul was always surrounded by groupies and that escalated rumors of him cheating to a tabloid exposé with photos of him in a hotel room with a barely legal nubile television actress.

Samantha had him served with divorce papers and, following a quiet divorce with a generous settlement, she returned to Florida and set up a freelance editorial service. Her reputation had preceded her, so she was never at a loss for clients wishing to break into publishing.

"I'm okay."

"Where are you? I called your folks and your mom wouldn't give me any information. I also called Jason at his office and he was just as mum. What's up?"

Ana and Jacob exchanged a long, penetrating stare. She placed her hand on the mouthpiece. "Can you please give me a few minutes of privacy?" she whispered.

Jacob shook his head. "Nope. My house. My phone. My rules. I get to monitor all incoming and outgoing telephone calls."

She glared at him. "That is so rude."

"That is your opinion," he countered.

"Ana, are you still there?"

She resisted the urge to suck her teeth—a habit her mother detested, and turned her back instead. "I'm still here. Look, Sam, I'm not going to be able to go down to Puerto Rico with you. And I was so looking forward to this trip."

There came a pregnant pause. "Is something going on that you can't talk about?"

Samantha was one of the most perceptive women Ana knew. There were times when she'd told the book editor that she could double as a psychic. Unfortunately, it wasn't the same when it came to Samantha's own future.

"Yes."

There was another pause. "Is someone there listening in on what you're saying?"

"Yes."

"The fact that no one in your family is talking and you can't tell me where you are reminds me of a mystery novel. I get it and respect that, but the only thing I want to know is if you're safe."

"Affirmative again," Ana answered, lowering her voice.

"Well, that makes me feel better and hopefully I can get a full night's sleep without waking up every few hours thinking about you. You know you're my girl, Ana. I never would've made it through my divorce without your support."

"Yes, you would've, Sam."

Samantha's husky laugh came through the earpiece. "I'm not going to debate that because I know I'll lose. I love you to death, Ana, but if there is anything I can do just call."

"I love you, too, but right now I'm in a very good place emotionally. If anything changes, then you'll be the first to know. Give my best to the rest of the gang and tell them I'll be with them in spirit."

Samantha laughed again. "We'll be certain to raise a couple of glasses of mojitos, piña coladas, cosmos and one or two extra-dirty martinis to toast your absence."

"And don't forget Jack and Coke."

"Please don't mention Jack and Coke. That's what got me into trouble where I'd lost my mind and wound up married to that fool."

Ana smiled. "Then scratch the Jack and Coke." She

quickly sobered when she shifted and saw Jacob frowning at her. "Look, Sam, I have to go. I'll call you in a couple of weeks." She ended the call, replaced the receiver on the cradle and then turned to meet her protector's angry scowl. "What's the matter now?"

The seconds ticked as they engaged in what could only be determined as a stare-down. Ana knew instinctually that Jacob hadn't wanted her to make phone calls, but there was no way he could completely shut her off from the outside world.

"I would prefer that you not make any calls, and if you do then limit them to a minute or less."

A smug smile touched her lips. So, she was right. He didn't want her using the phone. "That call was necessary because I had to tell my friend that my vacation plans had changed."

Crossing his arms over his chest, Jacob continued to stare at her, brows drawing together as he continued to frown. "What you're going to have to accept is that your entire life will change until the person or persons who want you eliminated is either caught or killed."

A shiver eddied up Ana's spine at the same time she closed her eyes. *Killed.* The single word was uttered as softly as a pleasant greeting. But then she couldn't afford to forget that the man with whom she would live with for who knew how long carried a firearm and had been trained to use it with deadly force when necessary. And she said a silent prayer that whoever was responsible for shooting Tyler would be apprehended alive. After all, dead people couldn't talk.

It hadn't been a week since that fateful day when she stood in the restaurant parking lot with her cousin, but Ana wanted it over. Perhaps when she went to sleep and woke up she would realize it'd been a bad dream. That she'd read one of the mystery novels Samantha had edited and everything that'd happened was because of an overactive imagination.

But she knew she couldn't blink and will it away because of the incredibly virile man standing only feet away. Despite the turmoil going on in her life that had impacted her family she did not want to think about sharing a roof with a man as attractive as Jacob. Why, she mused, couldn't he be short, fat, balding and smelling of liniment? But he wasn't, and that made her uncomfortable. She also wondered how long it would take before she would go completely stir-crazy from the inactivity.

Ana was used to getting up every morning and working out in her condominium's health club before she prepared to go into her office. She and Jason alternated chairing bi-weekly staff meetings where they brought everyone employed by the recording company up on what was going on with their artists. And once she'd taken control as CEO she'd established an open-door policy. There hadn't been a time when she did not entertain someone's suggestion, whether she believed it would or wouldn't benefit the company, whenever the executives held their brainstorming sessions.

"I know you see me as an imposition—"

"You're not," Jacob said, interrupting her. "If I thought of you as an imposition, then I never would've agreed to let you come and stay here."

"Why did you agree?"

He smiled, the expression reminding Ana of a ray of sunshine warming her face and she wanted to tell him that it was something he should do more often.

"Because there are very few things I wouldn't do for Diego."

Her eyebrows lifted at this disclosure. "Did you and Diego go to college together?" She'd asked because her cousin had attended college in Miami.

"No. Diego has three years on me."

Ana quickly did the math. Diego was going to celebrate his thirty-ninth birthday, so he had to be at least thirty-five or six.

"I'll be thirty-six September seventeenth," Jacob confirmed.

Her dimpled smile was infectious when he returned it with one of his own. "You read minds?" she asked.

He lowered his arms. "No, but I've noticed that you bite down on your lip when you appear to be thinking about something."

Ana's delicate jaw dropped. "I can't believe I'm that transparent."

"You really aren't. If you were, then I'd know what you're thinking."

"You really don't want to know what I'm thinking," she retorted.

There another lengthy pause as Jacob took several steps, stopping in front of her, while his gaze met and fused with hers. "I don't care. Nothing you say, or if you decide to throw a hissy fit, will get me to change my mind."

"What if I decide to seduce you? Will that get you to change your mind?"

She felt a rush of heat settle in her face as soon as the query rolled off her tongue, and Ana didn't want to believe where it had come from. She experienced a measure of redemption when he stared at her, apparently in shock.

"If you'd hoped to shock me, then you just did. But, even if I did permit you to seduce me nothing would change, Princess."

"That's where you're wrong. Everything would change." She had no intention of seducing him or any other man, but Ana was willing to bet her fortune that if they were to have an intimate relationship everything between them would change.

Chuckling softly, he winked at her. "We'll just have to wait and see, won't we?" His teasing mood changed like quicksilver. "And there will be no plans of seduction from either one of us. Diego asked me to protect, not take advantage of you."

"Do you always do what my cousin asks you to do?"

He shrugged a shoulder. "Within reason, yes. And the same goes for him."

"You're that tight." Ana's question was a statement.

"Very tight," Jacob confirmed. "Now that we've settled the notion of you trying to get one over on me, I'm going outside. Either you can stay here or sit outside and relax."

Chapter 4

Ana followed Jacob to the deck, her gaze scanning the spacious area. It was the perfect place to begin or end the day. Smiling, she inhaled a lungful of saltwater air. The views here were better than the ones from her condo. Lowering her body to the recliner, she turned on her belly, rested her head on folded arms and then closed her eyes.

Even though she felt a modicum of peace for the first time in days, Ana didn't want to accept that she was like someone who'd entered the Witness Protection Program. Cut off from her family, she couldn't go wherever she wanted, and she couldn't talk to whomever she wanted with Jacob listening in on the call. Prisoners were granted more rights than she was. At least they had privileges that included family visits and the right to confer with their attorneys.

Thoughts of her temporary exile were supplanted with the heart-stopping images of Tyler lying motionless on the ground, bleeding from his chest wound. His wife had kept an around-the-clock bedside vigil. Dana had put on a brave face when she gave Tyler an update on the antics of their children. She told Tyler he had to get well and come home and rescue their pets. Their children had given their chocolate-brown miniature poodles Mohawk haircuts, then painted their toenails fluorescent pink and green.

Ana wanted cry, scream or even throw something, but that would indicate weakness or lack of control, and for her that wasn't a thought or an option. As the youngest of four she always had to fight to assert herself, especially in a family where boys were groomed from birth to go into the family business, while the girls were left to their own career choice. The tradition had begun with her uncle Martin who'd succeeded Samuel Cole, the founder of ColeDiz International, Ltd. as CEO. Her father, David, gave up a musical career to take over the reins for nine years before relinquishing the responsibility to his nephew. Timothy Cole-Thomas ran the company for thirty-five years before stepping down at sixty.

Diego had broken with tradition when he'd asked her to come and work with him, but Ana loved the music industry and working with Jason. And for the first time she wondered, if she'd gone to work for ColeDiz would Tyler be in a hospital and would she be hiding out in the Keys until the person or persons responsible for the shooting were apprehended.

Twenty minutes later the aroma of grilling food wafted to her nostrils. Ana turned over and sat up. Jacob had put on another cap, this one newer and bearing a Miami Heat logo. He stood at the gas grill, basting ears of corn. "Do you need help with anything?"

Jacob's head popped up. "I'm good here, but I'd appreciate it if you'd set the table."

She pushed off the recliner, giving him a warm, friendly smile for the first time. "No problem."

It took several trips, but Ana brought out dishes, silver and glassware. The task would've been easier or faster if she'd had a serving cart. For someone who lived alone a cart wasn't a necessity, but necessary when entertaining. Her entertaining extended to having her mother and father over for dinner. She never assumed they were available because their social calendar was filled with an endless list of charitable fundraisers, political luncheons and dinner dances, and traveling abroad at least once a year. They'd talked about retirement for years, and when the opportunity presented itself they fully took advantage of every minute.

"Do you have a tablecloth?" she asked Jacob. He looked at her as if she'd asked for radioactive material.

"I hosed down the glass on the table so we don't need a tablecloth."

Ana made a mental note that if she were to go shopping with him she would buy a tablecloth. She'd given Jacob her credit cards, but she still had some cash in her wallet. "What are we drinking?"

"Mojitos." He gave her a questioning look. "If you don't drink, then I'll make one without the rum."

She wrinkled her nose. "I think I can handle the rum."

Half an hour later Ana sat across the table from Jacob enjoying the grilled, dry-rubbed red snapper stuffed with onion and peppers and topped with mango salsa. The spices lingered on her tongue until washed away with the expertly made mojito. A Greek salad and grilled corn with red chili butter rounded out what had become an incredible meal.

She raised her glass in a salute. "Hail to the chef."

Jacob modestly inclined his head. "I try."

"You do more than try," Ana countered. "Who taught you to cook?"

"My dad. He didn't know how to boil water before he married my mother. After a while he was a better cook than she was and she is definitely no slouch in the kitchen."

Propping her elbow on the table, Ana cradled her chin on the heel of her hand and closed her eyes. If the reason as to why she was hiding out in the Keys wasn't so serious, she would've believed her teenage dream had become a reality. She'd run away, believing she could spend the rest of her life living in the Keys, and apparently she'd gotten her wish, albeit on a temporary basis. Instead of running away, she'd been spirited away on a private jet. And she wouldn't spend the rest of her life here, only as long as it took to locate the person or persons who were attempting to eliminate her.

When her father was the head of the company he hadn't had to deal with some of the problems she'd faced. During his tenure the label's artists had problems with drugs and indiscriminate sexual encounters, not the high-profile feuds between artists and competing labels. The musicians during her father's era who'd died much too young either overdosed on drugs or committed suicide. Those in her generation usually met their end in a hail of bullets. Whatever happened to men settling their beef with fists instead of bullets?

She opened her eyes, staring at the colorful orchids growing in wild abandon. Palm and mangrove trees, frangipani and a profusion of flowering bushes surrounding the house provided a modicum of privacy from the neighboring houses. Her gaze shifted to Jacob as he stared at her. A hint of a smile tilted the corners of her mouth.

"It's really nice here." The temperature was at least ten degrees cooler than on the mainland.

Jacob took a long swallow of his drink, staring at Ana over the rim of the glass. "I like it."

"How long have you lived here?"

He set down the glass. "I bought the house about eighteen months ago. It really wasn't habitable, so I decided to gut it and start again."

A slight frown furrowed her smooth forehead. "Wouldn't it have been easier and less expensive to buy a house in move-in condition?"

"It'd been abandoned and was in foreclosure. I felt it was as good a time as any to take advantage of my GI bill. I made the bank what I felt was a reasonable offer and they accepted it."

"You were in the military?" Jacob nodded. "Army?" she asked, continuing her questioning. He gave her a look that raised the hair on the back of her neck. "Did I say something wrong?"

"Wrong branch."

The seconds ticked as Ana mentally went through the different branches of the armed forces. "If it's not the army, then it would have to be the marines."

"You've got it."

"I should've known. Every marine I've met is beyond arrogant. The exception is my brother-in-law."

"Merrick Grayslake is corps to the marrow of his bones. The difference is he's low-key about it."

Her eyebrows shot up. "You know Merrick?" Her sister Alexandra had married the ex-marine sniper who'd been recruited by the CIA as a field operative. He retired after a life-threatening injury; years later he reapplied, this time teaching courses in intelligence training.

Jacob winked at her. "Why do you keep forgetting that I'm family?"

She narrowed her eyes. "What are you talking about?"

"I'm your cousin S.J.'s godfather. And that makes me family." Diego and Vivienne had shorted Samuel Jacob's name to S.J. to differentiate between him and Tyler's son who was also named Samuel.

"If you're family, then why haven't you come to West Palm between Christmas and New Year's when everyone gets together?"

"I'd just gotten a promotion and unfortunately I couldn't get away. Diego and I always joke about living in the same state, yet we don't get to see each other as often as we'd like."

Ana ran her forefinger around the rim of her glass. "I always try and make time for my friends. We try and get together every other month for a girls' night out."

"Girls' night out or girls gone wild?" he teased.

She wrinkled her nose. "Very funny."

"I heard you mention Jack and Coke to your *friend*."

"What you shouldn't do is listen in on my telephone conversation."

"I told you before. My house, my phone and my rules."

Ana knew arguing with Jacob would prove fruitless and she chided herself for even attempting to engage him in conversation, because invariably he would pull rank and remind her that he controlled her life.

"Thank you for reminding me," she said facetiously. Pushing to her feet, she picked up her plate, then Jacob's. "You cooked so I'll clean up the kitchen."

Jacob stood up, gathering flatware and serving dishes. "I thought you told me you didn't know how to clean."

"I don't do housework and laundry, but I do clean up after myself whenever I cook."

"You can help clear the table, but I'll put everything else away."

Together they made short work of bringing in everything off the deck. Jacob rinsed and stacked dishes in the dishwasher while Ana went back outside. Sitting in front of the crate, she stared the large dog that lay with his muzzle between his paws.

"Hey there, big boy." The shepherd's erect ears moved in response. "I know you don't want to be in there, but it's not going to take too long before we become good friends." She continued to talk to the dog, unaware that Jacob was watching the interchange when he stood peering through the screened-in door.

He went completely still when she stuck her finger through the grating to touch Baron's paw. The canine responded by licking her finger. Jacob couldn't believe the dog hadn't growled or bitten Ana. Either she was a dog whisperer or Baron had sensed she didn't pose a threat to him. The large powerful dog belonged to a security expert hired by wealthy businessmen to safeguard their families when traveling on vacation. Brian had taken a week off to go on a fishing expedition and had asked Jacob if he would take care of Baron.

"He likes you."

Ana's head popped up, she staring at Jacob watching her. "He's magnificent."

Jacob nodded and smiled. "That he is." He slid back the door, stepped out and closed it behind him. "You like dogs." The question was a statement.

"I love them. I grew up with dogs, cat, birds, fish, guinea pigs and a few lizards and turtles. The only things my parents wouldn't let us have was snakes."

His smile grew wider. "It sounds as if you had a menagerie."

"It was more like a zoo."

Jacob thought about his own childhood growing up in Miami. He'd always wanted a dog, but because of his mother's allergies that wasn't possible. "I'm going to take Baron for a walk. Would you like to come with me?"

"Yes!"

Reaching down, he cupped her elbow, assisting her to stand. "You're going to have to wear a hat and sunglasses and hopefully no one will recognize you."

Tilting her chin, Ana met his eyes. "I can think of a better disguise."

"What's that?"

"A wig."

Crossing his arms over his chest, Jacob angled his head. "I'm sorry, but I don't happen to have any hairpieces lying around," he teased.

Ana assumed a similar stance, bringing his gaze to linger

on her chest. "There has to be a beauty supply or wig shop somewhere around here."

"I'm certain there is. But where, is the question."

"Do you have a computer?" Jacob nodded. "There's your answer. You can go online and search on Google to find shops in the Keys that sell wigs and costumes."

"I'm certain we'll find a few in Key West."

Ana's eyes lit up like a child's on Christmas morning. "When do we leave?" she asked. Her voice was filled with a lightness that hadn't been there in days. And despite her always wanting to visit Key West she couldn't forget the events that had brought her to this moment.

Smiling, Jacob shook his head. Her dimpled smile took his breath away. "Do you really want to visit Key West that much?"

"Some people want to climb Everest. Others want to see the pyramids, while I want to hang out in Key West."

"Why didn't you come down once you were emancipated?"

Ana lifted her shoulders. "After a while I shrugged it off as some form of childish rebellion. Maybe I'd wanted to prove to my parents I could make it on my own."

"Even if you'd managed to live on five thousand dollars for nine years what do you think was going to happen after the money ran out?"

"I would've come into my trust fund at twenty-five."

Jacob's expressive eyebrows lifted a fraction. "Your life would've been quite different from what it is now."

"I know that," Ana said wistfully. "I doubt whether I would've become involved with the record company. But now that I am I'll never forgive myself if Tyler doesn't make a full recovery." Closing her eyes, she combed her fingers through her short hair. "Basil Irvine lied through his teeth when he said there was no bad blood between his company and Serenity. If I'd been interviewed I would've let the world know exactly what went down between us."

Reaching out, Jacob held her shoulders firmly. "Stop beating up on yourself. There was no way you could know or stop what happened. Just be grateful that your cousin wasn't killed. Judging from what I know about your family, I'm certain they'll use every resource they have to uncover who's behind the shooting. But if I had to play devil's advocate, then I'd say it could've been a random incident where someone decided to use that parking lot for target practice. After all, there are a lot of crazies roaming the streets."

Ana's eyes met his. "If you find out anything about the sniper will you tell me?"

"I will tell you whatever Diego wants you to know."

"You didn't answer my question, Jacob. I'm asking whether you intend to withhold information from me."

"And I repeat—I will tell you whatever Diego tells me to tell you." When she tried extricating herself from his loose grip his fingers tightened. "Have you thought maybe you don't need to know everything that may take place?"

Her brow furrowed. "What are you talking about?"

He didn't want to tell her that her family had hired men who were trained to extract information from the most recalcitrant captive before turning them over to the proper law enforcement agency. His hands moved from her shoulders to her waist, slightly taken aback at her body's fragility. Lowering his head, Jacob rested his chin on her head. The floral fragrance clinging to her hair wafted in his nostrils.

All of his protective instincts surfaced when he said softly, "I don't want you to worry about anything. Let the professionals do what they do best. What you and I are going to do is have some fun. We'll drive down to Key West on Friday and spend the weekend."

Easing back, Ana flashed a bright smile. "Can we take Baron with us?"

"Sorry, Princess. Baron's going home Thursday night."

Her smile vanished quickly. "But that's tomorrow."

Jacob's arms fell away. "Then you'll have to make the most of your time together. Are you ready to take him for a walk?"

"Yes, but I'm going to have to borrow a hat from you."

"Come with me." Reaching for her hand, he led her into the house, up the staircase and into his bedroom. He opened the top drawer in a chest of drawers and took out a brand-new cap with a Miami Dolphins logo. He placed the cap on Ana's head, adjusting it low on her forehead, and peered under the bill. "Perfect."

Tilting her chin, Ana smiled up at him. "I have to get my sunglasses and change into a pair of running shoes, and then I'll meet you downstairs."

Ana suggesting a wig was a stroke of genius. A different hair color and/or length would work well in temporarily altering her appearance. Jacob knew staying inside the house would eventually grate on both their nerves. He would take her to Key West as promised and spend a couple of days in Old Town as their home base. Although it was mid-June and tourist season, he knew he would be able to secure lodgings with his aunt and uncle.

Anyone looking at them would've thought Ana and Jacob were out for an early-evening walk with their dog, but looks were definitely deceiving. She'd become a prisoner, exiled from her home and family. Baron was a highly trained dog that would attack on command, and Jacob a federal police officer trained to protect witnesses and prisoners. She'd exchanged her shorts and flip-flops for cropped jeans and running shoes, while Jacob had put on a loose-fitting shirt over his tee to conceal the holstered handgun at the small of his back.

"Have you made reservations?" she asked Jacob.

"Reservations for what?" he asked, answering her question with a question.

Ana gave him a sidelong glance. Walking alongside him made her aware of the differences in their height. She was five-four and he had to be several inches above the six-foot mark because her head only came to his shoulder. "You said we're going to spend the weekend in Key West."

"My aunt and uncle have a house in Old Town and they'll put us up."

She hesitated, almost tripping, but Jacob reached out, caught her arm and steadied her before she fell. Her heart was beating so fast Ana felt suddenly lightheaded. "Thank you." The two words were a breathless whisper.

"We're not going to share a bed, Ana. Not only are there enough bedrooms in the main house, but there's also a guesthouse on the property."

Ana was certain he could hear her sigh of relief. Her life was complicated enough without her having to share a bed with a man she hadn't known twenty-four hours. And even if she were forced to live with Jacob for more than a week or two, sleeping with him was not an option.

"How are you going to introduce me?"

Jacob stopped when the muzzled shepherd slowed to sniff tufts of grass growing between cracks in the sidewalk. "I'm going to tell them the truth." He held up a hand when Ana's jaw dropped. "My uncle is a retired undercover DEA special agent, so your true identity will not be compromised."

"How many family members or friends do you have in law enforcement?"

He thought about her question. "My father was a Miami-Dade cop and—"

"Was?" Ana asked, interrupting him.

"Dad was killed in the line of duty when he'd attempted to arrest a carjacker. What he didn't know was that the man's accomplice had come up behind him and shot him point-blank in the head."

Ana gasped, her eyes wide behind the lenses of her sunglasses. "What happened to the men responsible for his death?"

"Both were executed last year after they'd run out of appeals. And before you ask me, no, I didn't witness their execution. I'm not a proponent of the death penalty because it's not a deterrent. I believe life without the possibility of parole is much more profound psychologically than putting someone to death."

Again she wondered if he were a mind reader, because that was what she intended to ask him. "How's your mother?"

A wry smile twisted Jacob's mouth. "She remarried a widower with four young sons. I tried to tell her Henry was looking for a mother for his kids, but she wouldn't listen to me. His boys have been nothing but trouble for her, but my mother is one of the most soft-hearted people I've ever known. Dad used to tease her about feeding the neighbor's kids. They would come to the house because they liked Miss Gloria's cookies. It'd begun with cookies, and then graduated to sandwiches, and there were times when it wasn't unusual to find some of them sitting down with us at Sunday dinner."

Baron, finished with his exploration, started walking again. Ana slipped her hand into Jacob's, gently squeezing his fingers. She found it warm, the palm slightly callused; the roughness indicated he wasn't a stranger to hard work. "You say you know everything about me."

"I know enough," Jacob confirmed.

"But I know nothing about you," Ana countered.

"There's not much to tell."

"Then tell me how you met Diego."

He stared through the dark lenses at ripples of water in the canal. "I was sixteen when I met your cousin for the first time when he'd come down to Miami for spring break. My father and I had just come back from a baseball game and we were heading downtown when without warning bullets started flying. Rival drug gangs stood in the middle of the street dueling like in the Old West. My father stopped his car when he saw Diego on the ground covering his head. Several bullets had landed inches from where he lay. Dad pulled out his off-duty service handgun, shot one of the perps and managed to pull Diego inside the car to safety. I was in shock because it was the first time I saw my father shoot someone. Once Dad had driven a safe distance, he got out and went back. Diego and I sat motionless. We stared at each other for what seemed like an hour when it was only ten minutes. Once Dad returned uninjured, both of us started crying like babies. I tease Diego when I say that he cried more than me, but he counters saying that at least he wasn't slinging snot. I wish I'd had a camera phone, because then I would show him just how much snot he was not only slinging but also souping."

Throwing back her head, Ana laughed until she had to hold her chest. "That really must have been a sight. I can't believe my big bad boogeyman cousin was crying like a baby."

Jacob sobered. "It wasn't funny at the time. Not when you didn't know if you were going to have to take your last breath. Diego stayed with us that night and the next day Dad drove him back to where he'd parked his car. He told Dad that he owed him his life and if he ever needed anything he was to get in touch with him."

"I'm surprised Diego never mentioned the incident."

"I'm certain it's not something he'd want to relive. The three of us were sports fans, so every once in a while we'd get together and go to baseball, basketball and football games. When it came time for me to go to college, the bursar called my father and told him an anonymous donor had underwritten the cost of my tuition and room and board for all four years. We knew it was Diego, and it was only after my father passed away that he admitted to me it was the least he could do to repay him for saving his life."

A long silence ensued until Ana said, "It's always been that way with the Coles. You save one and the family will be indebted to you for life. It was that way with Matthew Sterling who helped save my uncle's life when he was left for dead in

Mexico. Uncle Matt also helped rescue my father when he was kidnapped and held hostage in Costa Rica. Daddy came home with a scar on the left cheek and a woman whom he'd managed to get pregnant while in captivity."

It was Jacob's turn to laugh, the unstrained deep sound coming from his chest. "I'll be damned. When did he find time to do that?"

"That's what my uncles wanted to know. My mother was three months pregnant with my brother Gabriel when she and my father married." A beat passed. "If you get me out of this situation without incident, then I'm going to owe you."

He shook his head. "No, you won't."

"Yes, I will. After all, you're giving up your vacation to look after me."

"The only thing I'm giving up is female company, because I still intend to go fishing."

Ana stopped again, turned and faced him. "What the heck am I if not female company?"

A slow smile touched his firm mouth. "Not the female company I'm thinking about. But that can change if you decide to sleep with me," he teased.

Her mouth moved but no words came out. It wasn't often that Ana was at a loss for words, but this was one of those times. "You are disgusting."

"Wrong, Ana!" Jacob spat out. "I'm not disgusting. I am a normal man with normal urges and making love with a woman just happens to be one of them. You can't be that naïve not to know what goes on between a man and a woman." He remembered her telling Sam that she loved him, and he didn't want to believe that she and Sam weren't sleeping together.

Heat flooded her face. "*¡Yo no dormiría con usted si fue el último hombre en la tierra!*"

He flashed a Cheshire cat grin. "Never say what you won't do, Princess. I bet if I was the last man on earth and you needed *some* you'd change your mind. But then you'd have to stand in line and wait your turn."

Her eyes grew wider. *"¿Comprende español?"*

He gave her hand a gentle squeeze. *"Sí, Princesa.* My best friend's grandparents had come to the States from Cuba and whenever I went to his house they would speak to me in Spanish."

Although fluent in the language Ana rarely got to speak Spanish. She never spoke it in the office and none of her friends spoke Spanish, leaving her to act as translator whenever they visited a country where it was the official language. *"¿Cuánto tiempo lleva antes que fuera con soltura?"* she asked Jacob.

"I was about ten before I realized I was fluent," he answered in English.

Ana narrowed her eyes. *"Inglés o español. Es todavía asquerosamente egotista."*

"I'm sorry if you believe I'm disgustingly egotistical, but I've never had any complaints."

"Do you mind if we change this conversation?"

He executed a mock bow. "Of course, Princess. Your wish is my command."

"Please don't call me that."

Jacob wanted to tell Ana that she was a modern-day princess. Not only was she born into wealth, but she'd grown up surrounded by people who took care of her every need. At twenty-five she wasn't faced with having to repay students loans because she had her trust fund. And she'd had a plum position waiting for her when David Cole stepped down as CEO of Serenity Records. Ana probably may not have thought of herself as spoiled, but there was no doubt she was privileged.

"I don't want to treat you as if you are on house arrest, and that's what you'll be if I call you Ana. With a wig, sunglasses and as Princess we should be able to go out in public and minimize the risk of someone recognizing you."

Ana knew Jacob was taking precautions to keep her identity under the radar but whenever he called her Princess his voice took on a patronizing tone. And she knew he was taking a risk whenever they left his home because there was the likelihood that someone could recognize her. High-profile performers who sought anonymity resorted to all types of disguises to avoid paparazzi, and most times they were unsuccessful.

However, she wasn't trying to avoid paparazzi, only the person or persons who'd taken out a contract on her life. Basil Irvine. The man's name continued to haunt her. Even if she'd only suspected Basil it was Jason who'd confirmed her fear and suspicion when he'd said, *"I know that bullet was meant for you."*

"You're right," she agreed, "but please don't sound so patronizing when you say it."

"I could always call you baby."

She smiled. "That's okay. I'll take Princess." Jacob calling her baby was a little too personal; it indicated they'd shared an intimacy that didn't exist.

Jacob led her to a bench in an area that overlooked the canal. Older couples and teenagers had come to sit, talk and watch the sunsets that appeared even more spectacular in this part of Florida. Baron lay down on the cool cobblestones and closed his eyes. Stretching out his left arm, Jacob rested it on the back of the bench, his fingers grazing Ana's shoulder.

"How often do you come down here?"

He let out an inaudible sigh. "Not often enough. This is the first time since I bought the house that I'll spend more than a couple of days."

Shifting slightly on the wrought-iron bench, Ana gave him a direct stare. "What do you do when you're not working?"

"I go to ball games."

Her eyebrows lifted at this disclosure. "How many games do you go to?"

Jacob smiled, the expression making him appear somewhat boyish. "I have season tickets for all of the Marlins, Heat and Dolphins home games."

"That's crazy."

"Why is it crazy? I happen to like sports."

"But...but it must take quite a chunk out of your salary."

He chuckled. "Even though I'm a civil servant, I don't have to concern myself with supporting a wife and kids. I don't smoke, drink to excess, gamble or dabble in drugs, so going to a game for a couple of hours is a lot better than lying on a couch spilling my guts to a therapist."

"Why aren't you married?"

Ana's question caught Jacob somewhat off guard, but then he quickly recovered. "I really don't know."

"Are you anti-marriage?"

Shifting on the bench, he turned to face her. "No. I suppose it's just that I haven't met a woman I feel I could spend the rest of my life with. When I put a ring on a woman's finger I don't want it to be for right now but forever, because I don't believe in divorce. I want what my parents had before my father died."

Ana turned to stare at the large orange sphere sinking lower and lower in the darkening sky. Jacob didn't believe in divorce or the death penalty. "Sometimes I think what your parents had and what my parents have doesn't exist anymore. Nowadays people marry with the notion that if it doesn't work out, then they'll divorce and try it again until they feel they can get it right."

"Why are you so cynical, Princess?"

"I'm cynical because I look at my friends and girls that I grew up with and most of them are divorced or on their second or third marriages."

"Are you telling me you don't believe in marriage?"

Smiling, Ana shook her head. "No. All I have to do is look at my family to know that marriage works. This is not to say there weren't divorces before they became Coles, but once they marry a Cole it is for life. I have a cousin who lives in Chicago who married, got divorced and then remarried his wife."

"That just proves that they were destined to be together."

"I agree."

"Are you going to marry Sam?"

Ana removed her glasses, staring at Jacob as if he'd taken leave of his senses. "What did you say?"

He leaned closer. "I know you heard me, Princess."

"Why would I want to marry a woman? I'm not gay."

"Sam is a woman?"

"Of course she's a woman. Her name is Samantha, but everyone calls her Sam for short." Suddenly realization dawned. "That's what you get for eavesdropping on my conversation," she said, accusingly. "My house, my phone and my rules," she intoned sarcastically.

Jacob cradled the back of her head. "Okay, Princess. You've got me. If you promise not to disclose where you're staying, then I'll allow you some privacy whenever you make a call. But, I'm going to have to know who you're calling in advance." He extended his right hand. *"Trato."*

Grinning, Ana took his hand. "Deal."

Chapter 5

Los Angeles

Camille parked her car in her assigned space behind her apartment building and cut off the engine. Reaching for her handbag on the console, she pushed open the driver's side door but it wouldn't budge. It wasn't until she glanced up that she saw the face of a man from her past. When he realized she recognized him he stepped back and opened the door for her. She got out of the low-slung vehicle. His top lip disappeared against the ridge of his upper teeth when he flashed a feral smile.

"How have you been, Doll Face?"

She hated his name for her, and she'd lost count of the number of men who'd referred to her as a black Barbie doll. "What are you doing here, Fletcher?"

Gerald Fletcher dipped his head and pressed a kiss to her cheek. He had to admit the woman responsible for him losing his government job was as stunning as she'd been when he first saw her in the club where he'd go whenever he was off duty. Her round dark brown face with perfectly symmetrical delicate features was hypnotic. He stared at the cloud of curly reddish-brown hair framing her face before his gaze lowered to the swell of breasts under a conservative white blouse she'd paired with a black pencil skirt. They lingered briefly on the expanse of slender legs in a pair of black patent-leather pumps. She'd cleaned up well.

"I came to see you, baby. Aren't you glad to see me?"

There was no way Camille was glad to see a man she'd slept with, and then robbed of his gun and wallet. It wasn't until she was on the other side of town and went through his wallet that she realized she'd just robbed a special agent with the Bureau of Alcohol, Tobacco, Firearms and Explosives. Camille kept the cash and sold his credit cards, government-issued automatic, ID and badge to a local hustler who used the gun and credentials when he went on an extended crime spree.

She swallowed to relieve the constriction in her throat. She couldn't see his eyes behind the dark glasses, but remembered their icy blue coldness. They were dead eyes, eyes that didn't look at you but through you. He came to the club on the days she was scheduled to work and instead of the dollar bills the club's patrons tossed up on stage Gerald always gave her tens and twenties. After she'd begun working the champagne room he continued to pay the required fee, but also added a generous tip for her services. It had been naïveté that had permitted her to fall under his spell where she'd agreed to sleep with him. Of course she didn't take him back to the apartment she shared with another exotic dancer after he'd given her a fistful of bills to *'make him feel real good.'* Once she'd counted the money she knew she'd be a fool to reject his offer. They'd checked into a rundown hotel and after she gave him what she called her special lovemaking he fell asleep. It was the last time she rolled a john; she quit dancing at the club, because the word on the street was that he was looking for her. It had taken him more than a year to find her and she didn't want to think of how he would exact revenge.

"No, I'm not," Camille whispered.

"Well, I'm glad to see you. It's taken a while to track you down," he lied smoothly.

"What do you want?"

Gerald cupped her elbow. "Let's go upstairs where we can talk in private."

"There's nothing to talk about."

The sinister grin was back. "That's where you're wrong, Doll Face. We have a lot to talk about."

Camille tried freeing her arm, but the effort proved futile when his fingers tightened like a manacle. "I don't dance anymore."

"I know that."

"I'm expecting company," she said quickly, hoping to change his mind if he thought she was going to sleep with him again.

"I know," Gerald repeated.

Her heart pounded so hard in her chest Camille was certain he could see it through her blouse. "You know?"

"Yes. You're expecting Basil Irvine. I can assure you I'll be gone long before he gets here."

"How do you know he was coming here?"

"People pay me well to know. Now, let's go, Camille, before I'm forced to break your arm. And that will pale in comparison to what you did to me."

She knew she didn't have much of a choice but to let him into her apartment. She'd thought she had left her old lifestyle behind. However, it was back in the form of Gerald Fletcher. "Please don't hurt me."

Placing an arm around her waist, he led her to the entrance to her apartment building. "I'm not going to hurt you. Not unless you don't do what I tell you to do."

"What's that?"

"Easy there, baby. I'll tell you everything once we're upstairs."

Ana felt as if the parole board had approved her request. It'd been four days since her life had changed forever, and even though she still wasn't free to come and go or do anything she wanted at least Jacob had relaxed the rules.

She lay in bed, staring up at the ceiling. After they'd returned from their walk Jacob had asked whether she'd wanted to watch a baseball game with him, but she'd refused with the excuse that she was tired.

It wasn't fatigue that plagued Ana and wouldn't permit her a restful night's sleep. It was guilt. She'd told herself she could play in the same arena where powerful men played and negotiated multimillion-dollar deals for centuries, yet the difference was a very powerful music mogul had found himself outsmarted by a woman. Instinct told her that if Jason had been the one to woo Justin the outcome would've been vastly different. It would've resulted in one man challenging another. The better of the two would've been declared the winner and the loser would've retreated with dignity.

Turning, she stared at the clock on the bedside table. It was nearly one in the morning and still she couldn't sleep. Tossing back the sheet and a lightweight blanket, Ann swung her legs over the side of the bed and turned on the table lamp.

Walking on bare feet, she walked out of the bedroom and made her way down the staircase. A cup of warm *café con leche* would be the perfect remedy for her restlessness. The hanging fixture, turned to the lowest setting, glowed in the hallway off the kitchen. There was another light—this one from under the range hood. She flipped a wall switch, flooding the kitchen with light.

The house was eerily silent as she turned on the single-cup automatic coffeemaker, dropped in a pod for a rich dark roast. Placing a large mug under the unit, she pushed a button. The aroma of brewing coffee wafted in the kitchen as she opened the refrigerator and took out a container of milk. The brew cycle ended and Ana added a generous amount to the coffee, then sugar. Stirring the mixture, Ana placed the mug into the microwave to warm it. The beeping sound echoed loudly and as she reached for the mug she felt movement behind her.

She froze, her fingers tightening around the handle of the mug. "Jacob? Is that you?"

A soft chuckle caressed her ear. "Were you expecting someone else?"

Turning, she saw him standing a few feet away. She forced her gaze not to stray below his neck. His body was so beautifully proportioned that her mouth went suddenly dry. He wore a pair of navy-blue-and-white striped pajama pants that rode low on his slim hips. "Oh…oh, no," she said hastily. "I couldn't sleep so I came down to make coffee."

Crossing muscled arms over a furred chest, Jacob angled his head. "I thought you said you were tired."

She knew she'd been caught in a lie and there was no way she could extricate herself except substitute that lie with another one. "I said that because I didn't want to impose on you."

Jacob lowered his arms and stared at the petite woman in a skimpy cotton nightgown ending at her knees. Her tiny compact body was definitely a turn-on. He smiled when noticing the bright pink polish on her groomed toes. "How would you be imposing?"

Ana lifted a bare shoulder. "You've made it quite known that I've ruined your vacation, so instead of compounding it I decided to make myself scarce."

He took a step, bringing them less than a foot apart. "Do you think hiding out in your bedroom is making yourself scarce? Even if I didn't see you every hour, I'd still know you're here."

With wide eyes, she said, "I bother you that much?"

A smile softened the angles in his face. "No, Princess. You're not a bother."

"Then what am I?"

"You're a reminder of how much I've cut myself off from the real world. I go to work, do what has to be done, then go to the gym to workout. After that I come home to shower off the reminder that I'm responsible for people who're locked up because they've committed unspeakable acts. After that I flop down in front of the television to watch a number of news channels and then it's ESPN for a few hours. I go to bed and then get up and do it all over again. If I'm not at a game, I may drive up to Winter Haven to visit my mother. So, you're not a bother but a welcome distraction."

Ana cradled the mug, enjoying the warmth seeping into her palms. "I've been called a lot of things, but never a distraction."

"Don't forget I said a *welcome* distraction." He peered down into her mug. "That looks like milk."

"It's *café con leche*. Are you familiar with it?"

Jacob nodded. "My friend's grandmother used to make it for me."

"Would you like to share mine? There's enough here for two."

"Seguro. Conseguiré otra taza."

She placed the mug on the cooking island, staring at the broad expanse of Jacob's shoulders and back. She wanted to tell him he should be arrested for looking so deliciously sexy. "I can't believe how well you speak Spanish."

"It helps whenever I'm on the job."

"Exactly what it is you do as a marshal?"

Jacob retrieved a cup from an overhead cabinet and poured some of the *café con leche* from Ana's mug into it. "I used to be assigned to the Violent Crime Fugitive Task Force before I was promoted to an administrative position."

"Do you miss not being in the field?"

He smiled. "Somewhat. Come with me. We can sit in the family room and talk."

The ball game had gone into extra innings and it was almost 12:30 a.m. when he'd finally turned off the television. After checking on Baron, who slept outside on the deck, he came back inside, activated the security system and took a shower. Jacob was already in bed when he detected the smell of brewing coffee. Slipping into a pair of pajama pants, he headed in the direction of the kitchen, surprised to find Ana there.

She'd admitted to not wanting to bother him when he wanted to tell her she did bother him in the worse way. Having her live under his roof was a constant reminder that it had been a long time since a woman had crossed the threshold to where he lived. Even in Miami he'd endured long droughts without female companionship. Jacob wasn't certain whether he was getting old, in a funk, or that his outlook on life had changed wherein he didn't want to contend with a merry-go-round of women in his life.

He'd had one or two serious relationships, but none progressed to the point where he considered marriage. He knew his mother was concerned that she would die without him giving her grandchildren; however, his comeback was that she had four other sons who could fulfill her most reverent wish. Her response shocked Jacob when she stated that her husband's sons were not her flesh and blood.

He didn't know what had made him so reluctant to commit, because his parents' marriage was filled with overt displays of love and affection. And if they did argue or disagree it was never when he was present. Stephen Jacob Jones's sage advice was: always let the woman believe she's right even if she isn't. After a while she'll realize she was wrong even if she won't openly admit it. That advice had made for a solid marriage for twenty-one years.

Touching a wall switch, the family room was awash in a soft glow from recessed ceiling light. The space had become his sanctuary. Someplace where he could relax and forget about everything going on outside. Something he wasn't able to do at his Miami apartment. The noise from pedestrian and vehicular traffic and the wail of sirens from emergency vehicles was a constant reminder that he lived in a thriving metropolitan city.

Here in the Keys the order of the day was to kick back and let the world pass leisurely by.

Ana stared at the room with a leather seating grouping, a large flat screen mounted above a fireplace, two walls with built-in bookshelves crowded with books, and a large colorful jukebox filled with CDs. Another corner near the sliding glass doors held a pool table, dart board and portable bar. A large Tiffany-style light fixture was suspended above the pool table. There was even a popcorn machine.

"Incredible," she whispered under her breath.

Jacob gave her startled look. "You like it?"

She flashed a dimpled smile. "I love it. It's the perfect sports bar. The only thing missing is peanut shells on the floor."

Throwing back his head, he laughed loudly. Here he thought Ana was a girly-girl, but apparently there was another side to her obviously feminine persona. Then he had to remember she was a female doing business in what was deemed a man's world.

"Do you play pool?"

"I've been known to dabble in it."

Taking her free hand, Jacob steered Ana to the sofa, easing her to sit before he sat beside her. Pulling up her legs, she pressed the soles of her feet against his thigh. "That noncommittal answer tells me you do."

"Let me warn you that I only play for money."

He took a sip of the perfectly brewed milk and coffee, staring at her over the rim. "I don't think so, Princess. There's no way I'm going to let you hustle me."

She pushed out her lower lip. "You took my credit cards, so I'm going to have to try to get some cash any way I can. How can I shop in Key West if I'm flat broke?"

"How much do you think you're going to need?"

"More than I have on me. And I could get a lot more if I had access to an ATM."

Attractive lines fanned out around his dark eyes when Jacob smiled. "Do you actually believe I'm going to give you back your credit cards?"

"You can't blame me for trying. You can call Diego and tell him to send Henri down with some cash."

"No."

"I may as well be broke."

"You're hardly broke, Ana."

"I feel broke."

Jacob ruffled her curly hair. *"Usted chica rica, pequeña y pobre."*

Ana swatted his hand. She resented the fact that he'd called her a poor little rich girl. "Does it bother you that I have more money than you do?"

He shook his head. "Not in the least. If I was concerned about becoming wealthy I never would've become a cop."

Ana sobered. "I'm sorry. I didn't mean to sound condescending and I'm not begrudging you for what you do, because I doubt if I could ever make it in law enforcement. My older brother's wife is an ex-DEA agent. She said there were times when she was so deep undercover that she actually identified with the people she'd been entrusted to bring down. Summer told me there was a drug dealer who had so much money stashed in a safe house that it was incalculable. She claimed it took two people three days, using a counting machine, to add up the money he'd made from selling two hundred kilos of nearly pure cocaine in a single month."

"I'm familiar with a few of those maggots."

"Just what do you do?" Ana asked Jacob between sips of coffee.

"As an assistant director I oversee staff that supervises the U.S. Marshal Service at four Miami federal detention centers."

"That's a lot of responsibility."

Jacob nodded. "It is, but it's a lot less dangerous than chasing down bad guys."

"I always thought of directors as older men with receding hairlines and beer guts."

"Shame on you, Princess. I never figured you'd be into stereotypes. We only look like that after retirement," he added, chuckling softly.

She rolled her eyes at him. "You're too vain to let yourself go."

"Why would you say that?"

"Didn't you say you work out?"

"I work out to relieve stress. I could always do sit-ups and push-ups at home, but I go to the gym because it has a lap pool."

"There's a pool and health club in the building where I live."

"Now that's convenient."

Jacob didn't know if Ana was boasting that by virtue of her wealth she could have anything within reason. She sent out her laundry, didn't clean her house and had her dry cleaning and groceries delivered. He didn't have unlimited funds at his disposal, but at least he could go to sleep at night knowing he earned his salary from doing an honest day's work.

He'd grown up with kids who wanted to make fast money

and a few of them were either in jail or in the cemetery. Perhaps if Stephen Jacob Jones hadn't put the fear of God in him that if he did mess up he would make certain to dispense his own brand of justice before turning him over to the proper authorities that kept him on the right road.

He set his cup on a side table. "Don't worry about money. I'll pay for whatever you want when we go shopping."

Ana leaned closer to Jacob in order to share his body heat. The air-conditioning in the room was much cooler than her bedroom. "I'll repay you once this craziness is concluded."

"Ana, Ana, Ana," he intoned. "Let's not talk about money anymore."

"But—"

"*¡Bastante! No más.*"

"Excuse me," she drawled facetiously.

"You are excused, sweetheart. Now, can we please talk about something else?"

She wanted to get up and leave, but didn't want Jacob to think she was the type to pout or run away. He just didn't know how independent she actually was. Even as a child she'd always wanted to do things on her own terms. Her favorite childhood catchphrase was "I can do it by myself." Her mother only had to show her once how to tie her shoes before she'd attempted it herself and got it right. It was the same with learning to swim or ride a bike. Wherein her brothers and sister took swimming lessons Ana decided to jump in and started swimming. Her parents may have thought she was gifted, but the reality was she'd watched and mimicked her older siblings. She'd learned to play the piano and a few other instruments. Fortunately for Ana she did inherit her father's gift for recognizing exceptional musical talent. What she didn't have, unlike Gabriel and Jason, was the gift for composing music.

"How many CDs do you have?" she asked.

"Probably close to 800." Jacob pushed off the sofa, walking to the jukebox and punching several buttons before he returned to sit beside Ana, pulling her feet to rest on his thigh. "Your toes are cold."

"That's because it's cold in here."

"Why didn't you say something?"

Ana flashed a sexy moue. "It's cold in here, Jacob."

"I've programmed the thermostat, but I can always make it warmer for you."

"That's okay. It's time I go back to bed."

Jacob increased his hold on her feet. "Don't go. Not yet."

She went completely still. "What are you going to do?" Ana didn't have time to react when she found herself scooped off the sofa as Jacob carried her across the room to a door that led into a space no larger than a dorm room. A queen-size bed took up most of the space. "What are you doing?"

Jacob placed Ana on the bed and covered her with a sheet and blanket. "I'm going to keep you warm while we talk and listen to music."

"Wait!" Her protest came too late when he turned on his heels and walked out of the bedroom. She didn't want to believe she was in the bed of a man she hadn't known twenty-four hours; a man who'd promised to protect her from someone who wanted her dead. But who, she mused, was going to save her from him?

Sitting up, she pressed her back to the mound of pillows piled against a brown cordovan leather headboard. The music from the jukebox flowed into the room from speakers concealed in the ceiling. Closing her eyes, Ana felt as if she was in Brazil. The musical selection was a fusion of samba and jazz. Her eyes opened when Jacob returned and touched the dimmer switch on the wall and crawled into bed with her.

"I thought we weren't going to sleep together."

He pressed a kiss to her hair. "What we are doing is sharing a bed. That's different from sleeping together."

"Same difference," she drawled.

Wrapping his arms around her shoulders, Jacob pulled her close to his chest. "Warmer?"

Ana smiled. "A little, but my feet are still cold."

"Do you want a pair of socks?"

"I wouldn't need a pair of socks if I was in my own bed."

"Put your feet between my legs. Is that better?" Jacob asked after he'd sandwiched her feet with his legs.

Ana tried making out his expression in the dim light. "Yes. Thank you." A beat passed. "I like the selection. It reminds me of Brazil."

Jacob rested his chin on the top of her head. "I see you recognize bossa."

"It's very distinctive."

He shifted into a more comfortable position when Ana rested her head on his shoulder. "That's a country I would like to visit."

"You could if you decide to come with me to Salvador da Bahia."

"Is that where your cousin lives?"

"*Sí.* She and her husband own a coffee plantation in the mountains. It's beautiful and primordial. I went there for Carnivale and partied so hard that I needed a vacation when I came back to the States."

Jacob played with the short curls clinging to Ana's scalp. "Do you want me to call Diego and tell him you want to go there?"

"No," Ana said much too quickly. "Even though I love Regina to death, there wouldn't be much for me to do there by myself. And I doubt that at fifty-something and a grand-mother that she'd want to hang out at night."

"What does her husband do?"

"Aaron's a pediatric microbiologist. He was born in the States, but raised in Brazil. He inherited the plantation from his aunt. It sounds kinky, but Regina was married to Aaron's father first. Theirs was a marriage in name only because she was nineteen and he was close to seventy."

"Damn! Talk about robbing the nursery."

Ana gave Jacob a playful tap on his shoulder. "It wasn't like that."

"Your family must have a lot of drama."

Smiling, she closed her eyes. "You just don't know the half of it. The Coles put the *d* in drama. It began with my grandfather cheating on my grandmother with his young secretary, and it was rumored that she'd set out to seduce him. When she discovered she was carrying his baby his chief financial officer offered to marry her and pass the baby off as his. It got real grimy when Teresa confronted my *abuela*, who was also pregnant at the time, boasting that both were carrying the same man's baby."

"That's drama taken to the ninth degree," Jacob drawled.

"You've got that right. That single act nearly destroyed my family. My grandparents were estranged for years even though they lived under the same roof. After they reconciled my father was born."

"I've heard that make-up sex is the best."

"You've heard or you know for a fact?"

"Sorry, baby, but I'm going to plead the Fifth. By the way, whatever happened to your father's half brother?"

"Joshua had remained the Coles' best kept secret until he turned seventeen. His mother approached my grandfather for the first time because she needed his help getting Uncle Josh into West Point. That's when my father, uncle and aunts discovered they had a half brother. Daddy said it wasn't easy for Joshua, because everyone blamed his mother for the affair when *Abuelo* was just as guilty. After all, he was a married man. Josh was about thirty before he was totally accepted as a Cole."

"That sounds a little pretentious, don't you think?"

"Of course," Ana agreed. "But you have to remember it

was another generation. Nowadays it doesn't matter whether you're so-called illegitimate or adopted, if you claimed one drop of Cole blood or the surname on your birth certificate says Cole, then you're one of us."

"Where does that put me on the family-tree schematic?" Jacob asked.

"As a godfather you're an unofficial Cole. Matthew Sterling was an unofficial Cole even before we knew that his stepson had married my first cousin. *Abuelo* named him in his will, along with his daughter and stepson. I know you don't want to talk about money, but if that's the only way we can show our appreciation then that's what we do."

"What if I want something other than money?"

Her eyes grew wider. "What would that be?" she asked after a pregnant silence.

"Maybe a kiss. Or even a hug before I take you back to your bed."

Another pause ensued. "Is that all you want?"

Jacob chuckled under his breath. "I can assure you that I can come up with something else, but I don't want you to get the wrong impression."

"And that is?"

"Take advantage of you."

It was Ana's turn to laugh. "No, you…" Her words trailed off when without warning she found herself on her back and Jacob straddling her.

Lowering his head, he fastened his mouth to the column of her neck, breathing a kiss there. "Thank you," he said in her ear.

A shiver of awareness eddied throughout her body when the heat from Jacob's body seeped into hers, and Ana was certain he could feel her trembling. It wasn't fear that had her heart racing but the sudden rush of desire heating her blood. His nearness was overwhelming as dormant feelings were aroused too, reminding her of how long it had been since a man had made love to her.

"Jacob."

"It's okay, Princess. Nothing's going to happen." He rolled off her body and the bed. Resting his hands at his waist, he watched as she slipped off the bed. His steady gaze bore into her. "Shall I walk you to your bedroom?"

Ana combed her fingers through her hair. She hadn't wanted to believe she'd spent the past twenty minutes in bed, wearing nothing more than a nightgown and bikini panties, with a man who disturbed her in every way. "I think I can find my way, thank you. Good night."

"Actually it's good morning."

She offered him a dimpled smile. "Good morning, Jacob."

He executed a mock bow. "Good morning, Princess."

Ana brushed past him, her skin tingling when it touched Jacob's arm. There was a maddening arrogance about her protector but there was also something maddeningly charming about a man who made her more than aware of why she'd been born female.

Careful, girl, or you'll find yourself in over your head. It was as if she could hear Sam's voice cautioning her about Jacob. And it wouldn't be the first time her friend had warned her about getting involved with a man.

She wanted to tell the voice in her head not to worry only because she doubted whether she would live with Jacob long enough to become emotionally involved with her protector.

Chapter 6

Ana woke feeling more tired than she did when she'd finally drifted off to the sleep. Rolling over, she peered at the clock on the bedside table; she'd slept away most of the morning. She closed her eyes again, trying to sort out her thoughts. Her mind was in tumult from a disturbing nightmare of someone chasing her. She wasn't certain whether it was a man or a woman because she couldn't see their face. Somehow she'd managed to escape her pursuer. Believing she was safe she'd turned a corner only to find a lurking dark-robed figure with a macabre grin waiting for her approach. She'd awakened in a cold sweat, shaking uncontrollably, while biting down on her fist to keep from crying aloud and possibly waking Jacob.

Ana remembered sitting up and resting her forehead on her knees, while waiting in the darkened room until fatigue claimed her enough to fall asleep again. The dreams returned; however, this time they were different. The erotic images of her in bed with a man, writhing under his kisses and caresses, his warm, moist breath in her ear and his hardness sliding in and out of her body had left her moaning, the area between her legs wet and pulsing, and her glorying in the aftermath of a long-forgotten orgasm.

Exhaling audibly Ana realized her body wasn't as tired as her overactive imagination. What she'd found puzzling was that she rarely dreamed or if she did then she hardly ever remembered them. But the nightmare and the erotic dream that followed were burned like a brand into her brain.

It was nearly eleven and she knew it was time for her to get out of bed. She couldn't recall the last time she'd slept so late. Even when she didn't have to go into the office she was up and working out at the health club. Her friends who'd dubbed themselves The Wild Bunch always complained about her getting up with the chickens after they'd partied well into the early-morning hours. What they hadn't understood was the internal alarm clock that went off whenever the sky brightened with daylight. The exception had been today. Swinging her legs over the side of the bed, she walked in the direction of the en suite bath.

Half an hour later Ana walked into the kitchen to find a note pinned to a corkboard. She read Jacob's barely legible scrawl: *Taking Baron to Miami. Will return for dinner.*

Ana smiled. That meant she would have the house to herself for several hours. Opening the refrigerator, she found the container with the ingredients for an omelet. She removed it along with two large eggs, butter and a loaf of wheat bread. Jacob kept a well-stocked refrigerator and freezer. There was another container, this one with marinating chicken. Most of the men she'd dated were so inept in the kitchen they had restaurants on speed dial. Then there was one guy she really liked who'd invited her to his home. Her liking quickly turned to revulsion when greeted with the clutter of take-out containers, pizza boxes and piles of dirty laundry scattered about the floor or tossed onto chairs. The "excuse the mess" was something she refused to excuse. And what she didn't understand was he could afford to hire a cleaning service, but hadn't deemed it a priority. When she'd asked if he ever cleaned his place his comeback was his girlfriends would pick up after him. Needless to say she never became his girlfriend.

The house appeared unnaturally quiet without Jacob or Baron around and Ana chided herself for not getting up earlier to see them off. Her gaze drifted to the wall phone, contemplating whether she should call Jason and tell him about her nightmare, then thought better of it. If Jason had believed her in imminent danger he would contact Diego, who in turn would call Jacob.

Somehow Ana managed to push the frightening images of the nightmare to the furthest recesses of her mind when she went through the motions of preparing what had become brunch. She ate her meal at the table in the kitchen, while thumbing through the current issue of *Time* magazine. If Jacob hadn't activated the alarm she would've taken her meal outdoors. After two cups of coffee, she cleaned up the kitchen, then made her way to the family room to watch television. Luckily she found a romantic comedy she hadn't seen and within minutes of the opening credits she found herself laughing so hard she had to raise the volume in order to hear the dialogue.

Jacob maneuvered into the driveway leading to Brian Murphy's modest home in an upper-middle-class gated Miami suburb. Brian had called him earlier to tell him that he'd returned from his fishing trip and would drive down later that afternoon to pick up his dog.

He and Brian had gone through basic training together at Parris Island, South Carolina, and although Jacob trusted the security expert, the trust did not extend to making him aware that Ana Cole was living with him—albeit temporarily.

Baron began barking as soon Jacob cut off the engine.

Brian came out of the house at the same time Jacob pushed a button to open the hatch. "Yes, boy, you're home."

Standing six-six and weighing close to two hundred and sixty pounds, Brian hoisted the crate with the large dog with the ease of lifting a newborn. Jacob winced when he noticed the summer sun had burned his friend's nose and arms. Seeing the sunburn reminded him to pick up sunblock for Ana.

Opening the crate, Brian hugged the shepherd when he bounded out, standing on his hind legs. "Welcome home, buddy."

Jacob watched man and dog become reacquainted, smiling. Twice-married, the ex-marine captain turned security specialist had professed he always got along better with animals than he did women, and it was apparent when seeing him with his pet.

Waiting until Baron trotted off and disappeared inside the house, Jacob extended his hand. "What did you catch?"

Brian's hamlike hand closed over Jacob's in a bone-crushing handshake. "A few yellowtail snapper, blue marlin and a mess of porgies. Come on in the house and take what you want."

"I'm going to pass on the fish. I just loaded up my freezer and I also plan to do some deep-sea fishing in another couple of weeks."

"Still, come on in and rest up before you head back."

Jacob shook his head as he stared at the behemoth of a man with the sandy-brown military-style crew cut and laughing brown eyes the color of copper pennies. Brian liked dressing up as Santa for the children whose parents were deployed, and anyone familiar with the former marine corps captain knew his benign appearance was merely a foil for a man trained in mixed martial arts.

"I'd love to but I have plans to visit my aunt and uncle in Key West." It was a half truth, because he and Ana weren't scheduled to leave until the next day. "Maybe next time, my friend."

"That's not going to be for a while. I have a client who's taking his wife to Mexico City next week to visit her relatives. They plan to be down there for six weeks. I'm also taking a couple of guys with me because of home invasions and the rash of kidnappings going on down there. You know, if you ever get tired of pushing paper, then let me know and I'll put you on the payroll, Jake. You can make more in three months than Uncle Sam pays you in a year."

"Thanks, but no thanks. I've grown to like pushing paper. It's much safer than tracking down fugitives or protecting rich folks."

Running a hand over the stubble on his chin, Brian gave Jacob a long, penetrating stare. "You have changed, haven't you?"

Jacob thought about Brian's query, wondering if he had changed. And if he did, then how much? And was the change good or bad? "I guess I have," he said after a noticeable pause.

"But it's all good, Jake. One of these days maybe I'll stop chasing the next rush."

It wasn't until he was back in his truck heading toward the Keys that Jacob thought about what Brian said about looking for a rush. He supposed the man was right because after graduating college he wasn't certain where he was going or what he wanted to be despite majoring in criminal justice. He'd always planned to join the Miami-Dade P.D., but with the elder Jones's murder Jacob knew he would not follow in his father's footsteps. After six months of floundering he decided joining the military would best suit his temperament.

He'd gotten up one morning, walked into the marine corps recruiting office and signed up. He went through basic training, giving the corps six years. Once discharged he was recruited to join the U.S. Marshal Service. Jacob had become what he'd tried to elude—a police officer. What he soon dis-

covered was that he loved law enforcement: tracking down
fugitives, stakeouts, and the ultimate gratification of capturing, cuffing and reading dangerous criminals their Mi-
randa rights.

One thing he knew: he was good at what he'd been trained
to do. So good that he was promoted and rose quickly through
the ranks. Being assigned a desk position was an answer to
his mother's prayers. Gloria's greatest fear was that his life
would mirror her husband's; that he would die in the line of
duty.

Jacob stopped at his apartment, and while there adjusted
the central air-conditioning. Jacob had asked his landlady to
periodically check on his place, and apparently she'd lowered
the temperature until it was bone-chillingly cold.

"Oh, Mr. Jones, you're back."

Jacob turned to find his landlady standing in the doorway. The middle-aged woman with a boyish-cut hairstyle
nervously touched the keys hanging from a large ring.

"I'm not really back, Mrs. Stokes. I had some business
nearby, but I'm leaving now."

Imogene Stokes smiled at Jacob. "I've been checking on
your place like you asked."

"And I thank you for that."

"Do you want me to get someone to come in and dust? I
know you like everything nice and clean," she added when
he glared at her.

"I'd rather you not." Mrs. Stokes knew he was adamant
about not letting strangers into his apartment, so he wasn't
certain why she would ask him that. "Other than you and
your husband, I don't want anyone else in my place. Am I
clear about that?"

Pinpoints of color dotted the older woman's cheeks. "Of
course, Mr. Jones. I would never let someone in your apartment without your permission."

A smile had replaced his scowl. "As long as we understand each other."

Imogene knew her best tenant worked for the Department of Justice, he paid his rent on time, came and went without much notice, and whenever he had company they never made a lot of noise like some of the other tenants. She knew he carried a gun and that was the reason why she'd rented him the apartment. Having someone around who was authorized to carry a firearm made her feel safer, and knew she could call on him for assistance in the event of an emergency.

"Have a good day, Mr. Jones."

"The same to you, Mrs. Stokes."

Waiting until the woman left and closing the door behind her, Jacob pulled out his cell phone, tapped speed dial and waited for a break in the connection. He'd dialed Diego's private number.

"Good afternoon, ColeDiz International. Mr. Cole-Thomas's office."

"Caitlin, this is Jacob. Is Diego available?"

"Hold on, Jacob. He said to put you through whenever you call."

He counted off the minutes until Diego's voice came through the earpiece. "Hey, Jake. What's up?"

"That's what I want to know. Has anything changed?"

"There's been no further info on the shooter."

"Any leads on who's behind it?" Jacob asked.

"Not yet, but contact has been made with one of Irvine's employees. Let's hope it provides a lead. How's Ana?"

"She's adjusting."

"I hope she's not being too difficult," Diego said with laughter in his voice.

It was Jacob's turn to laugh. "She's fine, Diego."

"That's a first."

"What are you talking about?"

"Ana's the type that if you ask her to slow down, she'll

speed up. If you tell her to go right, she'll go left. I suppose that's what makes her successful; she always pushes herself to the next level. I'd tried to get her to work for ColeDiz but she's too obsessed with the music industry."

Jacob didn't want to take sides only because he wouldn't have wanted anyone to determine the direction his life would take. Although his mother had always voiced her disapproval of him going into law enforcement he'd followed what he thought was his destiny. His paternal grandfather had been in the first graduating class to integrate the Miami-Dade P.D. His father had followed and his uncle had joined the DEA, and there cousins who worked for ATF, the FBI and other police departments in cities throughout the country.

Apparently it was the same with Ana. She'd made a decision to go into the music industry instead of working for ColeDiz. He admired her independence, her tenacity and that she'd retained her femininity despite the responsibility of running a company.

"What you should want is for Ana to be happy and content doing what she does best."

There was thirty seconds of silence before Diego said, "You're right, Jake." He launched into an update on what was going on with Serenity Records.

Jacob digested this new information. "Call me if anything else changes."

"I will," Diego confirmed.

He ended the call, pondering his response to his houseguest's cousin. Why, he thought, was he defending Ana when she was more than capable of standing up for herself? After all, she was neither afraid nor reticent when it came to speaking her mind. That's what he liked about her. It wasn't all he liked about her, but it was what he'd permitted himself to acknowledge.

Sitting together sipping *café con leche* was acceptable. Taking her to his bed wasn't, although nothing had happened between them. Even after she'd gone upstairs to her own bed the scent of her perfume lingered on the sheet and pillows, and it was as if she were still there.

Jacob knew he had to be very careful not to cross the line with Ana. Diego had asked him to protect her, not take advantage of her. He'd also taunted and insulted Ana when he'd talked about needing female company. Something he'd regretted mentioning because that wasn't his style. Leaving her alone in Long Key wasn't something he would've done under a different set of circumstances, yet he hadn't wanted Brian to know she was living with him. He locked up the apartment, planning to make one more stop before heading back.

Ana put aside the book she'd been reading when she detected the sound of a car's engine. Moving quickly, she raced up the staircase to her bedroom. Her heart was beating double-time when the bedroom door opened slowly. Never had she been so relieved to see Jacob when he walked into the room.

"What's the matter?" he asked.

She blew out her breath. "Nothing?"

He closed the distance between them, folding his body down on the bed beside her. "Why do you look as if you've just seen a ghost?"

Ana's eyelids fluttered wildly. "I heard a car and I decided to hide out—"

Jacob splayed his hand on her back. "No one's coming here unless they're invited."

Tilting her chin, she gave him a wide-eyed stare. "What about your neighbors?"

"They never visit because they believe I'm a grouch."

She smiled for the first time, bringing his gaze to linger on her mouth. "Are you?"

Jacob returned her smile with one of his own. "Yes. I go out of my way to perpetuate that because I don't want them in my business." He rested his chin on the top of her head. "I didn't want to leave you alone but I also didn't want my friend to know you were here. Even though I trust him I couldn't take the risk he'd inadvertently mention he'd met you. Now with the shooting you've become even more of a celebrity."

"I'm not a celebrity."

"You're a public figure, Princess."

"Unfortunately that has become a curse."

He massaged her back in a comforting gesture. "Don't let this get you down. The maggot that shot Tyler will be apprehended."

Ana relished the comforting warmth and strength in Jacob's body when he wrapped his arms around her body. "I hope you're right."

"Look at me, baby," he crooned. Waiting until she raised her chin, Jacob pressed a kiss to Ana's forehead. Angling his head, he brushed his mouth over hers. "I'm not trying to minimize what you're going through, but I believe the police are going to catch this creep because he's going to make a mistake. Either he'll try it again or the police will discover something they've overlooked." Easing back, Jacob felt as if he were drowning in pools of gold. However, he hadn't missed the puffiness around Ana's eyes or the faint dark circles that hadn't been there before.

"Do you trust me to keep you safe?"

A sweep of lashes brushed the tops of Ana's cheekbones when she lowered her gaze. "I think so."

"You can't think, Ana. You have to believe it."

She looked up at him and the sweep hand on his watch made a full revolution before she said, "I believe you."

"Good. Now, I want you to come downstairs with me to see what I bought you."

Ana followed Jacob, secretly wanting to trust and believe him. If she'd had a choice she would've remained cloistered in her parents' home. Her father could've hired a small army to protect the property, monitoring everyone coming and going. At least she would be with her loved ones. She even would've been able to conduct business from what had been her father's home/office.

The men in her family had gotten together to dictate her future for however long it would take to catch the shooter. Had they not realized that at thirty-three years of age she was more than capable of deciding her fate, and if she'd known what they were up to she would've fled Florida for Virginia. Living on a horse farm with Nicholas was preferable to living with a stranger—a stranger whose presence was a constant reminder of what she'd denied—that she was a normal woman with normal urges. She was no different than Jacob who'd admitted to her that he was a normal man with normal urges.

Jacob handed her a decorative shopping bag, watching her reaction when she recognized the contents. "Wigs! And sunblock."

"I bought three of them because I didn't know which one you'd want to wear."

Ana held up an auburn wig with gold highlights. "I've always wanted to be a redhead." She walked toward the half bath off the kitchen. "Come with me and let me know which one you like best." She put on the stocking cap, then the wig, staring at her reflection in the mirror over the vanity. Her eyes met Jacob's in the mirror. "What do you think?"

Moving closer, he rested his hands on her shoulders. The wig overpowered her small face. "The bangs are too long."

She took off the wig, handing it to him, then shook out another. This one was platinum blond. "I've never wanted to be a blonde."

Jacob winked at her. "What's the expression that blondes have more fun?"

"I wouldn't know. I've never been one." Ana slipped it on and stared at her reflection, somewhat stunned how much it'd changed her appearance. "I look like Tinker Bell." The pixie style was similar to her haircut.

"You look cute."

Turning, Ana met Jacob's eyes. "You really like it?"

He nodded. "It brings out the gold in your complexion."

"Let me try on the last one, then we'll make a decision." The final wig was sandy-brown, curly and framed her face as if it were her natural hair. "This is more like it. It doesn't even weigh as much as the other two."

Jacob turned Ana around to face him. She was right. The wig was the perfect fit for her tiny face. The corkscrew curls moved whenever she turned her head, as if they'd taken on a life of their own. Anchoring his hands under her shoulders he picked her up, swinging her around in the confined space.

"Please put me down, Jacob."

He lifted her higher. "Not yet." Eyes narrowing, he examined her face more closely than before. "Have you been crying?"

Ana tightened her hold around his neck. "No. Why?"

"Your eyes look puffy."

She wanted to ask Jacob if there was anything he didn't notice. "I didn't sleep well last night."

He set her on her feet, eyebrows lifting questioningly. "Is there something wrong with the bed?"

"No, the bed is fine." Ana decided it was better to tell him the truth because she'd discovered he had a mind like a steel trap. One lie would have to be covered by another and then another. "I did a lot of dreaming."

"Were they dreams or nightmares, Princess?"

Reaching up, she pulled off the wig and cap in one motion. "Both."

Jacob took her free hand and led her out of the bath and into the kitchen. "I'm not going to profess that I know what you're going through. And I don't want to minimize your situation, but I don't want you to beat up on yourself about something over which you have no control. You're safe and Tyler is getting better. I spoke to Diego and he said there's no word on the shooter, but he's optimistic they'll come up with something."

Ana's eyelids fluttered wildly. "What about Jason?"

"What about him?"

"Why wouldn't someone go after him? After all, he's also Serenity Records."

Cradling her face between his hands, Jacob pressed a light kiss on her soft, parted lips. "Jason has decided to close down the office for a month. He gave everyone four weeks' paid vacation."

Ana went completely still. "That's crazy! How can he shut down the company?"

"Easy, Princess," Jacob crooned. "All decision-making personnel are using video conferencing to connect with one another. Jason is using the studio at your parents' home to work with performers, so there's no lag time in getting their albums completed."

"But…why close the offices?" she stammered.

Pulling her closer, Jacob buried his face between her neck and shoulder. "Jason has contacted a real estate agent to look for a free-standing building closer to a residential neighborhood."

"Will it be in Boca?"

"I don't know. He also plans to wire it with a highly sophisticated security system. It's easier to monitor a single structure than a high-rise office building. All employees will have to swipe in and out, and all visitors—and that includes deliveries from shipping companies—will be on surveillance tape."

Ana exhaled an audible sigh. "It seems as if I've underestimated my brother."

"What makes you think he wouldn't be able to step up to the plate, Ana?"

Her smile faltered, she pulled back, staring up at Jacob. "Jason has always been about music. This is not to say he's totally ignorant when it comes to business, but he always seems so bored whenever we talk business. But he was quick to remind me that he does have an MBA."

Jacob wanted to tell Ana that her twin was a Cole, and that meant he'd grown up listening to his father, uncles and cousins discussing deals. If there was a gene for business acumen, if not all, then most of the Coles had inherited it.

"Jason will do all right without you there to hold his hand."

A flush darkened Ana's face. "It's not like that, Jacob."

"Isn't it? Who has the final decision when it comes to Serenity?"

A beat passed. "I do, but that's not to say I don't involve Jason."

"You involve him because you're partners. Have you ever thought that maybe he doesn't want to be involved? That he's content being the creative and artistic end of the business?"

Ana chewed her lower lip as she shook her head. She recalled the times when she had to ask Jason something twice during an executive staff meeting. It was as if he'd been daydreaming. The first time she noticed it and called him out on it his excuse was that he'd been out late the night before and was practically falling asleep. The next time she knew he couldn't use the same excuse because they'd had dinner with their parents and she'd slept over.

Her eyes narrowed as she gave Jacob a penetrating stare. "What are you saying?"

"What do you want me to tell you?" He'd answered her question with a question.

"Are you saying I shouldn't involve Jason in the business component?"

"That has to be your decision, sweetheart."

Ana ignored the endearment. "Maybe you're right. My aunt Josephine's grandson interned with us one summer, and he would be the perfect replacement for Jason." Her expression brightened. "As soon as this madness is over I'll talk to Jason about inviting Graham to join us."

"Where is he now?"

"He's working for ColeDiz."

Jacob grimaced. "Won't that cause a rift with Diego?"

"Not really. Diego knows Graham's not happy working for ColeDiz. He constantly tells Diego he's a composite of his twin cousins—equally comfortable with music and business."

"You're lucky, Ana, because you don't have to go too far to look for a competent executive."

She angled her head, appearing to be deep in thought. "I suppose you're right. All I have to do is raid ColeDiz and endure Diego's wrath for taking his people. His style is very different from his father's. He hires only the best and pays them well to ensure their loyalty. I've heard he's not easy to work with or for, but there's one thing I can give him credit for."

"What's that?"

"He's a risk-taker. He's diversified ColeDiz, and he's now a cotton broker. Diego paid cash on delivery to a Ugandan cotton grower, making it the biggest family-owned agribusiness in the States. Joseph is now involved in setting up a tea plantation in the South Carolina Lowcountry."

"Where do you stand in all these business machinations?" Jacob asked Ana.

Her smooth brow furrowed. "I don't follow you."

"Have you thought about what's going to happen if you decide to marry and start a family? Will you still be involved with Serenity, or will you take time off to raise your child or children?"

"Why shouldn't I be able to balance marriage and motherhood?"

Jacob shook his head. "That's not what I asked you. Do you intend to push out a baby, hand it over to a nanny, then put on your power suit and go into the office?"

Ana's jaw dropped as she struggled to form her words, while not losing her temper. Closing her eyes, she counted slowly to five. "I wasn't raised by a nanny and I'd never let someone else raise my children. My mother was a stay-at-home mom. She didn't go back to work until all of us were in school, and that was part-time. When I woke up I saw my mother and when I went to bed her face was the last one I saw. So, please don't imply that I'd neglect my babies."

"Good for you. Unfortunately, that's not the case with mothers who *have* to work."

Her expression changed, a smile ruffling the corners of her mouth. Ana didn't know what it was but whenever Jacob challenged her it got her to thinking. "You just gave me an idea." His smile matched hers, her gaze fixed on his sexy mouth.

"What's that?"

"If the building Jason's buying is large enough, then we can set up an on-site child care center. It would save employees the cost of sending their children to daycare or sitters."

"There you go," Jacob said, smiling.

Going to tiptoe, Ana brushed her mouth over his. "Hanging out with you is good for me."

Cradling her waist, he pulled her close. "Why?"

"You challenge me to think outside the box."

Staring down at her through lowered lids, Jacob's eyes caressed her face. "Is that good, Princess?"

Her lush lips parted in a smile. "Very good."

"What you don't realize is that you already think outside the box. It's just that you need someone to bounce your ideas off of, and right now I happen to be that person."

Ana sobered, wondering why Jacob was being so self-deprecating. "You're wrong, Jacob. You are good for me."

Jacob didn't have a comeback. He may have been good for Ana, but he was struggling with the notion of her being good for him. She'd lived under his roof for twenty-four hours and during that time there was never a moment when she wasn't in his thoughts. Even if he closed his eyes he could recall everything about her. He knew the exact timbre of her voice when annoyed. Then there was her smile: warm, inviting and incredibly sexy with a matched set of dimples.

Diego had mentioned about her being difficult. Jacob knew she was used to giving orders, not taking them, and it had taken Herculean self-control for her not to get in his face whenever he told her what to do. And he was more than aware that Ana had tempered her attitude because she was still traumatized. He respected her strength when he'd re-called some men who'd cracked completely, becoming bab-bling idiots when they saw someone shot down in front of them. Jacob wasn't certain whether she was still in shock or in denial. Whatever it was she'd handled the situation better than he would've thought she would.

She claimed to have had a nightmare and that meant she had internalized everything. What he had to do was make life as normal and stress-free as possible. Jacob had called his aunt and uncle to let them know he was coming down and bringing a friend. His aunt told him she'd already rented the guesthouse, and that he would have to stay in a room in the main house. She'd also mentioned that if he was coming with a woman, then they would have to share the bedroom. It was the second high season in the Keys, so with the in-flux of Europeans, bargain-seekers and lobster divers rooms were scarce.

"You may change your mind when I tell you that we're going to have to share a bed tomorrow. My aunt's place is booked up with the exception of one bedroom suite."

"Did you tell her you were bringing someone?"

"I told I was bringing a woman with me."

"And what did she say?"

"She said she's giving us the suite because then we won't have to share a bathroom with the other guests."

Ana wondered how many times he'd brought a woman

with him while visiting his Key West relatives. "I guess it's okay," she said glibly. "I doubt if we're going to spend that much time in bed, so let's not sweat it."

Either she was a consummate actress or Ana was truly indifferent whether they would sleep together or not. Jacob wanted to believe it was the latter, because he definitely wasn't indifferent. There was something about her face and luscious petite body that had him harboring impure thoughts—thoughts that translated into making love to her.

He glanced at the clock on the microwave. "It's time I start dinner."

Ana affected a sexy moue. "I made a side dish of apple and fennel slaw."

Grinning, he ruffled her hair. "Well, look at you. As soon as you learn to do laundry, then you'll be ready to become the perfect housewife."

She stuck her tongue out at him, while scrunching up her pert nose. "I still don't do housework."

"You don't have to, sweetheart. That's what cleaning services are for."

"Are you saying if I learn to do laundry, then you'll consider me marriage material?"

"No, I'm not. Even if you couldn't boil water, wash dishes or pick up a sock you'd still make some man a wonderful wife."

Resting her hands at her waist, Ana angled her head and stared up at him. "Thank you, Jacob. That's quite a compliment coming from a confirmed bachelor."

"I've never professed to be a confirmed bachelor. I haven't married because I haven't met the woman I'd want to spend the rest of my life with."

"I have four single girlfriends I could introduce you to."

Jacob wanted to shake Ana for being so obtuse. "No, thank you." He wanted to tell her he didn't have a problem meeting women. It was just that most of the women he'd been in-

volved with bored the hell out of him and he could only take
them in very small doses.

Ana lifted her shoulders. "Well, if you change your mind
then let me know and I'll hook you up."

"Which part of 'no, thank you' don't you understand, Ana?
I don't want or need your help in finding a woman."

She glared at him. "Your neighbors are right. You are a
grouch."

That said, she walked out of the kitchen leaving him to
stare at her back. There was no need for him to get so hostile
because she'd offered to introduce him to her friends. Most
men would've been jumping for joy. For them the more the
merrier, but not Mr. Jones. She swore that it would be the first
and last time she would ever broach the subject with him.

Chapter 7

Ana sat beside Jacob, staring at the passing landscape out the side window. The Keys were like another world. Despite her seeing a few mansionlike structures, the topography appeared virtually untouched, creating a primordial world with exotic plants and flowers, subtropical birds, mangroves and coral reefs. Something startled a flock of white herons when they rose majestically from their nesting site to take to the air. Boats, ranging from rowboats to luxury yachts dotted the waterways. Those sailing were either fishing or sunbathing, and a few were photographing the spectacular water views.

The excitement she'd expected to feel because she was going to see Key West for the first time wasn't there, and it had everything to do with Jacob. Over dinner the night before he was practically monosyllabic and after they'd cleaned up the kitchen she'd gone upstairs to her bedroom and read for hours.

Thankfully she'd slept throughout the night, waking alert and rested. She made her bed, showered and dressed for the day. When she'd gone downstairs Jacob was nowhere in sight. The security system was still armed and Ana had assumed either he hadn't gotten up or he'd gone out again. She doubted the latter because there was no note tacked to the corkboard.

Not waiting for him, she made fresh squeezed orange juice, diced pineapple, mango, papaya and white grapes for a fruit salad. The aroma of brewing coffee had filled the kitchen when he walked in wearing a Hawaiian-print shirt, faded relaxed jeans and running shoes. He looked different and it wasn't until he sat down at the table across from her that she realized he hadn't shaved. The stubble on his lean jaw enhanced his overt masculinity, but she wasn't about to tell him that.

He'd thanked her when she'd placed a dish of fruit at his place setting. They ate in silence and as she cleared the table to stack the dishwasher he'd announced they would be leaving in less than an hour, so she should pack what she wanted to take with her.

His neighbors were right. Not only Jacob was grouchy, but he was also moody.

Jacob stared through the windshield when he'd wanted to take furtive glances at Ana. Her face framed by a profusion of brownish-gold curls made her look like a fragile doll.

He smiled despite his lingering annoyance that she'd offered to hook him up with one of her girlfriends. Attracting a woman had never been a problem for him. Finding one for other than sex proved a bit more challenging, and now that he was getting older sex didn't top his priority list when it came to women. Jacob wanted and needed someone he could talk to after the lovemaking ended. He hadn't lied to his mother when he told her he had yet to meet the right woman. Some he'd dealt with were either too immature, while others were much too needy. Nothing grated on his nerves more than a whining, needy woman.

Early in his career with the marshal service he'd believed

he'd met *the* woman. Jacob had seriously considered proposing marriage, but she'd ruined everything when she'd begun to complain that she didn't get to see him enough. When he'd tried explaining to her that when assigned to the Violent Crime Fugitive Task Force he didn't know when he'd be called away, Delia morphed into someone he hadn't recognized. Her accusations that he was cheating on her escalated into uncontrollable shouting matches. Jacob knew he had to end their relationship, knowing he wouldn't be able to cope with a jealous girlfriend and remain focused.

"What do you want to do tonight?"

Ana turned to look at Jacob. "Hallelujah! He speaks," she spat out sarcastically.

A hint of a smile flitted across his mouth. "Don't push it, Princess."

"What do you expect me to say? You barely grunt at me, and now you're asking me what I'd like to do."

He smiled, giving her a quick glance. "I'm sorry for being a grouch."

A beat passed before Ana said, "Apology accepted."

"Thank you, Princess. I'll ask you again. What would you like to do?"

"Can we stop to see the Hemingway museum?"

Jacob nodded. "That can be arranged. What else?"

"I'd like to eat at Jimmy Buffet's Margaritaville Café."

"That's also doable. Anything else?"

"I suppose we can visit some of the more popular bars and clubs."

Jacob's straight white teeth were a startling contrast to his brown complexion when he laughed. "Now you're talking."

Ana removed her sunglasses. "How long do you plan to stay?"

He met her eyes. "As long as you want."

She placed her hand over his when he gripped the steering wheel. "I'd like to take a tour and do some shopping."

Reversing their hands, Jacob cradled her much smaller hand, giving it a gentle squeeze before kissing her fingers. "That's going to take at least three or four days. Are you certain you don't have anything pending on your calendar?"

This was the Jacob she liked—smiling and teasing. "Very certain."

"Good. I suppose this means we're free to go and do anything we want."

Ana closed her eyes. "I wish I could turn back the clock to when I was sixteen and planned to live the bohemian life in Key West. Even though Daddy cut short my dream I still felt freer than I do now." She opened her eyes to find Jacob staring at her with a strange expression on his handsome face.

"This too shall pass," Jacob said in a quiet voice. He wanted to tell Ana she had to be patient, because eventually the shooter was going to make a mistake. Most criminals did. "You still could live a bohemian lifestyle. The first thing you'll have to do is move out of your luxury condo, buy a loft and decorate it with vintage posters of singers and musicians dating from the 40s to the 80s. Of course, you'll set up a salon with a gathering of writers, musicians, political dissents and deadbeat intellectuals."

Ana laughed softly. "Why stop at the 80s?"

"Disco, baby. Most contemporary pop music is an amalgamation of prior decades. R&B vocal groups like Jagged Edge and Boyz II Men and a few of the others are nothing more than a throwback to doo-wop with emotional ballads and a cappella harmonies."

"What about rap and hip-hop?"

"I found early rap rather primitive with all the sampling. Thankfully it has evolved where it's now much more sophisticated. As for hip-hop, I've always liked it."

"Who're your favorite R&B singers?" she asked.

Jacob angled his head. "It has to be Anthony Hamilton. He's probably more blues than R&B."

"Who else do you like?"

"Maxwell, but unfortunately I have to wait years for him to put out a new album."

Ana and Jacob spent the next quarter of an hour discussing musical genres until she eased her hand from his, put on her glasses and returned her attention to staring out at the landscape. Traffic was heavier than usual for that time of morning, but he was in no hurry to reach their destination, estimating it would about take nearly forty minutes to make the fifty-five mile drive from the Long Key Channel to Key West. After all, he had nothing but time on his hands and it was the same with Ana.

Tapping a button on the steering wheel, he tuned the radio to a satellite station featuring songs from the early 2000s. The voices of Destiny's Child singing "Say My Name" came through the speakers located throughout the SUV.

Ana and Jacob shared a smile when they sang along with the girl group. He felt a chill eddy its way down his back when Ana sang Faith Hill's "Breathe." She had a rich wonderful alto singing voice. It was his turn to showcase his singing talent with the "Thong Song."

Ana gave him an incredulous look. "I can't believe you know every word."

"That's because I have it in the jukebox."

"I suppose you know the number, too."

Jacob winked at her. "Damn straight. In fact, I know most of the numbers to my favorites. All of the CDs are grouped by genre—blues, R&B, classical, jazz, Latin, country, pop, rap and hip-hop, show tunes and movie soundtracks."

He tapped another button, lowering the volume, and told Ana that his father and uncles had formed a band when they were in their teens, playing at weddings and small local clubs whenever they needed a backup band. They told anyone who wanted to sign them that they were twenty-one and twenty-three so they could play in bars and clubs. He'd grown up listening to their jam sessions and the one time he'd sat in playing guitar was a night he would remember forever.

"Are you good?" Ana asked.

"I do all right."

"That's not what I asked you."

"I can read music, and with a lot of practice I can memorize a piece." He gave her a sidelong glance. "What are you hatching in that beautiful head?"

Ana knew what she was going to propose to Jacob would extend their friendship beyond her current predicament. "I'd like you to audition for Jason. He's always looking for session players. You could come into the studio and he'll record what you play, then he'll integrate it into a number of tracks. Of course you'll be paid and your name will be listed in the credits."

"Whatever happened to synthesizers?"

"Jason's an old-school dinosaur. He's like my father. They believe in using the actual instruments."

"No, Ana."

Shifting on her seat, she gave him a pleading look. "Please don't say no until you talk to Jason. He'll set up a time that's convenient for you to visit the studio. I know once you two start jamming together you'll change your mind."

"I'm not going to promise anything except that I'll think about it."

Ana felt as if she'd won a small victory. Serenity was always looking for new talent whether in front of the microphone or as backup singers and/or musicians.

"Idiot!" Jacob shouted when a driver cut in front of him. Instinctually his right arm went out to shield Ana when his foot slammed down on the brake to avoid rear-ending the sports car. "Are you all right?" Heat raced up his arm when his hand unintentionally cupped her breast. He pulled his hand away. "Sorry about that."

"It's okay," she whispered.

Ana pressed her back against the leather seat, her heart pumping wildly in her chest. If Jacob's reflexes were any slower there would've been an accident. She'd told him it was okay when she wasn't okay. For a nanosecond her body had reacted not to the vehicle's sudden stop but to the warmth of his hand on her chest. Her nipples had tightened and she prayed he wouldn't notice them through the fabric of the tee.

An uncomfortable silence filled the interior of the truck as they passed Marathon and approached the Seven Mile Bridge. How, she mused, was she going to share a bed with Jacob and remain indifferent?

Whenever he touched her she felt like a pat of butter on a hot surface, melting under his caress. Then there was his kiss. Chaste kisses that were more to comfort than seduce; kisses and caresses that had triggered her erotic dream.

Why, she mused, couldn't he be old with ill-fitting dentures and smelling of liniment instead of young and virile; and despite his occasional gruffness he was as slick and charming as a hustler smooth-talking an unsuspecting victim that a counterfeit designer handbag was authentic. Maybe, she prayed, a guest would check out earlier than planned and they wouldn't have to not only share a room but also a bed.

Ana knew she wasn't a prude, but there was no reason why temptation had to be so overtly delicious. She took a surreptitious glance at Jacob's hands and the length of his fingers, recalling the time when she and her girlfriends had traveled to Jamaica on vacation; they'd sat around the pool looking at men in their swimsuits, while attempting to make the correlation that the size of man's hand was indicative of the length of his penis. After too much sun and countless glasses of rum punch and incessant giggling they were incapable of arriving at a consensus.

She missed her girlfriends, their spontaneous laughter,

and their unwavering support. There was never a time when they weren't there for one another whether it was emotionally or financially.

Jacob maneuvered onto the driveway leading to a large two-story house with shuttered windows and a wraparound porch. Towering centuries-old trees shaded the structure from the brilliant summer sun. Shutting off the engine, he got out and came around to assist Ana at the same time the door to the house opened. His aunt stood on the porch, waving.

"That's my aunt. Her name is Mathilda, but everyone calls her Mattie. Go inside and out of the heat. I'll be in as soon as I get the bags."

Ana wasn't conscious of the heat until Jacob mentioned it. The humidity clung to her bared skin like a wet blanket. Sitting in the air-conditioned vehicle made her oblivious to the outside temperatures. The mouth-watering aroma of grilling meat wafted in the heavy air. She glanced up at the house. It was as if she'd stepped back in time when the Spaniards, and subsequently the English, built grand homes to showcase their status and wealth in the New World.

Mattie was a tall, slender woman with short straight silver hair; her complexion reminded Ana of aged parchment. Upon closer inspection she could see the older woman's strong Native American features. Mattie looked refreshingly cool in a sleeveless blouse, cropped cotton pants and espadrilles.

"Come and let me get a good look at you," Mattie crooned in a slow Southern drawl. "In all the years my nephew has come to visit he has never brought a girl with him." Her warm brown eyes studied Ana, giving her a long, penetrating stare. "You're kinda small, but still pretty as a picture. Now, give your Aunt Mattie a hug."

Ana found herself in a comforting embrace, she returning it with one of her own. "Thank you for having me."

"There's no need to thank me, gal. If you're Jacob's girl, then you're family."

Help me out here, Jacob, her silent voice implored him. Ana chided him for not making the introductions first. Jacob must have heard her silent supplication because he appeared like a specter with their luggage: two garment bags, her carry-on and his duffel. Leaning down, he kissed his aunt's cheek.

The warmth of Mattie's smile reached her eyes. "Please come in and rest yourselves. She held the screen door for her nephew and his girlfriend. "You're going to have to hold this door whenever you come in or leave, because it slams and makes enough noise to wake the dead. But whenever I ask Ray to fix it he acts like I'm speaking a foreign language. He'd rather blow on that darn horn than do anything around the house."

Jacob smiled at his aunt over his shoulder. "If you get the toolbox I'll fix it."

Mattie let the door close slowly to avoid it slamming against the frame. "That's all right. I'm going to call the handyman, and only after I give Ray the estimate will he actually pick up a hammer and do something. He hates giving away his money to folks when he can make the repairs himself."

Ana glanced around the entryway in the house with ten-foot ceilings, gleaming parquet floors and a curving staircase leading to the second floor. A large crystal vase on a round mahogany table was filled with a profusion of colorful fresh flowers. Their footsteps were muffled on the carpeting covering the staircase as she stared down at chairs, loveseats and tables in the expansive living room. The furnishings were distinctly from a bygone era.

She followed Mattie and Jacob down the long hallway. Doors to most bedrooms were closed, but the ones that were opened revealed spaces with four-poster beds draped with mosquito netting, matching armoires and upholstered armchairs with matching footstools. Ana wondered if the furnishings were antiques or reproductions. Regardless of their authenticity they were exquisite.

An inaudible gasp escaped her when she walked into the bedroom suite she was to share with Jacob. A king-size decoratively carved four-poster mahogany bed was draped with sheer netting embroidered with minute sand-colored butterflies. The butterfly design was repeated in the tapestry-covered seat cushions on two pull-up chairs at the small round table in a corner, mahogany bench at the foot of the bed and the two facing club chairs in front of a fireplace. A cushioned window seat spanned the length of floor-to-ceiling windows, and shutters rather than curtains or drapes were installed to provide maximum privacy.

Mattie gestured to a door on her right. "There's a full bath with a dressing room through that door. If I'd known you were coming three days ago I wouldn't have rented out the guesthouse. You would've had a lot more privacy."

Ana wanted to tell her they didn't need privacy. Jacob's declaration *"there will no plans of seduction from either one of us,"* came back in vivid clarity, and she knew even if she pranced around butt-naked nothing sexual was going to go down between them.

Jacob set the luggage on the floor near the armoire with the same carvings etched into the bedposts. "That's okay, Aunt Mattie. We're going to be out most of the time."

"I hope you save some time for me and your uncle before you go back. By the way, I've opened the windows to let in some fresh air. If it gets too hot for you, close them and turn on the air-conditioning. The thermostat is on the other side of the armoire." She exhaled a sigh. "I guess I've talked enough. I'll let you two settle in."

"Where's Uncle Ray?" Jacob asked his aunt.

"He should be back soon. He went to the store to pick up some more wood chips for the smoker. Ray bought a smoker a couple of months back and he smokes everything from brisket to ribs, fresh ham, chicken and sausage." Mattie flashed a wide grin. "I must admit I've gotten used to eating smoked meat. Cooking outdoors is preferable to heating up the kitchen, where it takes hours to cool down."

Jacob shared a glance with Ana. "What's on today's menu?"

"Brisket and ribs. Do you intend to stick around for dinner?"

When Ana nodded, Jacob said, "Yes."

"Do you need any help in the kitchen?" Ana asked.

Crossing her arms under her breasts, Mattie surveyed the woman who looked as if she could really use a home-cooked meal. She was more fragile-looking than skinny. "Do you eat what you cook?"

Ana couldn't stop the rush of heat suffusing her face and chest. "Yes, ma'am. I do eat. Tell her, Jacob," she pleaded when Mattie shot her a skeptical stare.

"She eats," he said in agreement.

Mattie smiled. "If that's the case, then you can help me. I'm cooling some white potatoes for a salad. You do know how to make potato salad?"

"Yes, ma'am."

"Enough of that ma'am business. Either you call me Mattie or Aunt Mattie. The choice is yours."

Ana felt properly chastised, and when she cut her eyes at Jacob she wanted to kick him for smirking. "Okay, Aunt Mattie."

Mattie inclined her head in acknowledgment. "Take your time settling in. If you don't find me in the kitchen, then I'll be out back."

Waiting until Mattie left, closing the door behind her, Ana turned to face Jacob. "When are you going to tell her?"

"I'm not going to tell her," he countered. "I'll tell my uncle and he can explain everything to her."

Ana's expression mirrored confusion. "Why not your aunt?"

"My uncle will tell her what he feels she should know. It was that way when he worked undercover and it has continued to this day. They've been married for nearly forty years, and apparently whatever they've agreed to works."

"Do they have any children?"

Jacob shook his head. "No. Years ago they'd talked about adoption, but once Uncle Ray went undercover they decided it was best they didn't. Ray was afraid if anything had happened to him then Mattie would be left to raise a child or children alone. I'm going to warn you that they're like a couple of newlyweds. They can't keep their hands off each other."

Ana thought about her own parents who'd complained that they couldn't wait until their children left home so they could run around the house stark naked. Gabriel was the first to leave, then Alexandra. She had been next.

Only Jason remained. And it was good that he hadn't given up his apartment in the house where he'd grown up. It was his home base and that made it easier for him to continue re-recording sessions using the studio set up in the Boca Raton mansion.

Ana had always felt like the more dominant twin because of Jason's low-key personality; but he'd risen to the challenge when he closed down the office, and was negotiating the purchase of a building that would prove conducive to maintaining maximum security.

Any of the performers coming to her parents' home in the gated community would have to go through a series of checkpoints before gaining access to the in-home recording studio. Her father had mentioned dismantling the studio and replacing it with an in-home health spa, but hadn't as long Jason continued to live there. Whenever Jason hadn't come into the office he could be found in the studio listening to and editing countless hours of recordings until they were able to meet his exacting standards.

It had taken less than a week for Ana to grasp the enormity that Serenity Records could survive without her micromanaging every phase of its operation. Business would continue with video conferencing and the projected launch date of new music would be met. What she'd failed to realize, until now, was that the company continued with business as usual whenever she went on vacation, and now that she was exiled it would do the same.

Reaching up, she took off the wig, fanning her face with it. "It's hot enough without wearing this."

Jacob gave her a sidelong glance. "I guess you can go without it when we're in the bedroom. But, I'd like you to wear it whenever you step outside this door."

"Copy that," she quipped, using military jargon. "I'm certain hearing that takes you back to your days in the corps."

"Not back in the day, sweetheart. Once a marine always a marine."

"Were you special operations?"

Bending from the knees, Jacob opened the duffel bag. "I was assigned to MSG. I'll tell you about it later."

Ana joined him, unzipping her carry-on. "Does your aunt serve meals to her guests?"

"No. She just offers rooms at daily or weekly rates. A lot of folks with large houses do the same. It's an excellent way of earning extra income."

"I'm going to put away our clothes, then I'm going to take a shower and get into something cooler." Her tee, jeans and running shoes were not conducive to the tropical temperatures.

"Why don't you go and take your shower first," Jacob suggested. "I'll hang up your stuff."

Ana smiled. "You don't mind?"

He made a sucking sound with his tongue and teeth. "Of course not."

She removed a set of underwear, and then took out a smaller bag with her grooming supplies. Kicking off her shoes, she placed them neatly in a corner. "I'll see you later," she said as she headed toward the bathroom.

"Princess?"

Ana stopped, but didn't turn around. "What is it?"

"Do you mind if we stay here tonight with my aunt and uncle? I'd like to do some catching up."

She turned slowly, her gaze taking in everything about the man she'd felt so comfortable with that they'd planned to not only live together for an undetermined length of time, but she would also sleep with. Ana wasn't as indifferent to Jacob as she projected. In truth, she'd come to like him—a lot. Now that she understood his rationale for not using a phone or her credit cards she'd come to respect his somewhat dictatorial edicts. And it wasn't as if he'd been paid to protect her, but had agreed to do it as a favor to *her* cousin. He'd given up his vacation and altered his life for her, and the least she could do for him was be obliging.

She smiled sweetly. "Of course not, sweetheart. I don't mind at all."

Jacob was still standing in the same spot, staring at the door to the bathroom when it closed behind Ana. He was trying to process her calling him sweetheart. Was it a slip of the tongue because on occasion he'd called her sweetheart? Or was she softening and finally willing to accept their unconventional relationship?

What Jacob had to keep reminding himself was why Ana had come into his life. Why she was living with him. But then there were times when he wished they could've met under a different set of circumstances. That there was no threat on her life and instead of becoming her bodyguard he could date her in the conventional way.

Although he called her Princess there was nothing about her indicating she was spoiled. It hadn't been her choice when she was born into a wealthy family where there were certain tasks she didn't have to concern herself with. Whether pampered or protected, she definitely wasn't spoiled or lazy. She offering to help his aunt in the kitchen was a testament to that.

He'd dated a woman who wouldn't bend over to pick up a straw because she said she'd achieved diva status. He knew a few who wore rhinestone tiaras to demonstrate to the world that they were princesses. To him they were phony illmannered princesses with bad attitudes.

There were times when he knew Ana wasn't pleased with what he'd said, but she'd quickly diffused what could've become a volatile and hostile confrontation by walking away. It was probably the same strategy she used in business. Retreat, restrategize and prepare for the next battle.

She and Basil Irvine had waged a war to sign Justine Glover. Irvine had won the first battle, but Ana had achieved the ultimate victory once she'd convinced the young singer to sign with her label. Oh, Jacob mused, to have been the proverbial fly on the wall when it was announced that Glover had signed with Serenity.

The sound of running water came through the door and Jacob placed the garment bags on the bench at the foot of the bed, unzipped them and began hanging up garments in the armoire. Ana's slacks, dresses and blouses hung from the rod next to his shirts, slacks and lightweight jackets. The carry-on bags were next. A knowing smile parted his lips when he held up a pair of bikini panties with a matching bra. There was hardly enough fabric to cover her private parts. Pretty—yes. Practical—definitely not.

Ana finally emerged from the bathroom, a trail of perfume wafting behind her, wearing a white bra with matching panties. If Jacob had eaten he definitely would've lost the contents of his stomach when the muscles violently contracted. The triangle of silky fabric barely covered the area at the apex of her thighs and the swell of firm breasts were close to escaping the confines of the lacy cups. He turned away inasmuch as not to gape at her, but also as an attempt to conceal his growing erection.

He smothered a savage curse. How was he going to sleep in the same bed with a woman so uninhibited that she thought nothing of flaunting her body? *It can't happen. It's not going to work.* The traitorous thoughts pelleted him like sharp needles. Jacob had told himself that he wouldn't make love to Ana, and he'd reassured Diego that his cousin would be safe with him. He'd promised his friend that he would protect Ana from whoever wanted her dead, but who would protect her from her protector?

Resisting the urge to grab his crotch, Jacob managed to sit down, cross his legs, while praying his hard-on would go down before Ana noticed it. "Is this what I can look forward to everyday?"

Ana looked at him, but was unable to see his expression in the shadows because he'd partially closed the shutters. "What are you talking about?"

"Watching you model your underwear."

She sucked her teeth. "Please, Jacob. I'm certain you see a lot more skin on the beach. It's not as if I'm wearing a thong."

"What did I tell you about having urges?"

Ana opened the armoire, reaching for a loose-fitting white linen sundress. She peered around the door. "If you have urges, then you should do something about it. And I shouldn't have to tell you how to relieve your sexual frustration."

Jacob leaned forward, glaring at her. "I don't like to do *that*."

Stepping in the dress, she adjusted the bodice. Bending slightly, she picked up a pair of black patent leather sandals, pushing her feet into them.

"Since we're not going to have sex, I'm willing to help you with your dilemma."

"How's that?"

"I'll help you do the deed. And I'll close my eyes when I do it so as not to embarrass you." Ana clapped a hand over her mouth to keep from laughing aloud. She knew she'd shocked Jacob when she'd offered to masturbate him when she heard gurgling noises. It served him right for insulting her. "Come now, sweetheart. We're both adults who're definitely not new at this, so what you do say?"

Somewhere, somehow Jacob recovered his voice. "I'm not going to let you jerk me off."

Ana closed the door, moved closer, seeing his pained expression and clenched fists. "It's up to you. I'm just willing to help you out."

"I don't need your help," he said between clenched teeth.

Fluffing up her damp hair, Ana walked over to where she'd left the wig, shaking it out. "I think it would be cooler if I didn't wear the stocking cap." She put on the wig, adjusting it. "I'm going downstairs." Wiggling her fingers, she crooned, "See you later, sweetheart."

It was much later after Ana left the bedroom that Jacob wanted to shout at the top of his lungs that she was a tease. A beautiful, uninhibited tease that had him close to ejaculating when he'd fantasied about her hand between his thighs.

She had the face of an angel, the body of a goddess and never in his wildest imagination would he have believed she was a sexy irritant that had him thinking about pleasuring himself. It was something he hadn't done in a very long time.

Pushing off the chair, he crossed the room, closed the door and walked in the direction of the bathroom to hopefully exorcise the image of the woman whose very presence had become mental torment.

Jacob was back in control when he went downstairs and found his uncle in the backyard adding seasoned wood chips to the smoker. The two men exchanged strong hugs, with Ray kissing his nephew's cheek. The resemblance between them was remarkable, and Jacob knew what he would look like in his sixties. Ray's once dark hair was now salt-and-pepper, matching his cropped beard.

He thumped Jacob's back. "You look good. It can't be work, so it must be that little girl in the kitchen with Mattie."

"It's not like that, Uncle Ray."

"What aren't you telling me, son?"

Jacob gestured to the chairs positioned around a table under a copse of palm trees. "Please sit and I'll tell you everything."

"Something tells me I'm going to need something stronger than water. I'm going to get a beer. Do you want one?"

"Sure."

He waited for his late father's brother to open a cooler and take out two bottles of ice-cold beer. Jacob didn't know why, but for the first time in his life he envied his uncle's lifestyle. Raymond Jones had married a woman he claimed to have fallen in love with on sight. Ray had returned from his second tour of duty in Vietnam and had driven down to the Keys to blow off steam. Mattie, who'd worked in her father's restaurant, apparently hadn't been able to take her eyes off the young soldier in his uniform. He explained what each of the medals pinned on his shirt represented, and before he walked out he left Mattie a generous tip and his Purple Heart with a promise he would come back to pick it up once he received his official discharge papers. Six months later he was back, asking for his medal and her hand in marriage.

Ray enrolled in college, and after graduating he joined the DEA, working undercover for more than a decade until he finally was assigned a desk position. The day he celebrated twenty-five years with the agency, he filed for retirement. Mattie, who'd continued to run her father's restaurant after he passed away, sold it and bought the large dilapidated house in Old Town. It took more than a year to renovate it, and to earn extra income they rented out rooms during the tourist season.

Jacob gave his uncle a half salute, then put the bottle to his mouth and took a long swallow. He studied the label. "This is really good."

Ray nodded. "It's a little more expensive than some of the more popular brands, but I always say you get what you pay for. Now what's up with your girlfriend?"

Jacob stared at a tiny brown lizard sunning itself on a rock. "Did you hear about the sniper shooting in Boca Raton?" Ray nodded again. Pulling his chair closer, Jacob rested his elbows on the top of the table and told his uncle everything, while watching the gamut of emotions crossing the elder Jones's face.

"She's looks so different from the photographs of her they show on television."

"That's because she's wearing a wig."

Ray shook his head. "Damn! I just can't believe someone would want to kill her for what amounts to her closing a deal. What the hell is wrong with these so-called music moguls? The artists they sign are no better. The list goes on and on with hip-hop artists who die much too young. There's not only Tupac and the Notorious B.I.G, but Freaky Tah, Big L and Scott LaRock. I don't believe any of them were thirty when they died."

"I see you still keep up with everything and everyone in the music industry."

Attractive lines fanned out around Ray's dark eyes when he smiled. "What can I say. I'm still a frustrated wannabe musician. Not a day goes by when I don't blow a few tunes on Sally. If it hadn't been for Mattie and playing my sax I would've lost my mind a long time ago." He took another swallow of his beer. "I would tell any special agent considering going undercover to really think about it."

"That's because you stayed under too long," Jacob remarked, deadpan.

"That's true," Ray agreed. "Now, back to Ana. What's

going to happen if they don't find the shooter before you go back to work?"

That was something Jacob didn't want to think about. The longer it took to apprehend the shooter the more danger it posed to Ana. "Her father's going to send her to Brazil."

A frown creased Ray's forehead. "Who or what's in Brazil?"

"She has a cousin who lives there with her husband. Ana says they have a coffee plantation somewhere in the mountains."

There came a pause as Ray stared at his nephew. "Do you know what I can't understand is how someone knew she would be at that restaurant on that particular day."

"It's common knowledge that it's her favorite restaurant and with vanity plates reading SERENITY she was an easy enough target."

"All of that will have to change, Jake."

He nodded in agreement. "A lot of things *will* change once this is over."

"What's your stake in this other than you're doing a friend a favor?"

Jacob sat up straight. "I'm not following you."

"The girl is living with you. And you bring her here and I have to assume you'll both sleep in the same bed. What's up with that?"

"It's not like that."

Leaning back against the chair, Ray affected a half smile. "Do you have ED?"

"Hell, no!"

Ray sobered. "Your daddy's gone, so I'm going to talk to you as if you were my son. Be careful, Jacob. Promises and the best intentions are forgotten once a man's sap starts rising. And, if you do get involved with Ana you have to remember who her people are. You hurt that girl and they will come after you and it's going to be all she wrote."

A muscle jerked in Jacob's jaw when he clenched his teeth. "I'm not going to get involved with her."

"That's what I said when I came back here to pick up my medal from Mattie. I dated her every day for a week and it took seven days for me to realize my life wouldn't be complete without her. It was the same with your father and mother. One glance and he knew she was the one."

"Where is all of this coming from?"

"Mattie told me how you look at Ana. It was the same way I look at her and the way Stephen used to look at Gloria. It appears as if the Jones men haven't quite learned not to be so transparent. The only other thing I'm going to say, then I'll shut up—she's quite a catch. Excuse me, but I have to check on my meat."

Jacob sat there, staring at his uncle when he opened the door to the smoker. The sweet scent of apple-infused wood chips and the succulent aroma of smoked meat floated in the air. What had Mattie seen that he wasn't aware of? He'd admit he was physically attracted to Ana, and that was it. Or was it more?

He went through a mental list of all the things he liked about her. What shocked him most was there wasn't anything he didn't like about her. She made him laugh—something he didn't do enough. And she'd shocked him when she'd offered to take care of his urges, something no other woman had ever offered to do. She didn't bore him and definitely wasn't needy. If the police or the investigators her family hired to find the shooter didn't come up with something concrete within another week Jacob wasn't certain how long he would be able to pretend he was unaffected by the woman he went to bed thinking about and woke up looking for.

There was no doubt he was in denial when it came to Ana Cole.

Chapter 8

Ana lay in bed waiting for Jacob. They'd sat on the porch swing watching fireflies, while listening to the cacophony of sounds from night creatures, and the radio on a nearby table was tuned to a station playing smooth jazz. She'd felt content, safe sitting with him in the darkness. Sharing dinner with their hosts in the backyard reminded her of the outings with her family whenever it cooled down enough to cook and eat outdoors.

She knew Jacob had told his uncle about her plight when Ray reassured her she was in good hands, that it wasn't the first time Jacob been entrusted to protect a witness. What she wanted to tell Ray was that not only was she a witness but also the target, but she'd promised herself that she wouldn't permit herself to dwell on what was but what would be. The shooter would be caught, prosecuted and imprisoned for a long time.

Dinner had become a festive affair with melt-in-the-mouth brisket and fall-off-the-bone ribs, savory potato salad, coleslaw and fluffy biscuits. Mattie had made a pitcher of white sangria with white peaches, grapes, pears and apples that complimented the delicious meat and side dishes.

Mattie told her the houseguests used a separate side entrance that locked automatically at ten each night; they had to use a special magnetic card key to gain entry after that time. Ray had given Jacob a set of keys to keep, so whenever he felt like coming to Key West the house would be available to him.

Ana knew she'd eaten too much, but after the first few forkfuls she couldn't stop, requesting a second helping of everything. She was certain she was going to gain weight with the inactivity. That didn't bother her only because she needed to weigh more than she did. Working out at her building's health club was only to relieve the stress she no longer had to concern herself with. Her eyes closed, her breathing deepened and within minutes she was sound asleep.

It was after midnight when Jacob climbed the staircase and walked into the bedroom at the end of the hallway. He'd waited as long as he could without falling asleep on the porch and become bait for the tiny insects waiting to feast on his skin.

He closed the door, locking it behind him. Ana had turned off the lamp, but had left the bathroom light on. Slipping out of his shoes, he left them on a mat near the door and tiptoed into the bathroom.

Standing in front of the mirror over the vanity, he stared at his reflection. The stubble made him look scruffy, sinister. He never shaved on his days off, but had done so because of Ana; when she hadn't commented on his emerging beard he decided to let it grow.

Jacob brushed his teeth and took a quick shower, and then returned to the bedroom and pulled on a pair of pajama pants. The pajamas were in deference to Ana, because he usually slept nude. He normally would've chosen the side of the bed closer to the door, but Ana had claimed it. Then he remem-

bered he'd concealed his handgun in the drawer of the bedside table next to where she lay. Not wanting to wake her, he
decided to let it stay where it was.

Everything in the darkened room seemed magnified: the
sound of her soft breathing, his own heartbeat echoing in
his ears, the hypnotic scent of her perfume and the warmth
of her body. During dinner he'd watched her, delighted she
was so comfortable with his aunt and uncle. She'd confirmed
what he already knew. She was a wonderful conversation-
alist, chatty enough to be charming and an intent listener
whenever someone else rendered their opinion. She and Ray
appeared to be kindred spirits when they discussed music;
he promising to play his saxophone but only if she accompanied him on the piano.

Mattie had whispered that she was a pleasure to have
around. This coming from Mattie was odd because those
familiar with her knew she didn't like anyone in her kitchen
whenever she cooked. Jacob smiled in the darkness. It appeared as if his charge had passed the test. She'd easily won
over his relatives just by being Ana.

He closed his eyes and soon drifted off to sleep.

Ana managed to get out of bed without waking Jacob. She
hadn't believed she would've been able to get a restful night's
sleep with him beside her, yet she had. In fact, she felt more
rested than she had in days.

Jacob had complained about her modeling her underwear
and she'd taken steps to counter that when she selected the
outfit she planned to wear for the day, leaving it in on a table
behind the decorative screen in the dressing room. Ana was
more than aware of the dangerous game she was playing with
Jacob by living and sleeping together, and felt the need not
to exacerbate the situation by teasing him.

There was nothing to keep her and Jacob from having
a physical liaison. After all, they weren't in love with each

other, which meant they could walk away unscathed. Yes, she liked him, but not enough to give him her heart although he claimed most of the attributes she liked and wanted in a man with whom she could have an ongoing relationship.

If they were to have a physical encounter, then she doubted whether it would continue after their current situation ended. If not, then they would remain friends. She brushed her teeth, washed her face with a special solution she'd purchased from her dermatologist to combat oiliness, then sliding back the shower door, stepped into the stall.

She glanced up through the skylight. A bright blue cloudless sky and warm temperatures set the stage for a day of touring and shopping. Turning on the faucet, Ana adjusted the temperature, luxuriating in the flow of warm water. Then she did something she hadn't done since before her luncheon date with Tyler—she sang. Singing in the shower was something Ana had done since she was a child. She had a good, but not great, singing voice. Gabriel had been gifted with an incredible set of vocal chords, as well as the gift to compose music. He'd earned a Grammy and an Oscar for a movie soundtrack.

For her it wasn't about writing music, playing an instrument, but training her ear to recognize something unique in someone's voice. It wasn't even about a vocalist's ability to carry a tune. It was about style. She'd grown up listening to her parents' music, marveling that singer/songwriters like Barry White and Isaac Hayes didn't have the most melodious voices, but it was their overt sexual tonality, blending with incredible background music that made them musical geniuses.

Broadway show tunes were her favorites. Her parents had always taken her to New York to see a Broadway show to celebrate her birthday. They'd check into a hotel several days before going to the theatre to go sightseeing and shop at boutiques and department stores. The show was always followed by dinner at one of her favorite restaurants. The tradition began when she'd celebrated her sixth birthday, continuing until she turned twelve. At thirteen she felt it wasn't that cool to hang out with her parents when compared to being with her friends.

Turning thirteen had changed Ana. She was a teenager, hosted sleepovers, was permitted to go to the local mall with her girlfriends, and it was the year she realized a boy who'd teased her relentlessly told his friends that he liked her. She may have reciprocated his feelings if he hadn't been so obnoxious. They were reunited for their tenth high school reunion and he'd apologized profusely, saying he had been too intimidated to approach her because of Jason. His disclosure shocked Ana because Jason, unlike Gabriel, never got involved with the boys or men his sisters dated.

Picking up a bottle of shampoo, Ana squeezed a glob onto her palm as she launched into "Don't Cry for Me Argentina." This was followed by a medley from one of her favorites: *Les Misérables.* She gasped, her breath catching in her throat and the words dying on her lips when the shower door opened and Jacob joined her.

His teeth shone whitely in his bearded face. "Good morning, Princess."

Turning her back, Ana attempted to shield her nakedness. "What the hell do you think you're doing? Get out!"

Jacob picked up a bar of soap. "I'm conserving water." Lowering his head, he kissed Ana's shoulder. "Don't worry, sweetheart. Nothing's going to happen, because you said you wouldn't let me make love to you even if I were the last man on earth."

"Just because nothing's going to happen doesn't mean we should shower together."

Standing under the showerhead, Jacob soaped his neck and shoulders. "Come on, baby. You can't be that shy. You had no problem modeling your Victoria's Secret yesterday."

"They were Eres."

"Never heard of it."

"Look it up," she snapped angrily. Ana couldn't believe Jacob would be so gauche as to barge into the shower with her. And she was being truthful when she'd told him that her underwear concealed more than what some women wore on beaches in some Caribbean islands where topless bathing was the norm and no one was bothered by it.

Swiping a handful of foaming shampoo off her head, Jacob rubbed it on his scalp. "I like your shampoo." He sniffed his fingers. "It smells nice."

"Why don't you use my bath gel while you're at it?"

"Nah. I don't need to smell like a girl. You better finish washing your hair before the water cools."

"I'll finish once you leave."

Jacob stared at her back, his gaze slipping lower to her tiny waist and even lower still to the roundness of her hips and slender thighs and shapely legs. Her body was incredible, her skin smooth and flawless. A slight frown formed between his eyes. "I don't believe you, Ana. You act the innocent, then you flaunt yourself in front of me while offering to jerk me off. Who the hell are you?"

Turning, she faced him. "You know who I am."

He shook his head. "No, I don't. What you're doing is playing a very dangerous game where you're going to wind up as the casualty."

Blinking furiously, Ana tried wiping away the shampoo trickling down her forehead that had gotten into one eye. Jacob captured her wrist and cupped his free hand under the water and splashed it on her face. "Finish with your hair while we talk."

Not venturing to glance below his neck, she massaged her scalp. "There's nothing to talk about."

Jacob continued to lather his body. "That's where we disagree. I said some things to you because I'd believed you were mature enough to deal with it. Case in point—human sexuality. I'm not going to hide the fact that I sleep with women, and that I enjoy sleeping with them. What I don't do is accept everything thrown at me because that has never been my way. I prefer to do the hunting instead of becoming the hunted. And, it's never slam bam thank you ma'am."

Placing her hand on Jacob's hairy chest, Ana gave him a gentle push as she turned her face upward to the flowing water. Reaching for another plastic bottle on the shower shelf, she applied a liberal amount of conditioner to the wet strands. "Why are you telling me this?"

"Because I want you to know where I'm coming from, Princess."

"And that is?"

"We have to stop playing games with each other. It's getting more and more difficult for me to keep my hands off you."

More surprised than frightened, Ana stared up into the deep-set eyes that reminded her of cups of rich dark coffee. A shiver of awareness raced through her body when she digested what she'd just heard. "You haven't touched me."

Jacob curved an arm around her waist, bringing them closer. "It's not because I haven't wanted to."

Large golden-brown eyes met his. "Is this about sex?"

His expressive eyebrows lifted a fraction. "And if it is?"

Ana closed her eyes against his intense stare. "That's all it can be because when this is over I'll go back to Boca Raton and you'll return to Miami to do whatever we were doing before this living nightmare disrupted our lives."

Jacob's expression changed, becoming a mask of stone. He couldn't believe Ana could talk about allowing him to make love to her as if she were negotiating a business deal. There was no warmth, only indifference.

He wasn't so naïve, believing even if he'd met Ana under an entirely different set of circumstances they could have a relationship similar to what Diego had with Vivienne before they were married. Firstly, he and Ana came from two different worlds where he wouldn't fit into hers and she in his. He also doubted whether she would give up or modify her career to share her future with any man.

Having her live under his roof, even for a short time, had changed him. It was nice having someone to talk to and share meals with. With Ana he never knew what to expect from her. There were times when she appeared mature beyond her years, then she would say something that indicated she wasn't as secure as she projected. He knew she missed her brother when she called him Jason rather than Jacob.

He wasn't a twin and he'd never had a brother so he was unfamiliar with the bond between siblings. His mother had miscarried several times before she had him, and he'd grown up hearing her refer to him as her "golden bead."

Jacob knew he was on edge from what had become a period of self-imposed celibacy, yet he didn't want to use Ana to slake his pent-up frustration. She didn't deserve that. He'd thought he was in control until she came prancing out of the bathroom in underwear that showed more than it concealed.

Raising his hands, he cradled her face. "I don't want to take advantage of you."

She flashed her trademark dimpled smile. "You can't, only because I won't let you." Going on tiptoe, she kissed his stubble. "Why don't we let things unfold naturally."

Even if they never made love Ana knew she would have wonderful memories of playing house with Jacob. He was different from the other men she'd known and she found herself looking forward to being with him. He was more complex than she'd originally thought, comparing him to a puzzle. She had to find all the pieces and put them together before the real man emerged.

Jacob smiled. "That sounds like a plan."

"Now please finish showering so I can wash my body."

"Do you want me to wash your back?" His smile was more of a leer.

Ana pointed to the bath brush hanging from a hook. "No, thank you. That's why I use a brush." She took a step back, her eyes traveling downward for the first time. Swallowing an inaudible gasp she suddenly wished she hadn't looked. Now she knew what Eve felt in the Garden of Eden when faced with temptation. Jacob's naked body was magnificent from head to toe. Raw desire raced throughout her body, making it difficult for her to keep her footing.

His leer widened. "Now that I know what you look like and you know what I look like I believe I have the better view."

"Please, Jacob," Ana pleaded. Her body was on fire and it had nothing to do with the water or the sunlight coming through the skylight.

He continued to stare at her, his gaze as tender as a caress. "No more teasing, Princess." Jacob hands went around her upper arms at the same time he angled his head and took her mouth in an explosive kiss that buckled her knees. The kiss ended as quickly as it'd begun.

Summoning strength from somewhere she didn't know existed, Ana was able to endure the length of time it took for Jacob to complete his shower. Her knees were still shaking when she rinsed her hair and stepped out. Smiling, she noticed he'd placed two towels within reach: one for her hair and the other for her body, aware it was to become a day of firsts. It was the first time she'd shared a bed with a man and they'd not made love. It was also the first time a man had ever showered with her.

Wrapping the towel around her head in a turban-style, Ana stared at her reflection in the full-length mirror as she blotted beads of moisture from her body. She'd reached a point with Jacob as to where they understood who they were and where they wanted to take their transient relationship.

They would continue to live together, but not necessarily make love with each other. However, if or when they did Ana prayed she would be able to walk away unscathed. Unlike her girlfriends, she'd always loved with her heart and not her head. It was why she'd become the Wild Bunch anomaly. Maybe she would be more successful with her relationship with Jacob.

Los Angeles

Webb watched his brother's approach. Raising his hand, he managed to get his attention. He knew by the expression on Basil's face that he was less than happy. Unfortunately, he refused to let go of the fact that he hadn't signed Justin Glover to Slow Wyne. Losing the singer to Serenity Records had made him virtually impossible to be around.

When Basil joined him in the booth in a secluded corner of the restaurant, Webb signaled for the waitress to bring his drink order. He clapped a hand on Basil's shoulder. "Either you lighten up or I'm going to forget you're my big brother."

A wry smile twisted Basil's full lips. "That will never happen."

Webb gave him a level stare. "Yes, it can if you don't let me take care of your problem."

Reaching up, Basil loosened his tie, and unbuttoned the top button on his shirt. He'd wanted to go back to his house and relax, but Webb had insisted he meet him for drinks. "You know we could've done this back at my place. Have you forgotten I have a fully stocked bar?"

"No, I haven't. There's a reason why I wanted to meet here." He leaned closer. "I know you're expecting to see your pretty little secretary later on tonight."

The intense gray eyes darkened until they appeared black in the dimly lit restaurant. "What does this have to do with Camille?"

"Do you know why I told you to invite her to spend the night at the Beverly Hills hotel with you instead of you going to her place?"

"No. Why?"

"Because the bitch has been taping everything you do and say."

Slumping against the leather banquette as if he'd been shot, Basil closed his eyes. "When?"

"When I got the footage back from Omar Thornton's place, and it was clean I knew the only other person you might trade secrets with is your so-called executive assistant."

"So you bugged her place without telling me." Basil's tone was accusatory.

"I knew if I'd asked or told you it wouldn't have gone down, brother."

"At least you could've warned me beforehand."

"There wasn't time. Our window of opportunity was so small that my men couldn't take the risk the maintenance staff would miss their uniforms. They had to get in and out in under half an hour. But, instead of planting bugs, we found a few. All they had to do was splice the feed and when I viewed the footage I discovered your girl has been running off at the mouth."

"Do you know who put her up to it?"

Webb touched his scarred cheek. "No. It doesn't matter because she's done."

Basil sat up straight. "What do you mean?"

"She's going to be out of town for a while. I know you liked her, brother, but she'd become a liability."

Basil noticed his brother said *liked* not like. He held up a hand. "Don't tell me anymore."

He did like Camille—a lot more than he had a woman in a very long time. She was beautiful, sexy and went out of her way to please him. He paid her well, bought her expensive gifts and gave her several hundred dollars whenever he spent the night as spending money. If Webb was being truthful, then Camille was no different from their mother—a woman who'd taught him it was dangerous to trust.

The waitress brought their drinks, smiling at him when she met his eyes. Reaching into the pocket of his suit trousers, he took out a solid gold money clip and handed her a hundred-dollar bill. "Keep them coming." Normally he wouldn't have more than two drinks, but this was one time he wanted to get drunk.

Webb gave Basil a sidelong glance. His brother had always taken care of him. Now it was time for him to take care of Basil. He knew the record mogul would drink until he wouldn't be able to stand. That's when Webb would call his men to assist him carrying Basil out a side entrance. He would spend the night at Basil's Beverly Hills' home until he sobered up. Then they would put their heads together to decide what to do next.

Chapter 9

Ana found Key West to be everything she'd hoped it would be—and more. The streets, restaurants and shops overflowed with locals and tourists. Brightly painted houses, some with lawns decorated with shells, beads and plastic pink flamingos were in keeping with many of the eccentric inhabitants living and working on the island.

The festive mood and energy reminding her of Carnivale. Hundreds of passengers disembarking from several cruise ships docked in the harbor also added to the throng of humanity, causing pedestrian jams along the narrow streets and alleys. There was something about the island that reminded her of some of the towns and cities she'd visited in Puerto Rico, the Dominican Republic and Salvador da Bahia.

Tugging on Jacob's hand, she pulled him into a gift shop. She knew he wasn't the least bit interested in shopping, but hadn't said a word in protest when she stopped to window shop, or if something did spark her interest enough to venture inside, while holding the bags with her purchases. She'd bought two bathing suits, several straw hats and gifts for her nieces and nephews, which left her with less than one hundred dollars in cash.

Jacob, attempting to shield Ana's body from the crush of tourists crowding into the small shop, asked, "What do you want now?"

She glanced up at him over her shoulder, trying to read his stoic expression. They'd left the house without eating breakfast, and it was now after two in the afternoon and he'd mentioned stopping to eat, but Ana had wanted to finish shopping.

"I saw a couple of toe rings I want to try on."

He stared down at her bare toes in a pair of leather sandals. "You don't even wear rings on your fingers, yet you want to put them on your feet?"

Ana followed his gaze, looking at her toes. There was a tiny chip on the big toe of her right foot and that meant she had to either find a salon for a mani/pedi or do it herself. A slight frown appeared between her eyes. For the first time since she'd come into her trust she was faced with a financial dilemma. Even when attending college and law school money was never a problem because her father paid her tuition, room and board, and deposited money into her checking account each month. Attending college and law school in D.C. had its advantages, because taxis and public transit had become her choice of transportation.

"What's wrong with toe rings?"

"Nothing," he said much too quickly. "I just didn't figure you would wear one."

Moving closer to Jacob, Ana kissed his stubble. "I'm trying to tap into my bohemian inner child." A pair of gold hoops had replaced the diamond studs, and today she'd worn a white poet's blouse, faded jeans and blue-and-white-striped espadrilles.

Splaying his fingers at the small of her back, Jacob steered Ana over to the showcase with an assortment of rings. After a brief wait, a saleswoman with a friendly smile came over to help them. He stared at the name tag pinned to the pocket of her blouse. Bernice's deeply tanned weathered face reminded him of the fishermen who plied the waters for revenue or sport.

"My girlfriend would like to see some toe rings," he said, smiling.

"Gold or silver?" the woman asked.

"We'd like to see both," he said before Ana answered.

Ana squeezed his fingers, garnering his attention when Bernice opened the showcase to take out two trays of rings. "I don't have enough cash to buy the gold ones," she whispered.

He winked at her. "Don't worry about it, baby. I've got this."

Perched on a high stool, Jacob slipped tiny gold and silver rings off and on Ana's middle toes. In a moment of madness he imagined slipping another type of ring on her hand: an engagement ring. He banished the thought as soon as it entered his head.

Marrying Ana Cole wasn't even a remote possibility. They were complete opposites who'd come from different worlds. She may have temporarily altered her lifestyle but it was just that—temporary. Once she returned to Boca Raton everything they'd shared would be relegated to her past.

Staring up at her, Jacob asked, "Which ones do you like?"

Ana, who'd perched her sunglasses on the top of her head, met his eyes. "I don't know. Which do you like?"

"I think the gold one with the diamond is cute."

She wiggled her toes. Blue-white sparks reflected off the minute stone from an overhead light. "I like it, too."

Turning around, Jacob said, "We'll take these."

Bernice pressed her palms together. "They're the perfect fit for her feet."

Ana wound her arms around Jacob's waist after he'd given the saleswoman his credit card. "Thank you, sweetheart."

Cupping her chin, he lowered his head and kissed her. It was more of a caress than an actual kiss, her lips parting under his tender sensual assault. The kiss, similar to the one in the shower earlier that morning, ended as quickly as it'd begun.

Jacob stared into the large eyes filled with an emotion he could only interpret as trust. He'd become familiar with the look when assigned to witness protection. He gave her a tender smile. "You're more than welcome, Princess. Where are we going next?"

Ana allowed Jacob to help her down off the stool. She slipped on her sunglasses. "Let's eat."

He cupped his ear. "I believe I hear a choir singing hallelujah."

Grinning, she swatted at him. "Very funny."

Jacob signed the receipt, and then pocketed it. He slipped on his sunglasses, grasped Ana's hand and led her out of the shop that was becoming more crowded with each passing moment. He knew where he wanted to eat. The restaurant was the perfect place to begin the day and end the night.

"Are you certain you don't want any more oysters?" Jacob asked Ana. He'd recommended they eat at the Schooner Wharf Bar not only because of its open-air dining but also because of the food selections. He'd ordered the raw bar combination of shrimp and oysters.

Chewing and swallowing a mouthful of avocado, she said, "Very certain."

Ana knew if she continued to eat off Jacob's plate she never would finish her own salad made with blue crab and avocado over mixed greens, tomato and corn and red-pepper relish, accompanied by honey-mustard dressing. It'd taken her a while to decide whether to order the salad or conch and shrimp ceviche. What had surprised her about the restaurant was happy hour was from 7:00 a.m. to noon, and again from 5:00 p.m. to 7:00 p.m. Her gaze lingered on the Schooner

Western Union, a 130-foot-long tall ship bobbing and rock-ing gently along the wharf.

"That boat is magnificent." There was a hint of wistful-ness in her voice, because seeing the ship was a reminder of what she would've shared with her girlfriends if she'd been able to accompany them on vacation.

"Do you get seasick?" Jacob asked when following the direction of her gaze.

"No. I'm quite comfortable on or in the water."

"Would you like to go on a sunset cruise?"

Her eyes sparkled, reminding him of polished smoky quartz. A fringe of lashes lowered once he gave her a long, penetrating stare. Jacob still hadn't figured out what it was about Ana that made him say and do things that were totally out of character for him. Barging into the shower stall had left him so off-balance that it'd taken a while to gather his wits. At first he'd tried telling himself that she deserved the intrusion because she thought nothing of teasing him. Well, it hadn't been the first time a woman had teased him and he knew it wouldn't be the last. But then he'd never reacted to them in the way he'd reacted with Ana.

He'd accused her of playing a dangerous game wherein there would be no winner. If they did make love Jacob knew it wouldn't be easy for him to walk away. After all, he'd ad-mitted to being practically family because he was her cous-in's godfather. There would be occasions in the future where they would run into each other at family gatherings, and he doubted whether the encounters would go as smoothly as he'd want.

In the past whenever he'd ended a liaison with a woman Jacob had always made certain beforehand that there would be no possibility of reconciling. That was not to say he was unwilling to try to work out whatever particular problem plagued their relationship, but he didn't believe in exacerbat-ing a situation that was certain to become even more problematic. He'd already admitted to himself that he liked Ana, but not enough to become *that* emotionally involved with her.

"I'd love to."

Jacob blinked as if he'd been in a trance. Why, he mused, hadn't he realized the warm, smoky timbre of her voice? It was slightly husky, the register sultry, seductive. "Do you have plans for tomorrow night?" he teased, his expression deadpan.

Ana laughed under her breath. "I'm going to have to call my boyfriend and ask him if he has made plans for tomorrow night. The last time I went out with a guy and didn't tell him there was hell to pay."

Propping his arm on the table, Jacob rested his chin on the heel of his hand. "What did he do?"

Ana scrunched up her pert nose. "He tied me to the bedposts with silk ribbons and fed me chocolate-covered strawberries."

Throwing back his head he laughed loudly, garnering the attention of diners from nearby tables. "That sounds a little kinky to me."

"It was."

He sobered quickly. "So, you like kinky?"

"It all depends on who's dispensing the kinkiness."

"Who are you, Ana?"

"What are you talking about?"

Jacob lowered his arm and leaned over the table. "When I told you I was horny you said I was disgusting," he whispered in Spanish. "Then you think nothing of walking around in lingerie that had me so turned-on I was afraid I was going to come right then and there. Fast forward—I get into the shower with you and you cover up your ta-tas and beaver like an innocent schoolgirl." A rush of color darkened her face, but Jacob ignored it. "You're what men call a tease. It's come here, baby, then you flip the script when you put up the sign that says look but don't touch. Is that what happened with you and that poor dude you brought to S.J.'s baptism? You told him or sent out signals that you were going to give him some, then changed your mind."

Eyes narrowing like a cat before attacking, Ana gave Jacob a withering glare. "You don't know what you're talking about," she countered in Spanish. "He was asking to take what friendship we had to the next level when he knew when we'd begun dating that we would never be more than friends. And for you information I don't tease men—"

"What do you call walking around in near-transparent underwear?" he asked, cutting her off.

Ana sucked her teeth. "That's your problem if you have so little self-control. Like I said, I'm certain you've seen more on the beach."

"But I'm not living with those women, *m'ija.*"

"We're not actually living together."

"What are we then?"

She smiled. "Roommates."

"That's BS and you know it."

"It's not BS," Ana countered. "Why are you trying to make more of what we have?"

"What is it we *do* have, Ana?"

A pregnant silence ensued as they stared at each other. "I don't know, Jacob."

"I do know that…" His words trailed off when a shadow fell over the table. Glancing up he saw someone from his past. Pushing back his chair Jacob stood up. "Kent! You old dog. What have you been up to?" He thumped the man's back at the same time giving him a rough hug.

"Other than couple of tours of Iraq, Afghanistan and a bum leg I'm as good as they come."

Jacob stared at the stocky blond man with whom he'd gone through basic training. "So, you stayed in?" he asked Wayland Kent.

Wayland ran a hand over his military-style cropped hair,

minute lines fanning out around large hazel eyes when he smiled. "I stayed in as long as I could. Got a medical discharge, sold my trailer, and me and the missus moved from Chattanooga, bought a houseboat, and we now live down here year-round. Are you still babysitting diplomats?"

Jacob gave Ana a quick glance. She'd concealed half of her face behind the oversize sunglasses. Although she went through the motion of eating her salad he knew she'd overheard Wayland's comment about him protecting diplomats. And it was the first time he'd ignored his instincts about bringing Ana to Key West. If they'd remained in Long Key, cloistered behind locked doors, then it appreciably decreased the risk of someone recognizing her or even having to explain her to those he knew.

Yet there was something about her exuberance when she saw places she'd read about and had wanted to visit for half of her life that held him enthralled with her childlike delight. Ana continued to mystify Jacob. It was as if she was a child in a woman's body. One moment she could be soft, teasing and without warning she'd become a siren, again teasing but this time it was so sexy and overt that he feared losing control. There weren't too many times in his life when he hadn't been in control. She claimed they were only roommates but he refused to acknowledge that. For him the sexual tension was so strong and thick it was palpable.

"No. I'm now a federal marshal," he said to Wayland.

"So you've gone from one babysitting job to another."

"Wrong, Kent. I'm now a paper pusher." He held out his arms. "Take a good look at a glorified bureaucrat in living color." Jacob told him about his position at the Miami-based detention center.

Wayland whistled. "You must have some serious juice to get desk duty. By the way, what are you doing down here?"

"I'm on vacation."

He leaned in closer to Jacob. "Aren't you going to introduce me to your lady?"

Jacob realized this was going to be the first test as to whether he and Ana would be able to pull off their prearranged subterfuge. "*Princesa. Esto es mi compañero marino viejo,* Wayland."

Ana extended her right hand in a limp gesture. "I'm *Princesa,*" she said in heavily accented Spanish. "Nice meeting you." The words had come out haltingly.

Wayland took Ana's hand, then looked sideways at Jacob. "Is her name really Princess?"

He nodded. "Yes, it is. And she is a princess."

"Why don't you and Princess come and stay with me and Adele for a few days? We can do some sailing, and if you're game we can get in a little fishing. Adele and me never had any kids, so we're like two big kids doing exactly what we want to do."

"I'd like to…but I don't think we can," Jacob stammered. He gestured with his head toward Ana.

"He's right," Ana piped up, still affecting the accent. "It's not what you think. *Jacobo no es mi novio.*"

"What is she saying?" Wayland asked.

Jacob picked up on her cue immediately. "Look, Kent. Precious and I just started seeing each other—"

Wayland gave him an incredulous stare. "You mean you two are not…"

"No, we are not," Ana hissed between clenched teeth. "I am no *puta!*"

Jacob approached Ana and rested a hand on her shoulder. "Wayland didn't say you were, *Princesa.*"

She threw up a hand in dramatic fashion. "Why do all men think just because they see a woman with a man that she is giving him her body?"

Red-faced, Wayland took a step backward. He motioned to a passing waitress for a pen, jotted his telephone number on a napkin and then handed it to Jacob. "I don't want to start something between the two of you, but here's my cell number. Give me a call whenever you have a chance and we'll get together. I still keep in touch with some of the guys from basic training. My boat is a 48-footer that can sleep as many as ten, so we could have quite a reunion."

Jacob pocketed the napkin, and then pulled his former corps buddy close. "I'm sorry about that," he whispered in his ear. "She can be a little overly dramatic at times. She was raised by her grand- and great-grandmothers, and they're very old-fashioned when it comes to premarital sex."

"There's no need to explain, Jones. Remember, Adele wouldn't give me any until I put an engagement ring on her finger. It has been worth it because we just celebrated our fifteenth anniversary."

"Congratulations, man. Give Adele my best and I will call you."

Ana watched from behind the dark lenses as Jacob and the man he'd introduced as Wayland say their goodbyes. She was hard-pressed not to laugh when the color in Wayland's face had turned a beet-red. Although she'd trusted Jacob enough not to accept the man's invitation to spend time on his houseboat, she wasn't certain whether upon closer inspection he would recognize her.

And despite the wig and sunglasses there was always the possibility someone would see through the ruse. The last thing she needed was for the media to report she'd been sighted in the Florida Keys, fearing once again a bull's-eye would be trained on her.

Jacob sat down again. "You missed your calling, *m'ija*. You're quite an actress."

A half smile parted her lips. "I had to come up with something quickly or blow it." Ana angled her head. "And it wasn't as if it was all a lie."

Lowering his head, Jacob kissed the wig. "Your accent was spot-on."

"That comes from having a Cuban-born grandmother. *Abuela* spoke English with a slight accent, but it would become more pronounced whenever she was angry or excited. She spoke Spanish to all of her children, and whenever we went to visit her she would speak Spanish to us because she claimed we should never forget that we're the descendants of what had been the Cuban upper class. Today that may sound a little pretentious, but if there had been Cuban royalty Marguerite Joséfina Isabel Diaz-Cole definitely would've been a princess."

"Diego started to tell me about his great-grandmother, but somehow we got distracted and he never finished the story."

"I'll tell you about her after we get back to the house."

"Talking about getting back," Jacob said, lowering his voice. "This is going to be our first and last public excursion. Once we return to Long Key you're going to have to be content to remain close to the house. I'm sorry—"

Ana placed her hand over his. "It's okay, Jacob. I understand the risk we're taking coming here."

He looked at her as if she'd taken leave of her senses. Again, Ana had surprised him with her unexpected acquiescence. Jacob didn't know why, but he'd expected her to debate why she shouldn't be allowed out in public with the wig and dark glasses.

"So, it's all right with you?"

She nodded. "When Wayland saw you my insides were quivering like frozen gelatin. I was so afraid that he'd recognize me and call out my name. I know I haven't been the most cooperative person you've ever protected, but all of that is going to change. I'll do whatever it is you want."

"Thank you, baby," he crooned.

She flashed her trademark dimpled smile. *"De nada,*

m'ijo." Her mood had changed like quicksilver. "I want you to promise me one thing, Jacob."

"What's that?" he asked, running a finger down the length of her nose.

"When all of this madness is over I'd like to come back here with you. Then I won't have to hide behind a wig and sunglasses, while pretending that I'm *Princesa."*

Jacob's mouth replaced his finger when he kissed her nose. "You can take off the wig and glasses, but you'd still be a princess. Do you want anything else to eat or drink?"

She offered him a bright smile. "No, thank you. I think when we get back to the house I'm going to take a shower and a nap."

Jacob returned her smile. "That sounds like a wonderful idea." He signaled their waitress for the check.

Ana lay beside Jacob in the red, white and yellow striped hammock strung between two live oak trees. She shifted onto her side and rested her head on his shoulder, one leg sandwiched between his, and an arm over his belly. Her sunglasses and the baseball cap Jacob had given her when they'd made their way down the staircase and out of the house were in the hammock near their bare feet. They'd returned to the house, showered separately, but instead of sharing the bed they'd decided relaxing outdoors was preferably to staying inside an air-cooled room.

"What are you thinking about, *m'ija?"* Jacob asked after a comfortable silence.

She emitted an audible sigh. "Would you believe nothing?"

He chuckled softly. "No. There's no way your brain isn't spinning ideas about Serenity."

"You probably won't believe it, but I haven't thought about Serenity since you told me Jason closed the office."

"Wonders never cease."

She tickled his ribs. "Very funny."

Ana fell silent again. She didn't know why, but she'd always felt as if Jason had little or no interest in running the company which was why she'd assumed that responsibility. There had been times when she'd wished he would take over and allow her to take a step back for more than the time she took when on vacation.

She would return and they would meet in her office where he'd brief her on everything that had occurred during her absence, then he would go into the studio, not reappearing until it was time for a staff meeting. There had been times when she would leave at seven or later and Jason would still be in the studio rehearsing, editing or writing.

"Tell me about your grandmother."

Ana smiled. Jacob asking about her grandmother shattered her musings about her brother. "*Abuela* was an only child. Her father owned one of the largest tobacco plantations and cigar factories on the island, and she'd grown up privileged and pampered. She'd just turned four when her mother died in a riding accent. When she was six her father sent her to a convent because he knew she would receive a quality education, but he also felt the nuns would teach her the deportment for a young woman of her station."

"Did it work?"

"The education part did, but whatever deportment she learned was undone by her aunt. When *Abuela* left home to attend the Universidad de la Habana her *tía* Gloria had become her chaperone. It was the 1920s and women were cutting their hair, raising their hemlines and smoking in public, and while Gloria was doing all those things, as well as wearing slacks, she never married. But there were rumors that she slept with both men and women."

"*¡Avergüence en ella!*"

Ana's soft laughter was smothered against the column of Jacob's neck. "Gloria *was* without shame. I'm certain my great-grandfather wanted to disown his sister, but couldn't. The straw that broke the proverbial camel's back was when photographs of *Abuela* wearing nothing more than a dressing gown were exhibited in a Havana art gallery. She'd become the muse of an up-and-coming artist whose work would eventually hang in the homes of well-to-do Cubans.

"My grandmother was tall, slender and unlike a lot of so-called modern women during that time. She refused to cut her hair. It was raven-black and reached her waist. She also was very beautiful, and when she stared out at the camera with her mysterious dimpled smile she'd instantly become the toast of Havana.

"When her father heard about the photographs he ordered her back to Piñar del Río, because she'd dishonored the family name. In order to save face he planned to marry her off to any upper-class man who represented the social elite, and his age was not a factor."

"That's crazy."

"It was the norm in those days when women had little or no independence. They were nothing more than chattel, but M.J., as she preferred to be called, threatened to take a lover, or even lovers, like her aunt."

"Did her father capitulate?"

"He had to. Grandpa had traveled to Cuba to buy a sugarcane plantation, but the Cubans wouldn't sell it to him because he was an American. At that time *Cubanos* felt they'd traded one oppressor for another after the Spanish-American War. Most *Cubanos* harbored a resentment of U.S. colonists buying up their land and the U.S. military paying next to nothing to set up a military base at Guantanamo Bay. No one would sell him a handful of Cuban soil, not because he was black but because he was an American.

"He left Cuba, went to Costa Rica and bought a banana plantation, then returned to Cuba to ask for M.J.'s hand in marriage. She was only twenty when she became Mrs. Samuel Claridge Cole."

"Her father approved of her marriage to an American?"

Ana nodded. "Yes. Grandpa was what people called a gentleman farmer and there was never a doubt whether he would be able to give M.J. the lifestyle to which she'd been accustomed. Her father must have breathed a sigh of relief when she did marry him because family honor superseded everything else. Her father and my grandfather were not only father and son-in-law but also business partners. Once he had grandchildren José Luís Diaz was heard to say that his world was complete. Before he passed away he had his lawyer draw up papers leaving all of his wealth to his daughter's husband. If he hadn't done that, then I suspect my grandmother would've left my grandfather when she discovered he'd fathered a child out of wedlock. But, she'd found herself living in a mansion with three young children and cash poor. I didn't understand her telling her daughters, granddaughters and great-granddaughters *'no permita que nadie le defina ni determine su destino,'* until Diego had asked me to come and work with him. He can be very persuasive but I know I'm not cut out to negotiate deals that involve produce and vacation properties."

"Don't let anyone define you or determine your destiny," Jacob translated literally.

"And it's been that way with every Cole woman, beginning with my father's sisters. My aunts are as tough as drill sergeants. Even those who marry Cole men follow the practice."

A beat passed, then Jacob asked, "Are you saying your grandmother didn't have a happy marriage?"

"No. Quite the contrary. My grandparents adored each other. They were married for seventy-five years, and after Grandpa died *Abuela* was never the same. As the family matriarch she was proud and controlling, but some of the light went out behind her eyes once she realized the man who'd been her rock was gone. When she talked about controlling one's destiny I think she regretted not finishing college. But, she didn't blame anyone but herself for that. She said if she hadn't posed for Antonio Santamaria her life would've been quite different. She probably would've married a man from her own country, had children and who knows whether she would've stayed or left the island after the overthrow of Batista."

Jacob rested his chin on the fragrant curls tickling his nose. "If she hadn't left Cuba then she wouldn't have had your father. Your grandparents created a dynasty they could be proud of."

"Grandpa wasn't perfect, Jacob. Not when he cheated on his wife."

"He's not the first and he definitely won't be the last man to cheat on his wife."

"I'd like you to answer one question for me, Jacob."

"What's that?"

"Why do men cheat?" It was the same question Ana asked Tyler.

"It's probably because they can, or they believe they can get away with it. Many of them do, because women tend to forgive them."

"I'm not that forgiving."

Jacob shifted on the hammock until he could see Ana's face. "Men have cheated on you?"

She nodded. "The first man I'd fallen in love with cheated on me. Then there was one I'd thought of as my soul mate and he also cheated on me. I'm what I think of as a cheater magnet."

Combing his fingers through her short hair, Jacob kissed Ana's forehead when she tilted her chin to look up at him. "No, you're not. You just haven't chosen wisely."

She smiled. "Now you sound like my father."

"Maybe you should listen to him. You're young, intelligent and beautiful and you probably attract men that want something from you."

"And that is?" Ana asked as a slight frown appeared between her eyes.

"Fame, sex or money. If they can get you to sign them to a record deal, then they're willing to do anything to get to that point. You're the gatekeeper and their meal ticket to a lifestyle most people fantasize about. There are also the parasites that don't have any musical talent but choose to feed off your fame."

"I've never advertised my love life."

"It doesn't matter if you do or don't. Every man who hooks up with you believes he'll be the one to capture the golden goose. And I'm certain you have men hitting on you all the time."

"No, I don't."

One of Jacob's eyebrows lifted questioningly. "You can't be that naïve. You don't believe that whenever a man shows an interest in you he wants something?"

"Why can't they just want me for me?"

"That's an age-old question not too many people can answer."

"What about you, Jacob? If we'd met under a different set of circumstances what would you want from me?"

Jacob pointed to the middle of her chest. "Your heart. Nothing more. Nothing less."

Ana's expression changed, growing serious, and she becoming increasingly uneasy under his steady gaze. Sunlight filtering through the leaves of the ancient trees cast long and short shadows over his handsome face. "That's it?"

"What else is there, Princess? I don't want or need your money. I'll never be able to match your earning power, but I make enough to support myself, a wife and children, if and when I decide to marry. I don't want fame, and if I need sex I know who I can call for that."

"So, you'd cheat on me, too."

"No, baby. I wouldn't cheat on you. Once I commit I'd never think of sleeping with another woman."

Her eyelids fluttered wildly. "How do you know that if you've never been married?"

"Because I'm too much like the Jones men in my family. We don't cheat on our wives."

"Look me up ten years from now and I'll ask you whether you've cheated on your wife. If you haven't, then you'll restore my faith in the opposite sex."

Jacob shook his head. He didn't want to believe a couple of indiscretions had soured Ana on men. Not all men were liars, cheaters, deadbeat dads, physically or verbally abusive. Most went to work, collected their paychecks, made love to their wives and loved and protected their children. That's how he'd been raised and that is what he would do *if* he ever married.

"Make it two years, *m'ija.*"

"Two years it is, *m'ijo.*"

Jacob sealed their promise with a kiss that left both of them breathing heavily and fighting for control of emotions and hormones that were running amuck. He could feel Ana's heartbeat keeping tempo with his own, and he knew if they didn't get out of the hammock he would beg her to let him make love to her where anyone could see them.

"I think it's time we go inside before we embarrass ourselves."

Ana nodded. "I agree."

Chapter 10

Jacob's cell phone rang and he went still. It was Diego's ring tone. Hopefully his friend was calling with good news. If they'd caught the shooter, then his time with Ana would be over. Just when he was getting used to her mercurial moods she would leave. He excused himself and walked off the enclosed back porch where he'd spent the past two hours with his uncle watching a baseball game between the Marlins and Giants.

He tapped a button. "What's up?"

"Where are you, Jake?"

All of his senses were now on full alert. "I'm at my uncle's house in Key West. Why?"

"I'm having the jet fueled as we speak. I need you to get to the Marathon airport within the next two hours. Henri will meet you. He'll have Ana's passport."

"Where are we going?"

"You know that private island I bought in the Bahamas for investment purposes."

"What about it?" Jacob asked."

"Well, you're going to live there for a while."

"What changed?" He couldn't believe he sounded so calm when his heart was pumping painfully in his chest.

"We managed to bug Irvine's girlfriend's apartment. Our man told us she also worked at Slow Wyne."

"Worked?" Jacob noticed Diego had used the past tense.

"Apparently someone discovered the bug but not before the investigators recorded his pillow-talk confession. He claimed next time his person wasn't going to miss."

"Did he mention Ana's name?"

"No. What we were able to record was him saying, 'that bitch at Serenity.'"

"Do you know who uncovered the bug?"

"Not yet." There came a pause. "Her body was found in the desert earlier this morning with a single gunshot to the head and her tongue cut out. The police haven't released her name pending next of kin, but our man has a reliable contact with the LAPD who identified her as Camille Nelson. Apparently she was an exotic dancer in her former life."

Jacob swore under his breath. Unfortunately the woman had become collateral damage. "What do you want me to tell Ana?"

"Tell her I'm meeting with the cotton broker in Uganda and I can't get away to take care of some problems at the resort. I'd like you to convince her that the two of you are going undercover as a couple, and that I need her to evaluate staff performance of the front desk, room service and the kitchen. I've already made reservations in the names of Mr. and Mrs. Jacob Jones. I told the manager you're family, so you won't be billed for anything. Meanwhile the investigators are going to step up the pressure on Irvine. We have to take down this sick sonofabitch before there's another murder."

There was edge in Diego's voice Jacob had never heard before. "It appears as if Irvine and/or his people are playing for keeps. Killing that girl execution style and cutting out her tongue is sending a message to anyone thinking of diming Irvine out. The man has to be psychopathic if he'd ordered a hit on a woman he was sleeping with. Do whatever you have to do to take him down, Diego."

That said, he ended the call and walked back to the porch. He sat down next to Ray. "Ana and I have to leave."

Ray removed his glasses and sat up straight. "Now?"

Jacob nodded. "Yes. My friend is sending his jet to pick us up at the Marathon airport."

"Can you tell me where you're going?"

"It's a private island in the Caribbean."

Ray stood up. "What the hell is going on?"

"I wish I knew, Uncle Ray." Jacob hugged him. "I'll be in touch when we get back."

"You tell your girlfriend she still owes me a duet."

"I'll let her know. Tell Mattie I'll see her the next time I come down."

Jacob was practically running when he took the stairs two at a time. Opening the door to the bedroom, he stood motionless, staring at the bed. Ana hadn't turned off the lamp on his side of the bed.

He knew he wasn't able to become actively involved in the investigation to identify the shooter. However, it had been different with Vivienne Cole-Thomas. Her late husband, a U.S. congressman had been killed in a hit-and-run. As the southeast regional supervisory deputy for the United States Marshal Service Jacob had worked closely with Vivienne to apprehend those behind the conspiracy responsible for the congressman's murder.

He hadn't hesitated when Diego asked him to step in and protect his cousin, but his friend had upped the ante because now they had to pretend to be married. Jacob wanted to tell Diego that he and Ana couldn't be any more married. They were living together and sharing a bed. All that was needed was a license, exchange of vows and consummating the union.

Jacob had had liaisons with women—some brief and others longer than he'd expected, yet none of the women affected him in the way Ana did. It hadn't been a week since she'd walked out of the terminal at the Marathon airport and somehow she'd managed to disrupt his very predictable lifestyle. And much to his surprise it had become a most welcome disruption.

He approached the bed and sat down. Ana's eyelids fluttered before they opened and she stared at him. "I tried waiting up for you. What happened?"

Jacob nuzzled the side of her neck. He wanted to tell her the game was on the West Coast, so it didn't start until late. "You smell good." He knew he was stalling for time.

"You didn't answer my question, Jacob. What took you so long?"

"You're going to have to get up and get dressed."

With wide eyes, she sat up. "Where are we going?"

He repeated what Diego had told him, deliberately withholding the information Diego had told about the body in the desert. Jacob suspected he wanted Ana out of the country before she saw news footage about Basil Irvine's girlfriend's murder.

"We're going down tonight."

"Is it that critical?" she asked.

"Diego believes it is. He's invested too much in this venture to have it fail."

Ana swung her legs over the side of the bed. "I suppose I'd better get dressed and packed."

She'd shocked him again. Jacob hadn't expected her to accept the justification for their unexpected departure from the Keys to the Bahamas without balking or further questioning. He rarely, if ever, lied, but apparently Ana either believed him or she'd reached the point in their relationship where she'd begun to trust him unconditionally.

Reaching for Jacob's hand, Ana held it tightly when the jet began its descent into Cannamore Cay. She didn't like flying at night, and especially with the aircraft landing on an island runway in the Caribbean. The island was made up of three hundred and sixty acres.

She closed her eyes, counting slowly. When Diego had disclosed that he'd bought an uninhabited island in the Bahamas she'd given him a look that spoke volumes because ColeDiz hadn't needed another vacation property. Then her cousin explained that Cannamore Cay wouldn't fall under the control of the family-owned conglomerate, but that he'd purchased it as a legacy for his children.

When Diego's driver met her and Jacob at the Marathon airport, Henri had handed Ana her passport. It was apparent her parents knew she was leaving the country because her official documents were stored in a safe at their house. They were driven to Jacob's Miami apartment where he'd retrieved his passport, then they were back in the air on their way to Cannamore Cay.

She opened her eyes as runway lights came into view and Ana felt as if she'd been holding her breath until the wheels to the sleek Gulfstream G550 touched the macadam, landing smoothly as if gliding on an icy surface.

"You can let go of my hand now," Jacob said in her ear. She was certain her nails would leave half-moon impressions on his skin.

Ana removed her hand. She stared at Henri who'd reclined his seat into a bed within seconds of takeoff and now was seated in the upright position when the voice of the pilot filled the cabin asking them to prepare for landing. When the taciturn driver/bodyguard met them at the Marathon airport he'd revealed that he would accompany her and Jacob to the

Bahamas, go with them to the resort and then return to the jet for the flight back to West Palm Beach.

The jet came to a complete stop and the copilot emerged from the cockpit to lower the steps. Whenever she had flown in the company jet it had been with a crew that included the pilot, copilot and one or two attendants. Tonight there were no attendants, just an armed bodyguard. Jacob told her he'd left his handgun in a safe in his apartment, and had only brought his passport, shield and photo ID.

A limousine bearing the logo of the island resort on the passenger-side doors waited as they disembarked. Henri and Jacob transferred their luggage from the jet to the trunk of the limo and minutes later they were seated inside the luxury vehicle and heading toward the resort that had taken more than two years to complete.

Henri closed the partition separating the rear of the limo from the driver. He handed Jacob an envelope, then ring boxes. "Starting now you're Mr. and Mrs. Jacob Stephen Jones. The envelope contains a valid marriage license." He held up a hand when Ana opened her mouth. "Please let me finish, Mrs. Jones," he urged in French-accented English. "Mr. Cole-Thomas arranged everything, including your marriage in absentia. If you have any questions, then you will have to ask him once you return to the States. He told me to tell you that the marriage is legal and binding, and he'll also arrange to annul it." He nodded to Jacob. "Mr. Jones, I suggest you put your rings on now."

Ana closed her eyes, unable to believe what Diego had concocted. There was no doubt her cousin had instructed his bodyguard to wait until they were on the ground in the Bahamas to mention the sham of a wedding. Diego had to know she would've never agreed to a marriage of convenience if he'd presented it to her before their abrupt departure.

Controlling and dictatorial; the two words didn't begin to describe the CEO of ColeDiz. Her hand was trembling

noticeably when Jacob reached for her left hand and slipped
an unadorned platinum band on her third finger. He handed
her his, and she repeated the gesture with the matching band.
Ana didn't want to ask Henri how Diego had gotten their
ring sizes because his answer would only add to her annoyance as to Diego's intrusion into her life. Had he, she mused,
even spoken to her parents about his plan, or had he come
up with it on his own?

A slight gasp escaped her parted lips, and she temporarily forgot about being Mrs. Jones when a two-storied
structure appeared, as if growing from the earth. Abundant
plantings around the main house and smaller matching structures claimed the ocean as their playground. Even in the dark
Ana recognized the exquisite architectural lines reminiscent
of the grand plantations built under British Colonial rule.

The driver maneuvered into a circular drive, got out and
opened the rear door. Henri alighted first, then Ana, and
finally Jacob. Flanked by the two men, she walked to the
entrance with automatic sliding doors. The lobby was an in-
door oasis with potted palms, trees and baskets of hanging
orchids and other exotic flowers growing in wild abandon.
A waterfall took up an entire wall, the sound of water flowing over rocks and into a large pool with schools of colorful
fish was visually hypnotic.

The colors of white and sea-foam green predominated,
contrasting with white wicker sofas, love seats, chairs with
seat cushions and accent pillows in the calming green hue.
A white concert piano was positioned nearby in an area with
a built-in bar and a dozen small round tables with pull-up
chairs.

A pale, middle-aged man wearing crisp white slacks and
a green floral shirt with large white leaves came over to
greet them. The green was the same shade as the seat cushions. Ana bit back a smile. There was no doubt Jacob would
feel quite at home at the resort with his colorful print shirts.

He inclined his head. "Good evening. I'm Shanley Osgood, resident manager of Cannamore," he announced in a clipped British accent. He extended his hand to Jacob. "Welcome, Mr. Jones. Mr. Cole-Thomas told me you were coming with your wife." He smiled at Ana. "Welcome, Mrs. Jones." He then nodded to Henri. "Sir."

Henri inclined his shaved head. "Shanley."

"I've taken the liberty of giving Mr. and Mrs. Jones the guest cottage near the garden. Will you need assistance bringing in their luggage?" he asked Henri.

"I believe your driver and I can manage," Henri replied.

Shanley ran a hand over his neatly brushed salt-and-pepper hair, then pinched the bridge of his nose. "I know you want to settle into your rooms, but I had the chef prepare a little repast just in case you wanted something to eat. The kitchen staff is available around the clock, so if you want or need anything just pick up the phone and dial the operator."

Jacob curved an arm around Ana's waist. "My wife and I are looking forward to some rest and relaxation."

"This is what Cannamore is known for," Shanley said with a practiced smile. "We do have a number of amenities you may take advantage of. There's a golf course and several boats available if you wish to go sailing. And of course there is gear if you wish to go snorkeling or scuba diving. Most of our guests request anonymity, and every staff member adheres to that rule."

Ana and Jacob shared a smile. "Thank you, Mr. Osgood."

"You're welcome, Mrs. Jones. If you're ready I'll show you to your cottage."

She held on to Jacob's hand as they followed the manager outside of the main house and along a lighted path to the cottage partially concealed behind an outcropping of trees. The fragrant smell of flowers and ripening fruit mingling with salt water wafted in the night air.

Shanley handed Jacob two card keys. "Our housekeeping

staff will not enter your bungalow if your doors are locked. If you need housekeeping you may leave it unlocked or hang the placard on the handle outside the door." He affected a slight bow. "Again I welcome you to Cannamore Cay."

Waiting until the manager retreated the way they'd come, Jacob swept Ana up in his arms. "Well, Mrs. Jones. Are you ready to be carried over the threshold?"

Her arms went around his neck. "I didn't know you were so traditional, Mr. Jones," she crooned.

Smiling, Jacob kissed her nose. "You just don't know the half, *m'ija.*"

Holding her effortlessly in his arms, he inserted the card key into the slot, waiting until the light glowed green, then shouldered the door open. Overhead lighting in the entryway glowed automatically. Slowly lowering Ana to stand, they walked into a living/dining room. Here sea-foam green was the dominant color with contrasting white accents. A sitting area with a sofa, love seats and chairs with footstools were positioned in front of a wall of glass that looked out on to the ocean. A flat screen and audio components sat on a mahogany credenza doubling as an entertainment unit. Large blocks of slate that made up the flooring were covered by area rugs woven in patterns to conform to the tropical setting.

Ana walked ahead of him, turning to her right and entering a fully functional, modern, state-of-the-art eat-in kitchen. She read the placard on the granite countertop: *This is an ecofriendly island. Please conserve water and recycle.* She opened and closed cabinets and closets. There were dishes, glassware, flatware and a stackable washer/dryer.

"Jacob, come and look at this." When he joined her in kitchen she stood to one side while he peered into the fully stock refrigerator.

He chuckled softly. "I think this is more than a little repast." The tray on the lower shelf was filled with sliced pineapple, mango, strawberries and cheese, a tin of caviar and several bottles of champagne. "Very nice. We're going to have to do a little celebrating before going to bed."

Ana closed the door to the refrigerator. "What are we celebrating?"

He wiggled his eyebrows. "Our marriage, of course. You are Mrs. Jones, aren't you?"

"You're enjoying this, aren't you?"

Jacob took a step until they were less than a foot apart. "I'm not complaining. We are on vacation. Or should I say our honeymoon?"

Ana stopped herself before she told Jacob that he, and not she, was on vacation. If she hadn't had to flee the country she would've been joining her friends when they sailed to Puerto Rico. "You're right. We are on vacation, so let's make the best of it."

He noticed she'd chosen to ignore his reference to honeymoon. "That's my girl."

"I'm going outside to look around."

"Don't go too far," Jacob warned at the same time a bell echoed throughout the cottage. "That must be our luggage."

It was only when Ana opened the French door to step outside that she realized that while she could see out the wall of glass she wasn't able to see in from the exterior, which eliminated the need for drapes, shades or shutters.

Strategically placed floodlights and solar lights lit up the path leading to the garden, while a full moon silvered the landscape. Sitting on a stone bench, Ana stared down into a man-made waterfall surrounded by palms and broad banana leaves. The sound of the incoming surf washing up on the beach, the incessant chirping of insects and an occasional croak from a frog had become a nocturnal symphony.

The peace that had evaded her for days, hours and minutes swept over her as she sat motionless, eyes closed, and inhaled all that was Cannamore Cay. Here she didn't have to hide under wigs and behind sunglasses. She didn't have to constantly glance around her to see who was watching her, while silently praying she wouldn't be recognized.

Ana inhaled a lungful of air, held it, and then let it out slowly and opened her eyes. She'd escaped death, been given a second chance to live, dream and maybe even fall in love where she would have her own happily ever after. The thumb of her right hand touched the ring. She'd never envied her older brother and sister, believing they'd chosen to alter their lives and lifestyles when both had fallen in love and married.

Gabriel had left Florida to live in Massachusetts, unaware he would fall in love with a woman who had been living a double life. Summer Montgomery had come to the high school where Gabriel was an artist-in-residence to teach musical theater, and as an undercover DEA agent to identify those responsible for selling drugs to students. Summer didn't vacillate, giving up her gun and shield once Gabriel proposed. She'd traded the excitement of undercover assignments for marriage and motherhood. They were now the parents of two sons and a daughter—all under the age of five.

Even her sister had settled into marriage and motherhood with the ease of a duckling taking to water. Alexandra had thrown all of her energies into caring for her daughter and son, decorating her home, while waiting for Merrick to come home where they'd share dinner as a family unit. Her brother and sister had what she wanted: to fall in love, marry, have children, while living her own happily ever after.

Meanwhile Diego had forced her into a marriage of convenience with a man who'd admitted he hadn't married because he hadn't met the woman with whom he wanted to share his life. When Henri had given him the envelope with their license Jacob had shown no visible reaction, leading her to believe he probably had known about the subterfuge.

It had taken an attempt on her life and exile for her to reassess her priorities. In less than two years she would celebrate her thirty-fifth birthday, putting her into the high-risk pregnancy category. And she wanted at least one child before forty, but that wasn't going to happen, unless she opted for adoption, if she continued to eschew a relationship and commitment. Ana knew her reluctance was based on the two men with whom she'd loved unconditionally.

There were things she was willing to ignore or dismiss but infidelity was not one of them. Perhaps it had something to do with her grandfather cheating on her grandmother. The one time she'd asked her grandfather why her father's brother's surname wasn't Cole, Samuel Cole had been forthcoming when he told her that sleeping with his secretary had been his greatest indiscretion because it had almost destroyed his marriage. It had also caused a rift between his children for three decades. In a moment of humility Samuel admitted he had grown to love Joshua Kirkland as much as he had his other two sons and daughters.

"Men hit on you because they want something from you." Jacob's words came back in vivid clarity. Why, she'd asked him. Was there something about her that made her a target for cheaters and users? Why, she mused, couldn't they be like Jacob? He claimed he didn't want anything from her except her heart. Had it been that way with him and other women? Could she offer him her heart and in return learn to trust again?

Trust. The five-letter word that was the foundation of any marriage or relationship. Her mother had told her without trust there couldn't be love.

She trusted Jacob when he'd said he would protect her, but could she trust him with her heart? Ana wasn't blind to his attraction for her, nor could she deny her growing feelings for him. She wasn't certain when her feelings had changed but she was tired of denying the sexual tension that was so apparent whenever they occupied the same space.

She hadn't meant to tease him when walking around in her underwear. After all, had they not beforehand established there would be no intimacy between them? That they would live together as friends or roommates until it was safe for her to return home?

But along the way something had changed. The occasional caresses and kisses had become more frequent, the stares between them longer and more longing. Now that they were a married couple, in name only, it made Ana wonder what it would be like if she were truly Mrs. Jacob Jones. Would she relocate from Boca Raton to Miami, or would Jacob be willing to move to Boca Raton? Would he want to start a family right away or defer to her decision to wait a couple of years? "Would he" and "what ifs" rushed over themselves in her head until she wanted to cry aloud, telling them to go away and leave her alone.

To even think about a real marriage meant she not only had to trust the man, but also be in love with him. Jacob had garnered her trust, but she doubted whether she would or could fall in love with him.

Ana was uncertain how long Diego wanted them to remain at Cannamore to measure quality review, but she intended to take full advantage of the island's natural beauty. She saw a shadow, and turning, she saw Jacob coming in her direction with a bottle of champagne in one hand and two flutes in the other. Shifting on the bench she gave him enough space to sit beside her. Her gaze was fixed on Jacob's hands when he removed the cork with a minimum of effort, half filled both glasses with the chilled pale bubbly wine, and handed her a flute.

"What are we toasting?" Ana asked when Jacob held his flute aloft.

"Me and Mrs. Jones. We got a thing going on," he sang in his rich baritone.

Ana's laughter was like the tingling of a delicate bell. "We both know it's wrong," she continued, singing the classic Billy Paul hit. They touched flutes, staring at each other over the rim in the silvered moonlight as they took a deep swallow of the premium wine. "You know that's a song about an extramarital affair."

Reaching for the bottle, Jacob refilled their glasses. "It doesn't apply to us because I will never cheat on you. However, for the present time we *are* Mr. and Mrs. Jones." His teeth shone whitely in his bearded face when he flashed a Cheshire cat grin.

"You're enjoying this faux marriage, aren't you?"

"I'd be a fool not to, *m'ija*. Where else would I get the opportunity to flaunt my beautiful wife? We're on a private island that is as close to paradise as we'll ever get with nothing more to do than have fun while we rate the quality of services."

Folding her legs under her body, Ana leaned against Jacob. "How long do you think that's going to take?"

"Probably a couple of weeks. You do your evaluation and I'll do mine, and then we'll compare notes."

"When do you want to make the comparisons?"

"Just before we're ready to leave."

Jacob couldn't tell Ana that if it took two weeks or two months to draw Basil Irvine out into the net the investigators had cast for him she would have to remain in the Bahamas; when it came time for him to return to his job he would be forced to leave her.

Once they'd arrived in Miami Ana had waited in the car with Henri while he'd entered his apartment to lock up his firearm, retrieve his passport and netbook. Instead of his cell phone, he intended to use email to communicate with Diego. He also packed another bag with the computer and several more changes of clothes that included dress slacks, shirts, a couple of lightweight jackets and dress shoes. Having two residences meant storing clothes in both places.

"What do you want to do tomorrow?" Jacob asked Ana when she smothered a yawn behind her hand.

"I don't want to do anything for a couple of days but lie on the beach." She yawned again. "Excuse me for yawning. Champagne always makes me drowsy."

He ruffled her hair. "That's all right." Jacob took a quick glance at the glowing numbers on his watch. It was after two in the morning. He took the flute from her hand. "Go on, *m'ija.* I'm going to sit out here for a while."

Ana lowered her legs, leaned over and touched her mouth to his. *"Bueñas noches."*

He smiled. *"Bueñas noches, mi amor."*

Jacob's "good night, my love" lingered with Ana long after she'd brushed her teeth, pulled a nightgown over her head and slipped into the four-poster California king-bed swathed in mosquito netting.

Her eyes had closed and her breathing deepened by the time *her husband* had gotten into bed with her. Unconsciously, she moved closer to him, sharing his body heat, pressing her hips to his groin. She moaned once when Jacob's arm rested on her waist, then Morpheus claimed her mind and body.

Streaks of light had pierced the night sky, heralding the beginning of a new day when Ana woke to find Jacob's erection against her hips. She knew he was asleep because of the soft snoring. Her heart stopped, then started up again when the area between her legs became moist, throbbing with a rising desire that eddied throughout her body. It was impossible to slow down the runaway beating of her heart, and she loathed moving only because she didn't want to wake him.

Each time he touched her, a delicious shudder had rippled throughout her body, bringing with it a welling desire to surrender to his subtle seduction. It had taken strength Ana hadn't known she had to demonstrate how much his presence *hadn't* affected her. This sexy, virile man, her so-called husband had her trembling like a frightened virgin about to embark on her first sexual encounter.

"Are you cold?" Jacob's voice sounded disembodied, as if it had come a long way off instead of a hair's breath away.

"No."

"Why then are you shaking?"

Ana swallowed to relieve the lump in her throat. What did he expect her to say? That she was so aroused that she feared climaxing? That she wanted him to make love to her and assuage the desire sweeping over her like a wildfire? The questions bombarded her as she tried forming a response, one that wouldn't embarrass her even further.

"I'm having a moment," she whispered.

Jacob rested an arm over Ana's waist, pulling her even closer. "What kind of moment?"

"The same moment you're experiencing right now."

A pregnant pause filled the room. "Oh, no," he crooned.

Ana smiled. *"Si, m'ijo."* Without warning, she found herself on her back and Jacob looming over her. Supporting his weight on his elbows, he covered her body with his.

"Don't move, baby."

She wanted to tell Jacob it was impossible not to move—especially with his hardness on her belly. "Why are you torturing me?"

"And you don't torture me?" he countered.

"Not deliberately."

"Deliberate or not, you do. If it's not in revealing underwear, then it's a pair of shorts that show more than they cover."

"I promise not to walk around in my underwear again if you promise not to barge into my shower."

Jacob buried his face between her chin and shoulder. "I can't promise you that."

"Why can't you?"

"Because one of these days before we leave here I am going to make love to you in this bed, on the beach, in the ocean *and* in the shower. And that's a promise."

There came another moment of silence. "You sound very confident."

"That's because I am, *m'ija.*" He rolled off her body and lay beside Ana. Reaching for her hand, Jacob held it gently, protectively.

They lay together, only the sound of their measured breathing punctuating the peaceful silence. The day of reckoning had come. Ana knew she and Jacob would make love. When, was the question. What she didn't delude herself into believing was their lovemaking would have anything to do with love. It was about sex.

Chapter 11

Los Angeles

Basil cradled his head in his hands. He'd taken enough pain-killers to stop his heart, yet the vise around his temples per-sisted. It had been years since his last migraine, and this time it was back with a vengeance. He knew the blinding headache was the combination of a mother of a hangover and stress.

First it was Justin and now Camille. Not only had he be-come a loser. He was now a sucker. He'd allowed himself get pulled in by a woman with a pretty face and perfect body; a woman who'd gotten him to forget any woman he'd ever slept with.

He raised his head, staring at the police detective who wanted answers—answers he was unable to give him. "I'm sorry, but I can't help you."

The veteran homicide detective stared at the music exec-utive, seeing grief etched into the man's features. He'd had enough experience and had interrogated countless people, studying and reading their expressions and body language. And after more than twenty-five years of law enforcement know-how he realized Basil Irvine was in pain. However, he wasn't certain whether the pain was physical or emotional.

"How close were you to Miss Nelson?"

"What the hell kind of question is that?" Basil snapped.

Detective Harrison did not drop his eyes. "I just need to know if your relationship with Miss Nelson went beyond the boardroom."

"If you're asking if I saw Camille outside the office, then the answer is yes. We went out to dinner and I'd occasionally stop by her apartment to discuss work. If you're going to ask if she ever came to my house, then the answer is no."

"Were you intimate with Miss Nelson?"

A feral smile parted Basil's full lips. "No," he lied smoothly. "I got involved with one of my employees years ago and it cost me my marriage. I swore I'd never do that again, and I haven't."

"We were told that you visited Miss Nelson's apartment on the day she went missing?"

"Who told you?"

"Just answer the question, Mr. Irvine."

There came a swollen pause as Basil continued to massage his temples. "When she didn't come to work I called her cell and then her home, but both calls went directly to voice mail. I waited until late afternoon, and when I still hadn't heard from her I went to her apartment, thinking maybe she'd taken ill or she'd had an accident. I rang her bell, knocked on her door and when I didn't get an answer I left."

"Did you ask the building superintendent if he'd seen her?" Danny Harrison knew the answer to his question, yet he wanted to see if Basil was going to lie. One lie meant he would have to cover that one up with another lie. And when he did he would spring the trap, ensnaring the music mogul. Instinct told him not only did Irvine know about Camille

Nelson's murder but he was also behind the attempt on Ana Cole's life.

Irvine's rise in the music industry hadn't been without controversy. There were rumblings about breach of contracts, artists not receiving their royalty payments, and there was still talk that it had been Basil and not his brother, Webb, who'd stomped a man to death in retaliation for the attack on Webb. The CEO of Slow Wyne was delusional if he believed himself untouchable.

"Yes, I did. He told me he hadn't seen her in several days. When I asked him if he would check on her he told me the only time he was authorized to enter a tenant's apartment was in an emergency. He told me just because she hadn't come to work he didn't believe that was an emergency."

Danny glanced over Basil's shoulder at the wall of glass behind the large, imposing man. "What did you do after that?"

"I gave the man my card and told him to call me if he'd heard from Camille."

His gaze shifted back to Basil. "Did you think something had happened to Miss Nelson?"

"I don't know what I was thinking at that time, Detective Harrison. All I knew was that an employee hadn't come to work. She hadn't given any indication she was sick, and she hadn't put in for vacation or a personal day."

"Are you always *this* involved with your employees? You visit their homes when they don't call or come into work?"

A rush of color darkened Basil's face. He'd had enough. "This interrogation is over, Detective. Now, I want you to get the hell out of my office and go and find who murdered my executive assistant."

The detective pushed to his feet. "I'll be back, Mr. Irvine."

Basil didn't bother to stand. "If or when you are it better be with a warrant for my arrest, because i'm not going to answer any more questions without my lawyer present. I'm certain you can find your way out."

"If I have to come back, then it'll be with a search warrant." Resting his hands on the marble-topped desk, Danny gave Basil a sly wink. "I know you're not telling me everything and that you know more about this than you're letting on. Have a good day, Mr. Irvine."

Basil's eyes darkened until there were no visible traces of gray. "I hope you're not threatening me, Detective Harrison. All I have to do is make one phone call and you'll find yourself back on the street directing traffic at a school crossing."

Danny stood up straight, sniffing. "I smell something. And it's fear. Make all the calls you want, but rest assured that if it's not me then it's going to be another cop that will bring you down. Good day, Mr. Irvine."

Basil was still sitting in the same position staring at the space where the detective had been when Webb entered his office. He flopped down on the chair the cop had vacated minutes before. Webb tented his fingers. When the detective had called, asking to speak to Basil, he'd retreated into an adjoining office, activating an audio and video feed.

"He's just blowing smoke."

Basil closed his eyes. "I don't think so."

"I can't believe you let him get to you."

"He was insinuating I knew who murdered Camille."

"He wasn't insinuating anything, brother. He suspects you and Camille had more than a boss-employee relationship and maybe the two of you had a falling out and either you killed her or had someone kill her."

Basil opened his eyes, glaring at Webb. "I didn't kill her."

"I know that and you know that. I know you're broken up over the girl, but you have to let it go."

"I can't let it go, Webb."

"Why not? She's no different from the others."

"That's where you're wrong. Camille was different."

Webb slowly shook his head. "She was a hooker and a hustler," he said, enunciating each word. "And don't ever forget that, brother. Who knows who she crossed in her past, and she paid for it with her life. Why don't you take a couple of weeks off, go somewhere and kick back. Call up some of your well-heeled friends who own places in the Caribbean and ask if you can chill out there until you're feeling better."

"I'll think about it."

"Don't think, Basil. Do it!"

Training his cold stare on the scars along the left side of Webb's face, Basil wondered when his younger brother had become the more dominant of the two. Had it come during Webb's incarceration when he'd had to develop his survival skills? However, with the blinding pain in his head and behind his eyes he wasn't equipped to verbally spar with Webb.

"Who's going to run Slow Wyne?"

The keloids that had ruined the handsome face of the slender, dark-skinned man in the charcoal-gray, pinstriped tailored suit looked like blisters whenever Webb smiled. Webb had prided himself on his good looks until another man who'd made it known that he would pay for getting his sister pregnant had followed through on his threat when he waylaid Webb and went to work carving up his face. Basil had come to his rescue, stomping the man to death. Webb told the police he'd killed the man in self-defense, but his plea fell on deaf ears because the prosecutor claimed he'd continued to kick the man even after he died, resulting in an unrecognizable corpse.

Even as he lay bleeding, while cradling the flesh hanging from his face like raw meat, Webb would never forget the sight and sounds of Basil kicking his attacker. It was as if his older brother had become temporarily insane. He knew women would never look at him in the same way they'd done as an adolescent, but that no longer mattered. He'd sworn a vow never to sleep with another woman as long as he lived.

"I will," Webb stated quietly.

The two brothers engaged in what had become a stare-down. "Okay," Basil finally agreed. "But first I have to tie up a few things."

"How long is that going to take?"

"No more than a week. I don't want to leave now, because the police will believe I'm running because I have something to hide."

There was another prolonged pause. "You're right," Webb said. "Maybe you should wait until that pig stops rooting around. Better yet, wait until they close the investigation."

"Have you heard anything since Serenity closed down?" Basil asked.

"Not yet. What I can't believe is that they would close their offices without setting up somewhere else. And where the hell is Ana Cole? It's as if she's dropped off the face of the earth."

Basil shook his head, groaning aloud. He couldn't even move his head with the stabbing pain making it virtually impossible to think. "I'm going to contact my inside person for an update."

Webb exhaled audibly. He knew Basil was playing a very dangerous game of revenge where there could only be one winner and one loser. His responsibility was to make certain his brother would not end up the loser.

"Be careful, brother. We can't afford to slip up now."

"Come on, baby. I won't let you fall."

Ana tightened her hold on Jacob's hand. They'd taken a golf cart to explore the west side of the island, and during their exploration they'd discovered water flowing down the mountains creating a waterfall that spilled into a lagoon. Jacob stepped into the crystal-clear water, and then swung her down beside him. The lagoon was at least five feet in depth and spanned the length and width of an Olympic swimming pool.

The heat of the brilliant Caribbean sun offset the chill of the water as Ana floated on her back, staring up at the canopy of ferns, vines, leaves and exotic flowers growing wildly and creating their private Garden of Eden. She watched Jacob duck under the water and swim laps. Ana joined him, matching him stroke for stroke. Her competitiveness surfaced and she streaked through the water like a colorful fish, Jacob in close pursuit.

She managed to make it to the opposite end, touching the bank, and before she could turn around Jacob was several strokes ahead of her. Seconds later it was a body's length and he stood, waiting and grinning when she finally caught up with him.

Gathering her close, Jacob anchored a hand under her chin, raising her face for a hot, explosive kiss that sucked the breath from her laboring lungs. Ana anchored her arms under his shoulders, holding on to to him as she went on tiptoe. Heat exploded inside her like an incendiary device. She was on fire! The kiss was nothing like the ones they'd shared before.

Jacob's hands moved up under Ana's shoulders, holding her aloft while his tongue slipped between her lips, suckling and tasting the sweetness of her mouth. He kissed her with all the passion he could summon for a woman, a passion he'd withheld from every woman he'd known and kissed.

It'd been three days since he and Ana had come to Cannamore; three days in which he'd become the husband of a woman who'd ensnared him in a web of longing that had him dreaming about her, lusting for her, and as much as he didn't want to admit it, he was falling for Ana—hard.

It had taken less than a week for Jacob to conclude Ana wasn't the spoiled little rich girl who pouted if she didn't get her way. She was unpretentious, generous, opinionated and wasn't prone to mincing words. And she wasn't into head games—something he truly detested. She also made him laugh—something he hadn't done enough.

He wanted to resent her intrusion into what he thought of as his predictable lifestyle. Whenever he woke each morning he knew exactly what he had to do and what was expected of him. That all changed the moment Ana walked out of the Marathon airport and into his life. Either he had changed or the woman with whom he went to bed and woke with had changed him. There had never been a time since his first sexual encounter that whenever he shared a bed with a woman he'd always shared her body. The exception was his *wife*.

Jacob hadn't begun to think of himself as a husband and Ana his wife until he went online and queried Diego about his supposed marriage to his cousin. Diego's reply came within minutes: *Rumors that Serenity has folded have gone viral. Jason is scheduled to give a formal press conference next week about the relocation. When asked about Ana's absence, he hinted she's away with her boyfriend. Enjoy your honeymoon.*

He hadn't shown Ana the email, but told her what Jason had said about her unavailability. When she'd complained that fabricating a marriage was definitely over-the-top, he'd countered that everything they did had to look real. Newshounds were usually relentless when it came to uncovering the truth.

Not only was he enjoying his honeymoon, but also his wife. Ana had gotten up earlier that morning, made breakfast, then joined him in bed while they ate pancakes, a fruit cup with diced mango, pineapple and freshly brewed coffee. He knew he could very easily get used to eating breakfast in bed with her.

It was with extreme reluctance that he released her mouth. Water had pasted her hair to her scalp and spiked her lashes. His gaze lingered on her thoroughly kissed, lush lips. Not only did he want to make love to Ana. He wanted to consummate their marriage.

Ana's eyes met Jacob's. Droplets clung to his bearded face. She felt the muscles in his biceps tighten when he lowered her until her toes touched the bottom. Her entire body was shaking and it had nothing to do with the cold water. Closing her eyes against his intense stare, she thought of the words that lay in her heart.

It hadn't mattered she'd only known him a week. It didn't matter that their marriage was not only arranged by a third party, but was also one of convenience. Here on Cannamore Cay she didn't have to hide from a nameless, faceless assassin but could dream about a future. Stepping away from Serenity had offered her a new perspective of a world beyond music. It was a world where she could fall in love and dream of marriage and children.

Living on the private island as Mrs. Jacob Jones was nothing short of fantasy. Falling in love with him would become an emotional disaster. Ana knew everything would end, including her marriage, once she returned to the States. She and Jacob had been married three days, and even after they annulled the union it still would exceed Britney Spears' celebrated fifty-five-hour nuptials.

"I want to go back now," she whispered.

Needing no further prompting, Jacob swung her up into his arms, carefully navigating the rocks until he placed her on the seat in the golf cart. Reaching for a pair of shorts, he pulled them on over his swim trunks. Ana realized they'd spent most of their time outside their cottage to resist the temptation of making love. After hours in the sun, swimming in the ocean and walks along the beach they were too exhausted to do anything but sleep once they retired for bed. Other than breakfast, they'd taken their meals in the restaurant with the resort's guests.

She didn't know how long she would be able to hold out not asking Jacob to make love to her. How long she would be able to deal with her own battle of self-restraint and survive without a meltdown. She kept telling herself that Jacob was a stranger in her bed, one who'd vowed to protect her, but who was going to protect her heart if and when she found herself in too deep?

What Ana felt and was beginning to feel for Jacob had nothing to do with appreciation. He was a constant reminder of what she'd denied because of the two men who'd forced her to put up a barrier to keep all men at a distance. Even her ongoing excuse that she was too busy for a relationship was beginning to wear thin.

It was his body heat, the now familiar feel of his arm resting over her waist, and the clean masculine smell of his freshly showered body that lingered with her even in her sleep. The erotic dream hadn't returned, because the man she wanted was her husband.

Her gaze shifted to the band on Jacob's left hand. "How much is Diego paying you to pretend we're married?"

Jacob maneuvered the cart over a grassy surface. Seconds ticked while he struggled not to lose his temper. "I thought we'd passed the stage where we'd no longer talk about money."

"We have."

"Then why did you bring it up, Ana?"

"I...it's just that when Henri gave you the license and the rings it was if you were expecting them. I know you told me Diego wanted to explain my disappearance, but I never would've thought you'd agree to a marriage of convenience."

"I couldn't agree because I wasn't asked. But if Diego feels this is the best way to deal with whatever is going on back in the States then I'm willing to go along with whatever he proposes. We are married, but that doesn't mean we have to stay married."

"You're right."

Jacob gave her a sidelong glance. "Thank you for agreeing with me. I never would've thought you would be an obedient wife."

"I hope you're not referring to obedient as in obey."

"Maybe yes, maybe no."

Ana rolled her eyes at him. "No wonder you're not married."

Jacob smiled. "That's where you're wrong, Mrs. Jones. We are married and I'm going to show you just how married we are."

She leaned against his shoulder. "What do you propose to do?"

"What I should've done to you that morning in Key West."

Ana knew he was talking about the shower incident. Jacob was right. If they'd made love that morning she wouldn't be able to stop repressing her urges. Her moments were coming more frequently and becoming more intense. The only thing that saved her from embarrassment was, as a woman, she'd been able to conceal sexual arousal wherein it was much more difficult for Jacob.

Ana was saved from replying when Jacob maneuvered to the entrance of the resort and a bellhop came over to greet them. "I'll take the cart back, Mr. Jones."

Reaching for a T-shirt, she pulled it on over her swimsuit. Resting her hands on Jacob's shoulders, she permitted him to assist her from the cart. Half a dozen couples sat at tables near the bar drinking and talking softly to one another. At night the area became an impromptu cabaret with a piano player taking requests while the bartender took drink orders. Accommodations at the main house contained ten one-bedroom suites and two two-bedroom suites. There were three private cottages set up as honeymoon retreats, each with a fully stocked refrigerator and pantry.

"Are you going to give me a hint what you're going to do?" Ana whispered to Jacob as they walked along the path leading to their cottage.

Throwing back his head, he laughed. "Of course not."

"Shouldn't I know what to expect?"

"No, *m'ija.* Surprises are always more fun."

Reaching in the pocket of his shorts, Jacob took out the card key and swiped it. Within seconds of the light turning green Ana felt her heart rate quicken. He opened the door, stepped inside and then beckoned her.

"Come inside, said the spider to the butterfly."

It was Ana's turn to laugh. She stared at the tall, bearded man with the intense dark eyes, amazed that she felt a closeness she hadn't thought possible. When he extended his arms, she walked into his embrace.

Jacob buried his face in her damp hair. "I'm not going to do anything you don't want me to do."

Ana pressed her cheek to the crisp hair covering her husband's chest. *Her husband.* That's how she'd begun to think of Jacob. With or without her approval or participation she'd become Mrs. Jacob Stephen Jones.

"I'll let you know when I don't like something or I want you to stop," she mumbled, pressing light kisses over his pectorals.

Bending slightly, Jacob picked her up. "I know you will."

For a reason she couldn't fathom, Ana felt making love with Jacob was the most natural thing in the world. It was as if they were destined to be together. She wasn't going to delude herself into believing she was in love with him, because she wasn't. However, with time she knew she could come to love him. Time—it had become her enemy. She didn't know how long she would have to remain in exile, and she also didn't know how long she would be able to enjoy the advantages of married life, which meant she didn't have to go looking for a date; she didn't have to deal with the pressure of trolling clubs to find a man for sex; she also wasn't faced with the angst following a breakup.

Jacob carried Ana into the bedroom, pushing aside the mosquito netting and placing her on the neatly made bed. He'd called housekeeping to have them change the linen, clean the bathroom and vacuum. Sitting on the side of the mattress, he stared at the golden orbs staring back at him. He smiled. Ana's expression was calm, serene. It was as if the day of reckoning had been in suspended animation until this time, and Jacob was astounded by a sense of self-realization that Ana possessed everything he sought in a woman. In the past he'd confused sex with companionship but their living together without the benefit of sex allowed him to appreciate his wife. His wife. He'd come to like the sound of the two words. He belonged to Ana and she belonged to him.

Jacob hadn't exchanged vows, promising to love, honor, respect and care for her in sickness and in death, but then again no words were needed. He went to his knees and brushed his mouth over hers. "How long has it been, baby?"

Ana knew he was asking about her having sex. *"Un par de años, papacito."*

He smoothed back the raven strands curling over the top of her ears. "Well, *mamacita*, I'll make certain to be gentle with you." It had been a couple of years for Ana, while it hadn't been that long for Jacob. Now, he was glad he'd waited. He rose from the bed, went into the bathroom and removed a supply of condoms from his toiletry bag.

Ana's eyes followed his every move when he returned, placing a condom on his pillow and the others in the drawer of the nightstand on his side of the bed. The visible, rapidly beating pulse in her throat indicated she wasn't as calm as her serene expression.

Smiling, he removed Ana's T-shirt and then the black maillot, his gaze worshipping her compact, curvy body. Spending time in the sun had darkened her olive complexion to rich henna. Her lashes swept down across a pair of high cheekbones, the gesture charming and wanton, and Jacob wondered, who was she? This woman who claimed his name. Was she as innocent as she now appeared? Or was she the siren who'd unwittingly seduced him with her sassy attitude and uninhibited exhibition of provocative lingerie? He'd lied to

Ana when he'd told her he wouldn't make love to her when his body said differently. The first time she'd strolled into the kitchen in Long Key, Jacob realized then that living with her wasn't going to be an easy endeavor. And within a week they'd traveled from Long Key as protector and protected, to Key West under the guise they were a couple, and now to an island in the Bahamas as husband and wife.

Jacob's gaze never strayed from Ana as he pushed his shorts and swim trunks down in one smooth motion, stepping out of them. He lay down, closing his eyes and permitting his senses to take over. Although fully aroused, he wanted to slow down his respiration to prolong their eventual coming together. Not only had it been months since his last sexual encounter, he couldn't forget that the woman beside him wasn't just an acquaintance but his wife.

His declaration that he wouldn't sleep with Ana came as much from his friendship with Diego as it did with his promise that he would protect and not take advantage of her. Now the circumstances were different because Diego had arranged their marriage in absentia and, as Ana's husband, he could and would consummate their marriage.

Jacob smiled when Ana held his hand, her thumb moving back and forth over his knuckle. "Are you all right, *mi amor?*"

"I'm wonderful," she replied in a breathless whisper.

Ana opened her eyes, staring up at the gossamer fabric shrouding the large bed. It was as if she and Jacob had escaped to an ethereal world where any and everything they could want was available to them. Cannamore Cay was a private paradise with exotic birds, flowers and fruit everywhere. Pristine white sand, blue-green ocean waters, lush mountains with waterfalls spilling into crystal-clear pools and lagoons and warm trade winds offsetting the tropical heat.

Ana hadn't lied to Jacob when she'd said she was wonderful. The reason she was hiding on a private island in the Bahamas was never far from her mind. Nor was the reality that it was she and not Tyler who'd been the target of an alleged hit.

If someone had predicted her life would take the turn it had Ana would've vehemently protested, calling them a liar. In no way could she have imagined having to flee her home and family because of a business deal. She and Basil Irvine weren't drug dealers fighting over turf, or heads of organized crime negotiating territory and/or who would control gambling, prostitution or drugs.

As if choreographed in advance, they turned and faced each other. A gentle smile lit up her eyes when she gazed into those of her husband. Even being addressed as Mrs. Jones didn't sound as strange as it had three days ago. If given a choice she would've hyphenated her last name. But that was beyond her control, and she realized Diego had her listed as Ana Jones instead Ana Cole-Jones because the name Cole would've raised a red flag.

Jacob ran a finger down the length of her nose. "You know this is going to change everything."

"The only thing that's going to change is our having sex. Everything else will remain the same."

Unconsciously his brow furrowed. "What about our marriage?"

A sweep of lashes concealed Ana's innermost thoughts. "There will be no marriage once we go back. I've accepted why Diego wanted us married, but I refuse to let him or anyone else determine my destiny. I will marry whomever I want whenever I want, not because someone else deems it."

"Even if your life depends on it?"

Ana's eyelids fluttered. "Yes. As the youngest of four I spent years fighting to be my own person. It was never Jason and Ana, but always the twins. Do you have any idea how aggravating that can be?"

"No, baby, I don't. I'm not a twin."

She rested a leg over Jacob's. "Please don't get me wrong.

I love Jason, but it gets a little tired when we're lumped together in the same breath."

"Like peanut butter and jelly, ham and eggs, and mac and cheese?"

"Exactly."

Jacob pressed a kiss to her forehead. "Don't worry about it. You've proven you can roll with the best of them. A lot of men can't do what you do and become successful."

"Why does it always come down to gender? If I were Clive Davis or David Foster no one would bat an eye, but because I'm a woman the spotlight is always there. As long as we're in the kitchen or bedroom, barefoot and pregnant, all is right with the world. But, if we dare step out of place or get out of pocket we're nothing more than a bitch."

Jacob's mouth touched hers. "That's enough beating up on yourself, baby. You're an incredible woman and if a man doesn't recognize that then he's a fool."

Ana kissed him, the touch of her lips as light as the brush of a butterfly's wing. "You're so good for my ego, *m'ijo.*"

"I don't want to be good for your ego, but good to you."

She smiled. "You are. You turned out to be a much better husband than I would've imagined."

His eyebrows lifted. "You had your doubts?"

"Initially I did. You were such a grouch."

"No!"

Ana giggled like a little girl. "Yes. But you managed to redeem yourself once I became Mrs. Jones."

"I told you the Jones men make good husbands. We support our women, protect them and remain faithful."

"I suppose I couldn't ask for more. We should—" Ana's words died on her tongue when Jacob flipped her over on her back, straddling her.

"No, you can't."

The sunlight coming in through the specially made glass and the sheer netting draping the bed wouldn't permit Ana to see Jacob's eyes clearly when he stared down at her. He'd awakened her mind and body to a rushing, heated desire that intensified whenever they shared the same space. The reality that he was a stranger, a stranger with whom she'd shared a bed and married had kept her from opening her heart to him. Always the realist, she knew they were playing a game that would end the moment the person responsible for wanting her dead was apprehended. There would be just right now for her and Jacob rather than a happily ever after.

She gasped again, this time when his erection brushed her inner thigh. At that very moment Ana wanted to surrender all she was and all she had to him. She clung to him, his touch warm and comforting. And when his mouth moved lower to her breasts she arched off the bed, swallowing the moans welling up in the back of her throat.

Ana clutched Jacob's shoulders tightly, pulling her lips between her teeth as he began his exploration. She tried but couldn't stop the whimpers and breathless moans when his mouth staked its claim on the soft, wet folds of her sex. Her head thrashed back and forth on the pillow as his tongue swept over the tiny bud of flesh in a flicking motion. It sent explosive sensations throughout her body, rocking her womb.

Jacob knew Ana was close to climaxing; he stopped and slipped on the condom. Spreading her legs with his knee, he penetrated her newly awakened body. Her moan of pleasure pounded the blood in his head, and he forgot everything. He forgot his marriage to Ana was one of convenience and why they were living on Cannamore Cay. There was only Ana Jones.

He felt her tight flesh stretch to accommodate his tumescence, then it closed around his swollen penis, holding him fast. His groans matched hers when they moved together, quickening and slowing until they established a rhythm that made them one.

Sliding his hands under her hips, Jacob pulled Ana even

closer, she rising to meet his powerful thrusting, matching the fury of desire that threatened to devour them whole. Without warning, desire, passion, possession and need collided in a fireball of ecstasy that shattered them into infinite pieces and left them struggling to breathe.

Tears leaked from Ana's eyes, sliding down her face and into the pillow under her head. Her heart felt as if it was going to burst from the most exquisite lovemaking she'd ever experienced in her life. It was as if her body had been dormant, waiting for someone to awaken her to the pleasure poets waxed about since the beginning of time.

She presented Jacob with her back to keep him from seeing her tears. Making love had changed her. As much as she didn't want to admit it, Ana was falling in love with her husband.

Chapter 12

Ana slipped her feet into a pair of strappy black patent-leather stilettos. It was Friday—date night at the couples-only resort. She'd chosen to wear a body-hugging, sleeveless sheath dress with alternating bands of black and white with an asymmetrical neckline.

Peering into the full-length mirror on the door of the armoire, she checked her face. A dusting of bronzer, a coat of mascara and cherry-red lipstick highlighted her eyes and mouth. Using her fingers, she fluffed up her short curly hair. The day before, she'd utilized the services at the on-site spa for an exfoliating facial, mani/pedi and full-body massage. Jacob had made his own appointment for a haircut, shave, manicure and pedicure. Instead of joining the other couples for dinner, they'd elected to call room service. After a sumptuous assorted cold fish entrée with marinated veggies and mineral water, they retired to bed and made love as if it would be the last time.

Ana still couldn't believe how easily she'd fallen into the

role as Jacob's wife. They could not have been better suited if they'd had countless rehearsals. His reflection appeared in the mirror behind her. Jacob had selected a pair of black dress slacks, black shirt and pale gray jacket. She smiled; he'd exchanged his predictable sandals and running shoes for a pair of black imported slip-ons.

"My, don't you look handsome."

He moved closer, circling her waist with his arms. "And you look delicious. Would you mind giving me a little sample of your goodies before we leave?"

"No!"

Jacob tightened his hold around her waist when she attempted to twist out of his embrace. "Why are you being so stingy?"

"I know you, Jacob. A sample will end up with us spending the night in bed and missing date night."

He pressed a kiss to her ear. "Don't tell me you're going to deny your husband his conjugal rights."

He loosened his hold and she turned around, meeting his eyes. Nearly four inches of heels put the top of her head at his nose. There was something about his cropped hair and clean-shaven face where he appeared younger, almost boyish. But Ana knew there was no boy in a man who was licensed to carry and discharge a firearm in the line of duty.

"If Diego hadn't bribed some court clerk to make up that license you would have no conjugal rights."

Jacob's impassive expression did not change. "Are you *that* certain he bribed someone?"

Ana sucked her teeth. "I wouldn't put it past him. I told you he isn't that far removed from my grandfather when it comes to getting what he wants."

Jacob's hands moved up, cradling her face. "Whatever he did is something we will not speak of again. Do I make myself clear?"

Her eyes grew wider when she realized he was chastising her. "Do not speak to me as if I were a child."

"I know you're not a child," he retorted between clenched teeth.

"Then don't treat me like one."

Jacob opened his mouth to read Ana the riot act, and then thought better of it. He didn't want to cause a rift in their fragile relationship by trading barbs. He doubted whether Diego would risk bribing a court official for his own benefit. It wouldn't be the first time people had married in absentia, and it definitely wouldn't be the last. It would be similar to Ana giving another person power of attorney to make decisions on her behalf.

He'd been just as surprised as Ana when Henri handed him the license and rings. What he did know about his godson's father was he would do anything within his power to protect his family. And Jacob knew it had exceeded the bounds of friendship when Diego had entrusted him with Ana.

"If you were a child I never would've made love to you," he said instead. Ana's mouth opened, but no words came out. Smiling, he cupped her buttocks, pulling her close, her breasts touching his chest. "Are you finished primping, *m'ija?*"

For a reason she couldn't fathom, Ana knew she couldn't stay angry with Jacob. Just when she thought she was going to verbally spar with him he switched gears, shutting her down. And it was impossible to argue with herself.

Resting her hand on his shoulder, she leaned in even closer. A smile played at the corners of Jacob's mouth, bringing her gaze to linger there. Choking sounds came from his throat when she cupped his groin, increasing the slightest pressure until he grew heavy in her hand. "Play with fire, *m'ijo,* and you'll get burned," she hissed.

Jacob didn't know whether to laugh or yell at Ana for giving him a hard-on. He picked her up instead and swung her around and around until she pleaded with him to stop. If he'd acted on impulse he would've stripped her naked and made love to her until she pleaded with him to stop.

"I warned you about teasing me," he said, glaring at her.

"I'm sorry."

Jacob slowly let her down until her feet touched the floor. "No, you're not."

"Yes, I am, *mi amor.*"

"Am I your love, Ana?"

She picked up her small evening bag off the nightstand. "Of course you are," she said glibly, winking at him over her shoulder. "I married you, didn't I?" She walked out of the bedroom, leaving Jacob staring at the seductive sway of her hips and sexy legs in the heels.

He caught up with her, resting his hand at the small of Ana's back and escorting her out of the cottage to the main building, through the lobby and into the restaurant that had been magically transformed into a nightclub setting with subdued lighting. Tables arranged with seating for two or four were covered with white linen tablecloths, bone china, crystal, silver, lighted candles and fragrant gardenias floating in bowls of rosewater. A live band with a male and female vocalist performed on a portable stage, while waiters moved quietly and efficiently around the room seeing to the needs of the guests.

Jacob escorted Ana over to a table for two, seating her. He lingered over her head longer than necessary inhaling the subtly sensual fragrance of her perfume. He pressed his mouth to her ear. "You smell as delicious as you look."

Reaching up, Ana placed her hand over his resting on the back of her chair. "Thank you, *mi amor.*"

Sitting opposite her, Jacob wondered if he was really her love, or was it just an affectation like baby or darling. Words that were bantered about all too often and much too loosely.

A waiter with a white napkin draped over the arm of his black jacket approached their table. He placed a menu on the table in front of Jacob, then Ana. "Evening, sir. Madam. I'm Lemuel and I will be your server tonight. The sommelier will be along shortly to help you with your wine selection. Meanwhile, you may look over the menu. If there's something you'd like that's not on the menu the chef will definitely be able to accommodate you."

Jacob nodded. "Thank you, Lemuel."

Waiting until the waiter walked away, he stared across the table at Ana. The light from the candle reflected off the diamonds in her ears. She looked nothing like the petulant woman who'd deliberately ignored her date at the baptism celebration that now seemed so long ago. She even looked different than she had more than a week before. Jacob had thought of her as a girl in a woman's body, but now she exuded a womanliness that was palpable, and he hoped it had come from being made love to.

He didn't know why their paths had crossed or their lives were intertwined, but Jacob didn't want to think about the time when what he had with her would end. In another six weeks he would have to return to Miami. Once there he would morph into the role as federal police officer responsible for the oversight of detention centers housing federal prisoners awaiting trial or deportation.

Pulling his thoughts away from the inevitable, Jacob studied the menu. One of the many perks at the resort was the staff's diversity, most of whom were multilingual, which helped bring a prompt resolution to any issues. Also, the various menus were never the same from day to day. Breakfasts were continental, American or the ubiquitous buffet with an omelet station. Lunch was usually buffet with offerings ranging from cold fish, meat, vegetable and fruit salads and a variety of miniature pastries. Dinner was less relaxed, requiring men to wear jackets and shoes, while their female counterpart usually displayed their tanned and toned bodies to their best advantage with revealing dresses and designer shoes.

His head popped up. "Are you hungry?" he asked Ana, staring at her bowed head as she studied the menu. They'd foregone lunch in lieu of making love.

She peered up at him through her lashes. "A little. I think I'm going to have steak tonight."

Jacob smiled. "What if we share the porterhouse for two?"

Ana scrunched up her nose. "Thirty-six ounces is a lot of meat."

"Not for this carnivore."

"I've noticed you haven't eaten a lot of meat."

"I go through phases when I swear off red meat for a month or two, then there're times when I really crave it."

"Well, right now I'm craving some moo," Ana joked. "But, then again the *perñil* looks as if it would be delicious."

"Why don't we order both?" Jacob suggested.

"No, Jacob. There's no way I'll be able to eat steak and pork and get a restful night's sleep."

"I'll order a smaller steak and that way you can order the *perñil.*"

Ana angled her head at the same time she lifted her eyebrows. "Are you still going to share your steak with me?"

The seconds ticked. Jacob stared at Ana as if she'd suddenly taken leave of her senses. "I've given you my name, and I'm sharing my life with you. Why wouldn't I share something as basic as food with you, *Mrs. Jones?*" He'd stressed the last two words.

Pinpoints of heat and embarrassment stung Ana's face. Why whenever Jacob chastised her did she find herself at a loss for words? She knew the answer as soon as the question formed in her mind. It was because he always told her the truth. Wherein she continued to think of their marriage as pretend, he didn't.

She knew if she'd met Jacob under another set of circumstances she doubted whether she would've slept with him so quickly. However, living with him had changed all that. He hadn't lied when he'd professed that the men in his family made good husbands, because within days of their *marriage* he'd become the attentive, loving husband. It wasn't what he wanted but what she wanted to do, eat or see. It was the same with making love. There hadn't been a time when he hadn't made certain she was fulfilled before he sought out his own. Jacob had gone from protector to friend, confidant, and now husband and lover.

"Thank you for reminding me."

Jacob reached across the table and held her hands, his thumb caressing the ring on her slender finger. "It's not about me having to remind you. It's about you remembering who we are."

Dimples kissed her tanned cheeks. *"Sí, mi amor."*

He gave her hand a gentle squeeze. "Now that we've settled that. How do you like your steak?"

"Medium-well."

The sommelier approached the table, listening intently when Jacob told him he wanted to order a wine that complemented wine and pork. The elderly gentlemen nodded and then walked away.

"Would you like to dance?" he asked Ana when he noticed her swaying along with a familiar love song. Other couples were already up dancing.

Ana flashed a smile. "I thought you'd never ask."

Pushing back his chair, he rounded the table and helped her stand. Wrapping an arm around her waist, he led her out onto the dance floor. She came into his embrace, her curves molding to his length.

Pressing his mouth to her ear, he kissed her. "I love this song."

"'Piano in the Dark,'" Ana whispered. "My dad played this song so much that my mother threatened to burn the CD. I think she was a little jealous of Brenda Russell even though she professed she was in love with Joe Esposito's voice when he collaborated with her on this record."

Jacob chuckled softly. "You really know your music, don't you?"

Ana closed her eyes. "I grew up with it. I woke up and went to bed with music. Daddy installed speakers in every room of the house, including the laundry room and pantry. Never mind he had a recording studio in one part of the house, he just had to hear music whenever he went."

"So, I guess it stands to reason why you went into the music business."

"Three of us did. Alexandra is an architectural historian. Although she likes music, she never was as passionate about it as my father and brothers."

Concentrating intently, Jacob spun her around in an intricate dance step. "You don't write it?"

"No. I leave the writing and composing to Jason and Gabriel. That's a gift I wasn't blessed with."

"What are you blessed with?"

Ana was going to say "you," but quickly dismissed the thought. She was blessed to have him accept the responsibility of keeping her safe. "I seem to have an innate gift for recognizing musical talent. As soon as a vocalist opens his or her mouth I know within under a minute whether they have something unique, special. It doesn't matter if you can imitate Aretha Franklin, have the range of the indomitable Whitney Houston, Christina Aguilera or Adele, a female singer must have something that sets her apart. It's the same with the male performers.

"That's why I fought so hard to sign Justin Glover. He wasn't just another pretty-boy with talent. He was the whole package. Justin can segue from R&B to rap, jazz and pop with the ease of taking a breath. When I heard him scatting I knew I would spend Serenity's last copper penny to sign him."

"Why did Irvine go after you and not the golden goose?"

"That's because if he gets me out of the way, then eventually he will get Justin to sign with his label."

"But, why you? Why doesn't he wait until Glover's contract is up, then go after him?"

The song ended and Ana stood in the middle of the dance floor, staring up at Jacob. Shadows from the dimmed overhead lighting flattered his lean face. "Irvine wants revenge because he'd heard I challenged his manhood."

Resting his hand at the small of her back, Jacob led her slowly back to their table. "How?"

"I said something about when he got up to put on his pants he should also remember to strap on his *cojones* if he planned to challenge Serenity."

"Oh, shit!"

Ana stopped short, Jacob stumbling when he nearly lost his balance. "What are you shitting about?"

"Did you or did you not say that?"

She lifted her shoulders. "I may have alluded to it. But only after he'd called me a bitch that had gotten out of pocket, and he was just the man to take care of me."

Jacob seated Ana, then pulled her chair close enough to his for their shoulders to touch. "Who was there when you said that?"

Exhaling an audible breath, she then bit her lip. "Of course Jason was there."

"Think, Ana!"

Her brow furrowed. "I guess it was the executive staff."

Beckoning to a waiter, Jacob asked him for a pen and a sheet of paper. "When that waiter comes back I want you to write down the names of the people who make up your executive staff."

"Why?"

"One of your employees is a rat, *m'ija.* Someone who knew you were going to be at that restaurant the day Tyler was shot."

Ana's eyes were as large as silver dollars. She shook her head. "I don't want to believe that."

"Why not?" Jacob whispered harshly.

"Because every employee has to sign a confidentiality agreement."

"Wake up, Ana. People take oaths every day, but that doesn't stop them from spying on their country or breaking the law."

Looping her arm through Jacob's, Ana rested her hand on the sleeve of his jacket. She didn't want to believe that someone at Serenity was leaking information to Slow Wyne. The employees had become her extended family. In fact, she saw them more than her own family members, with the exception of Jason. She tried thinking of a situation where the result ended with a disgruntled employee, but drew a blank.

"What are you going to do?"

"I'm going to get these names to Diego. He'll know what to do with them." Jacob kissed her hair. "I don't want you to concern yourself with this."

"But…I…I have to be concerned, Jacob."

"No, you don't. Right now Serenity is on hiatus, and that means Jason will only have to interact with a smaller number of employees."

"What about Jason? Who's going to protect him?"

Ana's wide-eyed look was one he would remember all of his life. It was the first time he saw fear in her. Occasionally he would detect it in her voice, but this time it was different. She wasn't frightened for herself, but her twin. "I'm certain Jason can take care of himself."

Jacob wanted to remind Ana that her family had enough resources to hire a small army of mercenaries to carry out their wishes. Her disclosure that she'd verbally emasculated Basil Irvine was the linchpin to identifying those responsible for shooting Tyler.

"I want you to promise me one thing, darling," he crooned.

Her expression softened, eyes glowing like amber in the candlelight. "What is it, *m'ijo?*"

"You're going to let me handle this."

There came a beat, then a smile when she said, "Okay. I promise."

He angled his head and kissed her, moaning softly when her lips parted. "That's my baby."

The waiter returned with a pad and pen stamped with the resort's name. Jacob tore off a sheet. "Thank you."

"Will there be anything else?"

"No. Thank you," he repeated.

Ana wrote down the names of three men and two women. "That's it."

Jacob folded the paper and slipped it into the breast pocket of his jacket. "I'll be right back."

Ana grabbed his sleeve. "Where are you going?"

Cradling the back of her head, he touched his mouth to hers. "I have to go to the cottage for something." Raising a questioning eyebrow, she met his steady gaze. "Don't run away."

Her dimples winked at him when she smiled. "Where would I go?"

Her question lingered with Jacob as he left the restaurant. Where would she go after leaving the Bahamas? Back to Boca Raton? Back to pick up the reins of operating Serenity? And back to a lifestyle that was as predictable as a sunrise.

He would also return to the States to resume his own familiar lifestyle, but with a difference. Jacob doubted whether he would ever forget Ana. Taking long strides he covered the distance between the main house and the cottage in record time. Retrieving the netbook he went online. The island had a cell-phone antenna, a satellite dish for limited television viewing, and the resort had what was touted as secure Wi-Fi connections, yet Jacob still felt uneasy about accessing the internet with what he considered sensitive information.

He connected to Diego's email and clicked on the instant-message feature. Jacob had to wait three minutes before Diego responded. Typing quickly, he listed the names Ana had given him. The coded messages went back and forth, until Diego asked how he was enjoying his honeymoon.

His hands stilled as he willed his fingers to type what lay in his heart. Then, as if they were detached from his body, he typed, *I love my wife. Later.* Logging off and not giving Diego the opportunity to reply, he sat motionlessly staring at the blank screen.

He'd admitted to his godson's father he loved Ana when he hadn't told her. He'd never been reticent when it came to speaking his mind, but staring down the barrel of a loaded gun was preferable to admitting those three little words to Ana.

The beginnings of a smile found its way to Jacob's eyes. It was apparent he was no different from his father—one glance and he'd known almost instantaneously the woman with whom he wanted to share his future. Ana was sexy, uninhibited and innocently seductive. And he suspected she had no inkling of how seductive she could be. She was also unpredictable and that kept him slightly off-balance. Unpredictable, independent, feisty and smart. These were characteristics he admired and looked for in a woman.

Jacob finally got up from the dining table to put away the computer. It was time he got back to his wife.

Ana averted her gaze when she heard the scathing interchange between the couple sitting at a table several feet away. What had begun as a disagreement had escalated into a noisy argument when the young woman stood up, called her boyfriend a drunken fool and then stalked out of the restaurant. *Good for you for walking out on that clown,* she mused, silently applauding the woman.

"Hey, beautiful. Wanna dance with me?"

She went completely still when the stench of stale alcohol wafted to her nose. Ana didn't want to believe the man had shifted his attention from his girlfriend to her. He was so close she could hear his raspy breathing. "No, thank you."

He leaned even closer and she shifted off her chair and onto the one Jacob had vacated. *Where are you?* the voice in her head screamed. Her husband had taken the most inopportune time to leave her alone. Ana didn't want to cause a scene, praying her unsolicited admirer wouldn't come any closer or attempt to touch her.

"Come on, baby. Don't be like that. Come on, dance with me." He grabbed her arm.

Ana fisted her hands. "Get the hell away from me."

"I—"

Whatever he attempted to say was cut off when he slumped, groaning in pain. Ana glanced up just in time to see Jacob catch him before he fell. The look in his eyes and the expression on his face didn't bode well for the inebriated man.

"Touch my wife again and I'll put your ass in the ground," Jacob threatened between his teeth. Supporting his sagging body, he steered him toward the entrance. He waved to the clerk manning the front desk. "Call security and have them take him back to his room." Within minutes two men appeared.

Jacob didn't wait around to see where they'd taken him because he wanted to get back to Ana. He found her, eyes closed and cradling a glass of water. The bottle of wine sat in an ice bucket next to a pitcher of water. Folding his body down to the empty chair, he whispered, "I'm sorry about that, baby."

She opened her eyes. "What did you do to him?"

"I turned him over to the security people."

Ana met his eyes. "Did you Taser him?"

"No! And where would I get a Taser?"

"He went down like he was hit with a bolt of electricity."

Jacob blew out his breath. "Let it go, baby. I rescue you from a drunk and you want to know what I did to him. He's lucky I didn't break his neck."

She shook her head. "I can't let it go, Jacob. What did you do to him?"

Waves of frustration washed over him. Ana was like a dog with a bone. She just wouldn't let it go. "I grabbed his midsection just below his heart. If I'd applied a little bit more pressure his heart would've ruptured. Now, are you satisfied?"

Ana knew Jacob was upset with her questioning him. "I'm only asking because I need to keep a low profile. I didn't leave Florida to become headline news in the Bahamas because of some idiot who just may decide to sue you for assault."

"Don't worry about him, *m'ija.* He probably won't remember anything after he sleeps it off."

The tense lines around Ana's mouth relaxed. She was more anxious than she'd originally thought. If the circumstances were different she was certain she could've repelled his advances, because it wasn't the first time she'd been harassed by someone who'd had too much to drink. Driving a heel into someone's instep usually got their attention.

Looping her arm through his, she leaned against Jacob's shoulder. "What is there about me that attracts crazies?"

Jacob pulled her closer. Ana didn't know how close he'd come to causing the drunk bodily harm. It was as if his protective instincts had gone into overdrive, superseding his promise to her cousin. "Even the crazies have good taste. You have to know you're hotter than a habanero pepper."

"Stop it." The shadow of a blush washed over her face, throat and chest.

"Well, you are. I really got lucky when I got you for a wife."

Ana closed her eyes. "And I got real lucky when I got a superhero masquerading as my husband."

Husband.

The word had flowed off her tongue as naturally as breathing. When had she begun to think of Jacob as her husband? She'd always believed she would meet a man, fall in love, marry, have several children and they would grow old together. What had been her predictable lifestyle was now a thing of the past. Even if she were able to return to Florida, Ana knew her life would never be the same because someone else had determined the course of her destiny.

"I'm no superhero, Ana. I'm just a man, a mere mortal who likes you more than he should."

Turning her head, she gave him a long, penetrating stare. "What you talking about?"

Jacob winked at her. "I like being married to you."

She smiled. "Same here," Ana agreed.

"What are we going to do about it? Do we try to stay together or do we call it quits before we get too involved?"

"We're already too involved, Jacob. We should've had this conversation before we slept together."

"Sleeping together should have no bearing on whether we decide not to annul our marriage. I've slept with other women and I knew I'd never marry them, and I'm certain it was the same with the men you've slept with."

Ana blushed again. "Men I should've never given the time of day."

"Don't beat up on yourself, sweetheart. I haven't always chosen wisely either. Maybe it took a third party to make a decision we were unable to make for ourselves."

"You're telling me this to say what?" Ana asked Jacob.

"I'm asking you to give me a chance to prove that I can be a good husband."

"You're already a good husband, *m'ijo.*"

Jacob clamped his jaw in frustration. Why was Ana making it so difficult for him? For them? "You're missing the point, baby."

Ana closed her eyes. She loved him, but doubted whether

she was in love with Jacob. She'd didn't want to be cynical only because she'd heard the word bantered around much too often and loosely. She loved music because it provided an emotional foundation and stability harkening back to her childhood. She loved her parents, her siblings and her extended family. The love she was beginning to feel for Jacob was different, and Ana didn't want to confuse it with sex or gratitude.

Her eyelids fluttered wildly. "Okay."

Jacob kissed the end of her nose. "What if we have date night back at the cottage? We'll order room service, watch a movie, then I'm not going to be responsible for what happens after that."

Ana gave him a dazzling smile. "Let's do it."

Chapter 13

Ana sat in the oversize claw-foot tub between Jacob's out-stretched legs. Bubbles from pulsing jets washed over her breasts as she sipped champagne from a delicate crystal flute. Their request to be served dinner in their cottage was nothing short of spectacular. Waiters had arrived with serving carts with table settings for two and dishes from which wafted the most delicious mouth-watering aromas. If Diego wanted feedback on his resort, then she would've given the service five stars.

One waiter lingered, serving and removing courses, while surreptitiously keeping his distance to not be intrusive. The roast pork was fork-tender; the steak broiled to the perfect medium-well. The piquant dressing on the mixed green salad with tiny mandarin oranges, *plataños maduro*—thinly sliced ripe bananas, and a dessert of caramel coconut flan set the stage for a candlelight dinner, followed by a black-and-white Hitchcock thriller, and finally a shared bath surrounded by dozens of candles.

"Do you plan on getting me buzzed so you can take advantage of me?" Ana teased Jacob.

He chuckled softly in her ear. "How did you know?"

"Because you've refilled my glass twice, and you know champagne makes me sleepy."

"All the better to eat you, my dear."

Staring at him over her shoulder, Ana flashed a lopsided grin. "Not if I don't eat you first."

"No, Ana. I won't let you do that."

She set the flute on a table next to the tub and managed to turn around without sloshing water over the rim of the tub and straddled Jacob's muscular thighs. "What are you afraid of, baby?"

His scowl deepened. "Nothing."

Moisture had curled her hair and spiked her lashes. Pressing her breasts to his chest, she whispered in his ear, "I think you are." Curving her arms around his neck, Ana rested her head on Jacob's shoulder. "I'm slightly tipsy."

Burying his face in her short hair, Jacob kissed her scalp. "Are you ready to go to bed?"

"Yes. But you're going to have to help me out."

Setting his flute on the table beside Ana's, he managed to stand up without dropping her and stepped out of the tub onto a thick chenille rug. Reaching for a bath sheet, he wrapped it around her body, swaddling her like a mummy. Supporting her body with one hand, he picked up another towel, then carried her out of the bathroom and into their bedroom. Ana had tied the mosquito netting to the posts, turned back the bed and adjusted the table lamps to the lowest settings.

"Don't go to sleep on me, baby."

Ana smiled, but didn't open her eyes. "I'm just resting my eyelids."

Leaning over her, Jacob pressed a kiss to each eye. He undid the towel, smiling. The sun loved Ana. It had kissed her body, the rich brown color of the skin on her arms and shoulders contrasting with the lighter hue on her small, firm breasts.

"Do you golf?"

Ana opened her eyes. "No."

"Have you ever tried it?"

"The closest I got to golfing is a driving range and I wound up with blisters."

Jacob dabbed her throat and shoulders. "That's because you didn't wear gloves. Will you go golfing with me tomorrow if I get you a pair of gloves?"

"Sure." Ana closed her eyes again, luxuriating in the feel of Jacob's hands on her body. "I don't know about you, but so far I'm giving Cannamore a top rating."

"I totally agree with you." Sitting back on his heels, he kissed her belly. "You're going to have to turn over so I can dry your back."

Ana sat up, wresting the towel from Jacob's grip. "Now it's my turn. Lie down, darling."

He stared at her under lowered lids. "I'm almost dry."

"Lie down, husband. On your belly."

"Aye, aye, wife."

Waiting until he lay as she'd instructed, Ana blotted droplets from Jacob's broad, muscled shoulders, down his straight spine and over his hips. His body was lean, strong and beautifully proportioned. She continued drying his legs and feet, lingering to dry between his toes.

She tossed the damp towel on the floor, then lay atop him, her face pressed to the column of his neck. "Am I too heavy for you?"

"You must be kidding. I can hardly feel you. But I do feel something else that's giving me a hard-on."

"Oh, really?"

"Yes, really."

Trailing her fingertips along his ribs, Ana blew in his ear. Jacob bucked under her. "Do you like that?"

"What do you think?" he asked, burying his face in the pillow. "What are you trying to do?"

"I'm seducing my husband. Do you have a problem with that?"

"No. But right now you have me at a distinct disadvantage."

Ana's mouth traveled downward from Jacob's ear to his shoulder. "I doubt that, *m'ijo.* You're at least a foot taller and probably outweigh me by at least fifty pounds."

Jacob chuckled. "Try eighty, *m'ija.* I'm six-three and weigh two-ten."

She didn't want to tell him that he was more than ninety pounds heavier than she was. She and her sister had inherited their mother's body type and metabolism. While in high school Ana was teased by girls who'd claimed she was bulimic; although she'd consumed her share of burgers, fries and shakes they hadn't known her twice-a-day regimen of swimming laps in her family's inground pool offset the calorie-laden diet.

"Don't move," she whispered, placing tiny kisses down his back. Jacob ignored her warning not to move when her hand slipped between his thighs, cradling his testicles.

A low growl echoed in the room when he suddenly turned over, nearly knocking her off the bed. He caught her before she landed on the floor.

Ana sprang up with the quickness of pouncing cat. She lay on his chest. Once more her hand searched between his legs, but Jacob outmaneuvered her when, using his superior strength, lifted her over his erection. With one sure thrust of his hips he was inside her.

She bit back a scream of ecstasy when she felt every inch of the hardened flesh stretching the walls of her vagina. There was something about this coupling that was so unrestrained and primal that she feared climaxing much too soon. Passion and lust pounded her head, heart and at the apex of her thighs. If Ana had any doubt as to whether she was in love with Jacob it fled at that moment.

What she felt for the man whose name she claimed wasn't about sex or gratitude. It was about Jacob himself. He was the first man she'd met who permitted Ana to be herself. She was more than aware of her strengths and weaknesses, and one was her teasing nature. There were times when she did tease men to see how far they would let her go. Most of them weren't as tolerant as Jacob, and for that she was grateful.

Then there were others who'd wanted her to sleep with them after one or two dates. Those who were willing to wait her requisite three months before sex she obliged. Others who claimed they weren't used to a woman using her body as a bargaining chip quickly moved on.

Her best-laid plans and prerequisites were forgotten when it came to the man making the most exquisite love to her she'd ever known. She loved his strength, the clean masculine scent of his body, beautifully formed hands and feet. Ana loved listening to his deep, soothing voice with a lingering hint of a drawl that indicated he'd grown up in the American South.

Bracing her hands on his shoulders, she stared at Jacob staring up at her. The carnality in his expression caused her to hold her breath until the constriction in her lungs forced her to expel it or faint.

Lowering her head, she lightly touched her lips to his before devouring his mouth, her tongue tracing the outline of his full, sensual lower lip. There was no teasing as her mouth and hands worked their magic, tasting, exploring and discovering a minute scar on his chest hidden by the mat of hair.

"What happened?" she whispered in his ear.

"Don't talk, baby. Just love me," Jacob groaned.

And she did love Jacob not with words but with the most intimate way possible—with her body. A moan slipped past her lips when his fingers tightened on her waist setting a rhythm as old as time when she rose and fell over his blood-engorged sex. In a moment of insanity she forgot about the men she'd met, those who'd cheated on her, and that they were making love without using protection. Her breath came faster and faster, moans escalating until Ana threw back her head and screamed as passion tore through her like a twister, shattering her into a million infinitesimal pieces.

Jacob managed to reverse their position without pulling out. He'd wanted to slow down the passion rushing headlong throughout his body, but the heat from Ana ignited an even hotter inferno. His thrusts grew stronger, communicating his need to possess her totally. If he could he would put her inside of himself if only to savor her essence every second, minute, hour, day, week, month, year, and beyond when both would cease to exist. He felt her hot flesh squeezing his as she climaxed, and unable to hold back his own rising desire he spilled his passions inside her hot, pulsing body.

Waiting until his heart resumed a normal rate Jacob rolled off her body, tucking her bottom against his groin. "Are you all right?"

Ana exhaled an audible sigh. "Yes."

"I didn't hurt you?"

"No, *mi amor.*" A beat passed. "How did you get that scar on your chest?"

"That's a long story."

"We have all night," she said softly. "In fact we have nothing but time. How many people can say that?"

"Not many," Jacob agreed. "I suppose there are a few things you should know about me."

"A few, Jacob?"

He kissed her again. "Okay. What do you want to know first?"

"The scar."

"That happened when I was twelve. A friend found his granddaddy's pellet gun and didn't know it was loaded. He pointed the gun at me and pulled the trigger. The pellet struck me in the chest. If it'd been an inch lower I wouldn't be here talking to you. The police would've charged him with reckless endangerment if my dad hadn't intervened on his behalf. He didn't want him to have a criminal record. Years later Dad blamed himself for interfering."

"Why? What happened to the kid?"

"The last I heard he's serving twenty-five to life for murder. He had a confrontation with his girlfriend's brother and in a fit of rage shot him in the head."

Ana shuddered noticeably. "That's horrible."

"That's because some people are horrible."

She listened intently when Jacob told her about her about his time in the corps. Before being assigned to a Foreign Service post he'd successfully completed a training program with the Corps Embassy Security Group. Her eyelids were drooping by the time he'd mentioned serving three twelve-month tours of duty at embassies in East Africa, Central Europe and South America. She was barely aware when Jacob pulled a sheet over them, then succumbed to a comforting, dreamless sleep.

Sleep wasn't as kind to Jacob. He'd disclosed things about himself only his parents knew. He turned off the lamps and settled down against the warm body of the woman who'd turned his orderly life upside down. He'd survived being shot, guarding U.S. embassies in regions where Americans were regarded as the enemy, and he'd tracked down fugitives who'd sworn they would never be apprehended alive.

He'd faced death and had confronted the devil several times in the guise of fugitive kidnappers, serial killers and pedophiles and had come out unscathed because of his mother's prayers. She claimed to have prayed for him every night since giving birth to him and continued to do so. It'd been too long since he'd prayed, and never for himself. It was time he began. And the prayers would not only be for himself but also Ana.

What he refused to think about was the fact she might be carrying his child. They had talked about giving their marriage a trial run, but not children. Jacob knew if this coupling resulted in pregnancy, then there would be no annulment or divorce.

Los Angeles

"Do not tell me you don't know where she is." A large vein appeared in Basil's forehead. His contact at Serenity had dropped the ball. "How can someone just drop off the face of the earth?"

"I'm sorry, Mr. Irvine," came a woman's voice through his cell phone's speaker feature. "I told you the office has been closed because we're relocating."

"Where?"

"I don't know."

Basil's hands fisted. "I don't pay you for 'I don't know.' I pay you well to give me information and right now I need to know where your boss is."

"If I knew I'd tell you."

"What about her brother?"

"He closed the office and gave everyone paid vacation. Jason said he'll contact everyone individually when he wants us to return."

"Have you spoken to your other coworkers?"

"A few. But they know what I know."

"Can you contact Jason?"

"I think so. I have his cell number."

Basil paced the length of the wall-to-wall windows. "Call him."

"And tell him what?"

He ignored the panic in her voice. "Tell him anything. Just find out where his sister is."

"I'll try, Mr. Irvine."

Basil stopped pacing. "Don't try. Just do it. You have less than a week to give me what I want, otherwise…"

"Otherwise what, Mr. Irvine?"

"Maybe your boss will discover they've employed a snitch. And you know what they say about snitches."

"I know. They get stitches." She paused. "I hate that I ever got into this."

"It's too late now, baby. You're a very pretty girl and it would be a shame if someone carved up that lovely face."

"I have to go now."

"Remember. One week."

Basil tapped a button, ending the call. He'd finally rid himself of the annoying, lingering headache, but his obsession with finding Ana Cole persisted. She reminded him of his mother although they'd looked nothing alike. He'd grown up abused and ridiculed by a woman who claimed he'd ruined her life when she discovered herself pregnant with a married man's baby. And she reminded him every day how much he looked like his father—a man she claimed she hated to her grave. Whenever he said something she didn't like she slapped him across the face. The taunts and slapping continued until he turned fifteen. By that time he was over six foot and had begun to put on muscle from a regimen of lifting weights. The last time his mother raised her hand to hit him he nearly broke her arm.

However, it had been different with Webb. His younger brother had been their mother's pride and joy. Although she hadn't married Webb's father, because he, too, was a married man, at least he stuck around, giving her money and buying her nice clothes until he was killed in a hit-and-run. By this time Basil had moved out and began hustling. He took orders from those in the neighborhood, stealing everything from clothes and jewelry to electronic equipment. One thing he refused to do was get involved in narcotics and instead of wearing flashy clothes or buying an expensive car, he saved his money. His goal was to become a successful businessman. Hard work, determination and years of sacrifice had paid off when he opened Slow Wyne in a small building in a rundown section of L.A. All of that changed once he signed artists whose first albums went gold weeks after they dropped. He moved Slow Wyne from the ghetto to a downtown high-rise, becoming a major player in the music industry.

"What do you think now, brother?"

Webb rolled his head on his neck. "You should've never threatened her. She's scared, Basil. And that means you can't trust her."

Sitting on the corner of his desk, Basil swung his imported leather-shod foot. "She's not going to mess up."

"I just hope you're right."

"I know you want me to drop this, but I can't. And I do need your support."

Stretching out his legs, Webb crossed his feet at the ankles. "Where is this coming from, Basil? When have I *not* supported you?"

A beat passed. "You're right. I'm sorry."

"Don't apologize. Just get rid of the bitch."

West Palm Beach, Florida

David Cole had to pry the cell phone from the hand of the young woman with a gun pointed at her head. He glared at her before setting it on a table out of her reach.

Her lower lip trembled. "Please…please tell him to put the gun down."

David nodded to the man who'd pressed the barrel of a small-caliber automatic at Charlene Brook's head. The threat to kill her if she didn't call Basil had worked. However, what the duplicitous woman didn't know was the gun wasn't loaded.

"Can I go now?" Charlene asked.

Martin Cole rose from a chair where he'd sat in the shadows of the library during the telephone conversation. As patriarch he'd convened all adult male family members to discuss Ana's exile. Missing were Joshua's son-in-law federal circuit judge Christopher Blackwell Delgado, FBI special agent Gavin Faulkner and CIA special agent Merrick Grayslake. These three had taken an oath to uphold the law and what the men cloistered in the West Palm Beach library planned to do was break it.

He gestured to the man who'd held the gun on Charlene. "Get her outta here. And make certain at no time she's left alone."

Charlene panicked. "I want to go home."

Martin's expression became a mask of stone when he glared at Charlene. The talented sound engineer had everything going for her with the exception of self-esteem. Tall, curvy with a flawless café au lait complexion, chemically straightened, shoulder-length auburn hair and catlike light brown eyes, Charlene had been seeing Basil Irvine and her treacherous actions were unforgivable.

"My niece also wants to come home, but she can't because of you. How twisted can you be that you set up Ana to be killed when she was nothing but good to you?" He waved his hand in dismissal. "Get her outta here," he said to the P.I.

"What do we do now, David?" Timothy asked his uncle.

Light from a floor lamp spilled over David's face, highlighting the thin scar running along his left cheek. "We wait. Ana's in good hands with Jacob." He frowned at Diego. "I still don't like that she was forced into an arranged marriage."

Joshua affected a smile. "Just think, little brother. If she decides to stay married, then you're ahead in the wager."

"Very funny, Josh," David drawled. "You wait until you're damn near close to ninety to become a flipping stand-up comic."

"Easy, *hermano*," Joshua said in a quiet tone. "Martin's closer to ninety than anyone else sitting in this room."

Diego laughed, then sobered. "I don't know what you old heads are talking about, but let's get back to why we're here. Ana being married to Jake is not an issue. I asked him to take care of her because I trust him with my life, Vivienne's and S.J.'s. This has been hard on all of us, the women in particular. Even though Tyler's home from the hospital, there is still the strain on Dana of having to take care of him and the children in her condition. Martin, I know you want them to stay here, but I'm willing to offer my house on Jupiter Island. I'll also arrange to have a nanny and housekeeper to help Dana with the kids."

Martin's expressive eyebrows lifted a fraction. "You'll have to talk to Parris about it. You know she loves having the grandkids around."

"May I make a suggestion?" Matthew Sterling asked, speaking for the first time.

David stared at the man who'd been former army special forces and a professional mercenary. Matt had not only saved his life, but also Joshua's. He'd cemented his tie to the Coles when his stepson married his niece. "Sure, Matt."

Gold-green eyes shimmered in a face deeply tanned from the New Mexico sun. "I agree with Diego about sending Tyler and his family to Jupiter Island. But you should also consider sending Parris and Serena along with them. That way they can become Dana's support group. You don't want her to have that baby before its due date.

"And we already know Irvine was sleeping with that girl whose body was found in the desert, and also who has been feeding him information as to Ana's whereabouts. The next thing is springing the trap, and we all know when it goes down Slow Wyne may end up with a few casualties."

"I don't care who lives or dies in the carnage," David snarled. "I just want my daughter home."

"When and where do you want me to hold the press conference, Dad?" Jason asked.

"Right here, tomorrow afternoon. We'll schedule it for noon."

Jason looped one leg over the opposite knee. He missed his twin more than he could've imagined. There were times when they didn't see each other for months, but he'd always been able to pick up the phone and speak to her. That had all changed because of a man and woman bent on revenge. Although he'd always eschewed violence he'd begun carrying a concealed firearm and wouldn't hesitate to use it if it meant protecting his sister.

"When's D-Day?"

All eyes were trained on Martin. "The last time I spoke to Simon he told me as soon as his people are in place he'll let me know."

"Let's hope it's soon, because Jake only has another three weeks before he has to return to work."

Martin nodded. "I'll let Simon know that."

All conversation came to an abrupt halt with a soft knocking on the door. David walked across the room, opening the door. He spoke softly to the woman. "Thank you." He closed the door and then turned to the occupants. "The caterers just sent word that everyone's waiting for us to join them for supper."

One by one the men stood up and filed out of the library where they'd sat earlier that year wagering which one of their children would marry first.

The heat and ocean breezes coupled with the gentle rocking of the boat lulled Ana into a state of total relaxation. She and Jacob had decided to go on a dinner cruise with ten other couples. The yacht, with a crew of eight, had set off late afternoon and was expected to return to Cannamore Cay around midnight.

It was the third week in July; five weeks since she hadn't slept in her own bed and with each passing hour she felt as if she were losing a piece of herself. If it hadn't been for Jacob Ana knew she would've gone completely stir-crazy. He'd helped her perfect her golf swing and whenever she was able to knock the ball into the hole it was cause for celebration. They'd traversed every mile of the island either on foot, by golf cart or jitney. The lagoon had become their private swimming hole, the beach the perfect place to read or picnic under a beach umbrella.

Shifting on the deck chair, Ana turned her back to Jacob. Without warning a wave of sadness swept over her. She missed her family, her home and the annual Fourth of July family cookout. There were so many things she missed that she'd lost count. She went still when she felt a hand on her back. "Yes?"

"*¿Es bueno, querida?*"

"I'm just a little tired," she lied smoothly.

Jacob pushed off his chair and came around to sit next to her. "Are you sure you're okay?"

Ana adjusted her sunglasses and then turned to face him. She couldn't see his eyes behind his dark lenses. "Yes. Why?"

Wrapping an arm around her waist, he kissed her ear. "You've been sleeping a lot lately. Is there something I should know?"

A smile trembled over her lips. "If you're asking if I'm pregnant, then the answer is no."

His eyebrows lifted. "Are you certain?"

"Quite certain."

A beat passed. "If you were, would you tell me?"

There came another pause. "Of course I would tell you, Jacob. Why wouldn't I?"

He blew out his breath. "I don't know. You've changed, Ana. You say you're too tired to make love, and when I suggest you see a doctor you claim you're okay."

"You don't trust me, do you?" Ana asked.

"Of course I do," Jacob countered.

"No, you don't. If you did then you'd believe me when I say I'm not pregnant."

He cradled her face in his hands. "I've been entrusted to take care of you, and that means I have to make certain you remain healthy."

"I am healthy."

"You've lost weight you can ill afford to lose, *m'ija.*"

"It's the heat."

Jacob gave Ana a long, penetrating look. She had an answer and/or comeback for everything. He hadn't lied when he said she'd changed. When he'd first met Ana she reminded him of a helium-filled balloon. If he hadn't held on to her she would've floated away. But now the air was slowly seeping out of her, leaving a mere shadow of the lively, feisty, teasing woman with whom he'd fallen in love. She may have looked the same outwardly, but something had transformed her. Lifting her effortlessly, he shifted her onto his lap.

He smiled when she curled into the curve of his body. Jacob realized this was the closest they'd been in weeks. They'd continued to share the same bed, yet it appeared as if they were separated by an invisible wall. Even their love-making had changed. It was more mechanical than natural, lacking in passion and spontaneity.

Combing his fingers through her hair, he pulled a curl. The shafts of sunlight played on the raven strands with reddish highlights. "What's bothering you, baby?"

"What makes you think something is bothering me?"

"Don't answer my question with a question, Ana. I know something is bothering you. We've spent practically every minute of every day of the past five weeks together, and I believe I know a little bit more about you than I did the day you walked out of that airport and into my life. So please, *m'ija,* don't insult my intelligence pretending you don't know what I'm talking about."

"I want to go home."

Jacob felt pain similar to what he'd experienced when shot with the pellet gun. He didn't want to believe Ana wanted to go home and put herself in the line of fire. "Can't you wait a little longer?"

"How much longer do you want me to wait? It's already been more than a month." Her words were monotone.

"A week." He knew he was buying time, but it would give those in Florida time to execute the plan they'd concocted to ensnare Irvine in a trap of his own choosing.

"You promise?"

He shook his head. "I can't promise, but let me contact Diego and ask if it's safe enough for you to return, but with restrictions."

Tilting her chin, Ana stared up at Jacob. "What restrictions are you talking about?"

A smile tilted the corners of his mobile. "House arrest."

Her smile matched his. "Will I have to wear an ankle monitor?"

"Yeah, baby. Me."

Ana tilted her head, dimples winking with the smile spreading across her face like the rising sun. "Thank you, *mi amor.*"

"You're welcome, baby." Jacob angled his head, brushing his mouth over hers. He held her closer, tighter, praying he wasn't being premature in his promise to take her back to the States in a week. However, he would promise anything just to have the smiling, teasing, sexy, enchanting woman who made him look for the next sunrise.

It'd taken Jacob a while to conclude he and Ana had become friends without benefits before becoming lovers. They shared a bed, were able to talk about anything, disagreed to disagree and along the way he'd fallen in love with her. It was only when he communicated with Diego that he was reminded why he and Ana were together.

He glanced around the deck. He and Ana weren't the only ones sharing a deck chair. Most the couples on the yacht were honeymooners unable to keep their hands off one another. The average stay of the resort's guests was a week, while those with deeper pockets extended their holiday. Jacob didn't know what Diego had told the resident manager but the very proper Brit was impeccably courteous at all times.

The sound of music flowed from concealed speakers, he recognizing the selection. "Dance with me, *Princesa*."

Ana smiled. It'd been a while since Jacob had called her Princess. Now it was my love, darling, sweetheart or the Spanish endearment *m'ija*. She in turn had called him my love more than his name. And he was her love. She loved Jacob and *was* in love with the man who had become her husband in every conceivable way.

Moving off the chair, she floated into Jacob's embrace. Sinking against his length, she lost herself in the man and the music. He'd promised her a week, a week wherein she would return from exile with a husband. So much for determining her own destiny.

Chapter 14

"I'm going to take a bath. Do you want to join me?" Ana asked Jacob.

He kissed the end of her nose. "No, baby. I'm going to take a shower." The dinner cruise was nothing short of spectacular. The weather changed with rising wind and choppy waters and by the time the ship docked at the island the rains came, soaking everyone to the skin.

Waiting until she disappeared into the bathroom, Jacob pulled out his cell phone. He knew it was late, but calling was faster and less conspicuous than sending an email at this hour. Doubting whether Diego would be up past midnight, he decided to leave a voice mail.

"Hey, buddy. This is Jake. Ana wants to come—" There was a break in the connection, then Diego's baritone.

"What's up, Jake?"

"What are you doing up so late?" he asked, buttoning his damp shirt and dropping it on the floor. His shorts followed.

"I was on the phone with our people on the West Coast. Why the call and not IM?"

"Ana wants to come home."

There came a pregnant silence before Diego asked, "Can you stall her?"

"One week, Diego. That's all I can promise. After that all hell is going to break loose down here."

"Has she gone off on you?"

Jacob shook his head, then realized Diego couldn't see him. "Not yet. I have to admit she's been pretty cooperative, but I'm not certain for how much longer. She's changed, and it's not good."

"My cousin is a sweet girl as long as you don't get on her wrong side. Someone should've warned Irvine before he went after her."

"I'm hoping he'll pay for it."

"Don't worry, Jake. He will. I know it's a long time for Ana to be cut off from her home, so I'm going to call our folks and tell them to push up the timeline for D-Day. Start packing and keep your phone charged. I'll call you before I send the jet to bring you back to the States. If I'm not onboard, then Henri will escort you to Ana's condo. I'd like you to stay there with her until it's over."

"I'll have to stop at my place to pick up my firearm."

"That's not a problem. You know the Coles owe you for taking care of Ana."

"No, they don't. We Joneses take care of our own."

"So, you weren't kidding when you said you love your wife."

"I adore her, Diego."

"Does she feel the same about you?"

Diego's question gave Jacob pause. Despite all of the endearments, Ana had given no indication she was in love with him. That no longer mattered. They were married and he had the rest of his life to get her to love him as much as he loved her.

"I think so."

"You think so? Don't you guys talk?"

Jacob smiled. Of course he and Ana talked, just not about their innermost feelings. "We have our own method of talking."

"Whoa! That's too much information."

"Well, you did ask, *amigo.*"

"My bad," Diego drawled. "By the way, Jason held a press conference where he revealed Ana was honeymooning with her new husband, and as a result of her marriage Serenity was not only relocating from its Boca Raton offices but also undergoing reorganization. Of course, there were a lot of questions he didn't answer and that didn't sit too well with the reporters. Gossip about the mystery man who'd gotten music's ice princess to say 'I do' has become headline news."

The realization of who he'd married hit Jacob like a bolt of lightning. Ana wasn't only a member of one of the wealthiest black families in the U.S., but she was also high profile. He'd always lived his life under the radar and without mishap. He was a solider, a federal police officer and the husband of a very wealthy woman with a recognizable name and face. When had he ignored what had been so obvious from the very beginning? He and Ana were native Floridians that came from different worlds. The most pressing question was would she be willing to live in his, because he knew for certain given his career it would be almost impossible to live in hers.

"I'd prefer if my identity be kept off the radar."

"No worry, Jake. Your name will not come up. And don't forget to be ready when I call you back."

"Copy that," Jacob said, using his old military jargon. He ended the call, then stripped naked, pausing to pick the discarded clothing off the floor.

* * *

Ana rested her head on a bath pillow and closed her eyes, luxuriating in the pulsing water flowing over her body. She felt alive—more alive than she'd been all week, and she knew it had something to do with Jacob's promise that he was going to take her back to Florida.

A smile softened her features. She was going home, home to where she would sleep in her own bed; home where she would prepare meals in her own kitchen, and home where she'd sit on the balcony drinking a chai latte while watching the sunset. Her eyes flew open when she realized she hadn't thought about Serenity.

Had being away from the company changed her that much or was it because of the problems with Slow Wyne that had soured her on the music industry? Ana shook her head as if banishing the thought. She couldn't walk away from Serenity, not when it was in transition. Jason had decided to relocate, but where? And would he reduce or increase the number of employees? She also had to decide whether to take a less than hands-on role, and if she did then could she convince Graham to leave ColeDiz and join Serenity.

Although Jason had decided it was best Serenity go on hiatus, Ana knew he would never dissolve the company. Like ColeDiz, Serenity was a privately-held, family-owned conglomerate. Music had been and still was her father's life despite being a retired musician and former CEO, and she knew it would be the same with her.

Then there was the matter of she and Jacob. They'd decided to try and make a go of their arranged marriage, however, there was still the issue of where they would live. Boca Raton and Miami were less than fifty miles apart but would he expect her to move in with him, or would he be willing to relocate to live with her?

His apartment wasn't in Key Biscayne or Coral Gables but in a neighborhood undergoing gentrification. She had to think of the time when they would eventually have children, and for Ana a quality education was definitely a priority. She didn't want private schools to become a necessity, but an option. She and her siblings had attended Boca Raton public schools where they weren't ferried to and from classes in chauffeur-driven limos or forced to join the social clubs that were so much a part of the lives of the affluent residents in their upscale neighborhood. Serena Cole's mantra was that she wanted to have normal kids living normal lives.

Ana knew if she and Jacob were going to remain together the subject of parenthood and parenting would have to be discussed beforehand. She wasn't certain whether she would be like her mother, establishing boundaries and limits when necessary or if she'd leave that responsibility to Jacob.

She wanted to raise her children the way she was raised with respect but also with enough independence to explore their gifts and talents. Ana was certain of one thing. She didn't want her son or daughter to go into law enforcement, only because she would wear out her knees praying nothing would happen to them.

Get a grip, girl, she mused. Why was she ruminating about children when she knew she wasn't pregnant? Or was it wishful thinking?

Reaching for a bottle of scented bath gel she squeezed a generous glob on a bath sponge and began lathering her body. Jacob walked in, gloriously naked, at the same time she stood up and rinsed her body with a retractable nozzle.

Leaning over, he patted her bottom. "Hey, skinny mama."

"Please hand me a towel." Ana took the bath sheet from his outstretched hand, wrapping it around her body and tucking the ends over her breasts. "I'm hardly skinny."

Jacob lifted her from the tub, setting her down on a thirsty bath mat. "You've been eating like a bird. Take tonight. You hardly tasted the soup, managed one forkful of the lobster and steak entrée, and even refused the key lime pie. You've been picking at your food for the past week, yet you tell me there's nothing wrong with you."

Sitting on a padded bench, Ana applied a light layer of scented body crème to her neck, shoulders and arms. "I always lose my appetite whenever I'm stressed."

Jacob walked over to the free-standing shower behind a frosted-glass enclosure. "What are you stressed about?" he said over the sound of running water.

She removed the towel and continued moisturizing her body. "I told you before I want to go home."

"You're going home."

Ana froze, her heart pumping wildly against her ribs. "When?"

"As soon as I get a call from Diego. Hopefully it will be either later this week or early next week. We need to pack, only leaving out what we're going to wear for the next day."

Pressing a fist to her lips, she whispered a prayer of thanks. "Thank you, Jacob."

"You're welcome, baby."

She heard the sound of his mechanical toothbrush, followed by gargling. "I'll be in bed waiting for you."

"What took you so long?" Ana asked when Jacob got into bed and nuzzled her neck.

His hand rested on her bare hip. "What's this? No nightgown."

She giggled. "I thought I'd save you the trouble of having to take it off."

"Are you trying to seduce me, Mrs. Jones?"

"Of course not, Mr. Jones. There's never a need for me to seduce you because you're always hard and ready."

Jacob's unrestrained laughter filled the bedroom. "She's back," he crooned. "I love it when you talk dirty."

"That's because you're a dirty old man."

"Dirty I'll cop to. But not old. At least not yet. When I'm

not able to get it up, then I'll have to acknowledge that I'm getting older. Thanks to modern medicine there're pills to counter erectile dysfunction, so that means I can keep going like the Energizer Bunny until I'm at least ninety-five."

Turning over and facing Jacob, Ana pressed a kiss to his shoulder. "If you think I'm going to allow you to climb up on me when I'm ninety, then you're as crazy as a loon."

Jacob sobered. "Are you saying we can expect to celebrate a sixtieth wedding anniversary?"

She closed her eyes. "No, I'm not saying that. I told you before that I'm willing to give our marriage a chance. But there are a few things we need to talk about."

"What are they?"

"Children."

"What about them?" he whispered.

"Do you want children?" A swollen silence followed her query and Ana thought perhaps Jacob hadn't heard her.

"Of course I want us to have children," he finally said. "Do you?"

"Yes." She'd noted he'd said children and not child. "Now that we've settled that, the next question is where are we going to live?"

"I'd like you to move in with me. I know it's not as luxurious as your Boca condo, but at least you'll be able to keep out of the spotlight."

"Is your apartment large enough for the both of us?"

"I have a bedroom, living/dining area, a serviceable kitchen and I don't have to share the bathroom with other tenants."

A noticeable shudder shook Ana when he mentioned sharing a bathroom. "My condo has a manned gatehouse, semi-private elevators that serve only two residences per floor. I have a large bedroom with walk-in closets and en suite bath, gourmet kitchen, a living and formal dining room and another full bath. And because I have a corner residence there are gorgeous wraparound balconies with unobstructed ocean and city views."

"If I move in with you, then it would mean I would have to commute to Miami."

"And if I move to Miami, then I'd have to commute to Boca," Ana countered. "What if we compromise?"

"Compromise how?"

"What if we move midpoint?"

There was another pause. "What do you consider midpoint?" Jacob asked.

"Fort Lauderdale. I'll put my condo on the market and have my real estate agent look for something in Harbor Beach, Rio Vista Isles, Las Olas Isles or Bay Colony."

Jacob felt himself withdrawing from Ana even though he hadn't and couldn't move. It was apparent she'd planned their future without his input. "I can't afford to live in the communities you just mentioned."

Placing a hand over his chest, Ana swirled the crisp hair around her finger. "Yes, we can, baby."

He caught her wrist. "No, we can't. I'm not going to pimp my wife."

"You're not pimping me, Jacob. We have enough money to live wherever we want."

Jacob's hold on her wrist tightened. "Wrong, Ana. *You* have enough money to live wherever you want. I don't. I work for the government, and that means I fall into the ninety-nine percent category. You on the other hand can count yourself among the one percent—"

"Why are you turning this into a social debate? This is not about the haves and have-nots, Jacob. It's about you and me and our future. And if we have to argue about money, then maybe we should live in separate residences."

"That's not going to happen until after they catch the person or persons who want to kill you. Until then we'll live together."

Ana's temper rose quickly. "You may have the upper hand here in the Bahamas, but once I set foot on U.S. soil we're done, Jacob."

"That's not for you to determine."

"We'll see."

Pulling her hand from his firm grasp, she turned over, presenting Jacob with her back. She'd had enough. From the moment that bullet hit Tyler her life hadn't been her own. She'd been held captive at her parents' home, then at Long Key and Key West. And now it was Cannamore Cay where she was married to a man not chosen by herself, but others. Ana had believed she and Jacob were able to make the best of a situation in which they'd no input; a situation that had and would change them forever.

Ana was no different from her girlfriends who went on constantly about meeting Mr. Right. She wasn't a serial dater, but she'd gone out with enough men to know what she expected from them and what she refused to accept. *No permita que nadie le defina ni determine su destino.* Never had her grandmother's words rung more true than they did now. Her father had determined her destiny when he'd taken the keys to her condo and car; then Diego decided it was best she go into exile in the Florida Keys with a man who was more a stranger than family friend. Her exile was exacerbated when she and Jacob took up residence on a private island in the Bahamas as husband and wife.

Like most normal women Ana had hoped to fall in love and marry, but not through a marriage of convenience. After all, it was the twenty-first century and they lived in a country where arranged marriages were peculiar to the culture.

Annulment. The word was as stinging as a slap. Once married, no one in her family had ever had an annulment. Nor did they divorce. There was an unspoken adage that Coles marry for life.

A wry smile twisted her mouth. Regardless of the circumstances that brought them together, the only thing standing in their way for a happily ever after was her wealth. It was something she'd accepted and couldn't change. Either he dealt with it or they could say goodbye. Ana Juanita Jones née Cole intended to end her marriage to Jacob Stephen Jones.

Jacob's cell phone chimed Diego's ring tone and he stared at it for several seconds before picking it up off the countertop. "What's up, buddy?"

"We'll touch down at eight. Be ready."

"Copy that."

He ended the call and made his way to the bathroom. It hadn't taken a week but three days for Diego to arrange their return. Leaning against the door frame, Jacob stared at his wife as she brushed her hair. He smiled. The chic hairstyle was missing, replaced with black curls that made her look like a fragile doll.

"M'ija?" She turned on the stool in front of the dressing table. Her golden eyes appeared unusually large and haunted in her small face. It was good they were going home because Ana was disappearing before his eyes. "We're leaving."

With wide eyes she continued to stare at him. "Now?"

Jacob smiled. "Yes, now."

Ana sprang off the stool, launching herself at him. He caught her in midair. "Thank you, darling. Thank you, thank you," she repeated over and over while kissing his face.

"Slow down, baby. Let's get ready to blow this nightclub."

It was Diego who descended the steps to the jet. Casually dressed in a pair of taupe slacks, a short-sleeved shirt and tan woven-leather sandals, he extended his arms to Ana. Smiling, she went into his embrace. *"Hola primo,"* she whispered.

Holding her at arm's length, he angled his head. "Beautiful tan. A little thin. But none the worse for wear."

She exhaled an audible sigh. "I have Jacob to thank for that."

"We have Jacob to thank for a lot of things. Somewhere

along the way he's become the Coles' guardian angel." Diego glanced over Ana's head. Jacob and the limo driver were unloading bags from the trunk. "Let me help with the luggage so we can lift off." He kissed her forehead. "Go on up and get belted in."

Ana walked slowly up the stairs and entered the luxurious aircraft. She recognized the flight attendant. Linda Franklin was one of four ColeDiz flight attendants that were a part of the crew for the Gulfstream corporate jet. Linda was in the galley with an onboard chef.

The flight attendant, carrying a travel mug emblazoned with the ColeDiz logo approached her. "Mr. Thomas told me you like your coffee light and sweet."

"Thank you, Linda."

The tall, slender redhead nodded. "Congratulations on your recent marriage."

Ana forced a smile she didn't feel. "Thank you." She took a sip of coffee, savoring the rich taste. She recognized the blend. It was Jamaican Blue Mountain, touted as the best coffee in the world. ColeDiz owned coffee plantations in Jamaica, Mexico, Belize and Puerto Rico. The flavor was also served at the Cannamore Cay resort. She'd drunk half when Jacob and Diego entered the aircraft. Light coming through the oval window reflected off the band on Jacob's hand as he sat opposite, leaving Diego to sit in the adjacent row.

Linda, carrying a tray, handed each man a similar mug. "Breakfast will be served as soon as we're airborne."

Ana stared out the window at the stretch of white sand and beyond the vibrant blue-green water. Even though she'd averted her gaze she could feel the intensity of Jacob's stare. It was over. The make-believe and the fairy-tale marriage would end once they were back in the States.

The fasten-seat-belt sign was illuminated and Ana placed her mug into a holder, then fastened the belt around her waist. Pressing her head against the back of the leather seat, she closed her eyes as the sleek jet taxied down the airstrip, picked up speed, and within minutes they were airborne. She opened her eyes, staring down at the rapidly fading island landscape as the jet increased its altitude. Once they obtained cruising speed, Diego turned his seat to face her and Jacob.

"We're going to touch down in Miami where Jake has to pick up a few things. Then Henri will drive you to Boca where the two of you will stay until—"

"No, Diego—" Ana interrupted.

Diego held up his hand. "Please let me finish, Ana."

She gave him a long, penetrating stare. One thing she didn't want was for her and Jacob to continue cohabitating. With a great deal of reluctance, she said, "Okay."

"I'm bringing you back to Florida against my better judgment. But knowing you'll be with Jake belies some of my apprehension. We still haven't finished our investigation but we're closer than we were a month ago. I'd like you and Jake to stay at your condo until this is over."

"Are you saying I can't leave?"

"Yes. You're a newlywed, so you're still on your honeymoon."

When she glanced at Jacob she was unable to read his expression. "What about visitors?"

"I would limit visitors to members of the family."

"You bring me out of exile to make me a prisoner in my own home." The familiar mask of brooding settled on Diego's features. "I understand your concern for my wellbeing," she continued, "but somehow you forget I'm not a child. You, my father, Uncle Martin and Joshua get together, make decisions, and then expect me to follow them without question. I would've liked to have known in advance that I was going to get a husband."

"You never would've gone along with it, Ana," Diego argued softly. "But you have an out. You can annul it." His gaze shifted from her to Jacob who shot him a lethal stare.

"Why do I feel as if I've just come down with a case of foot in mouth? *Lo siento*," he apologized softly.

Ana and Jacob shared a glance. She wanted to tell her cousin that she had fallen in love with her husband, didn't want to end her marriage, yet dissolution was inevitable. He was willing to share her life but not her wealth.

The awkward moment was shattered when Linda approached with a serving cart. She pushed a button under the burl armrests of the saddle-tan chairs that converted to beds. Activating the retractable tray tables, the attendant covered the trays with damask tablecloths.

Working quickly and efficiently, she set out plates of fluffy mushroom omelets with strips of crisp bacon, crystal goblets with freshly squeezed orange juice, freshly baked scones and cups of coffee. Prerecorded music flowed throughout the cabin during their mile-high breakfast.

Ana managed to eat most of her omelet, while drinking two glasses of orange juice and a cup of coffee. The anxiety that had weighed on her like a lead shield lifted the closer they came to the U.S. coastline. The blue-green waters of the Caribbean Sea faded as the colder gray water of the Atlantic Ocean came into view. She recognized the island of Cuba and the Florida Keys as the jet began its descent.

The fasten-seat-belt sign chimed, and Jacob moved across the aisle to sit with Diego, and within minutes all evidence of breakfast disappeared. "Ana and I have a few things we're going to have to work out before deciding whether we want to stay together, so I'd appreciate it if you don't get involved in what's going on between me and *my* wife." His voice was low, words cold and biting as needle pricks.

Diego went still, his gaze meeting and fusing with Jacob's. It was the first time in more than twenty years that he felt less than comfortable with his friend. He'd had to pull strings and make promises he hadn't wanted to make in order to secure the valid marriage license, yet never in his wildest imagination would he have suspected that the two would've become that involved with each other.

Diego was also more than aware of Ana's proclivity for dismissing men from her life for the slightest provocation. Although he counted Jacob as his closest friend and confidant they'd usually avoided talking about the women in their lives. He owed Jacob his life, that of his wife's and now his cousin's. Jake was his son's godfather and legally married to Ana. That made him family.

"I respect you telling me how you feel, and I promise not to interfere. I'm going to say one more thing, then the subject's moot."

"What is it?"

"Ana's father. He was totally opposed to you marrying her, because he wanted that choice to be hers. I managed to convince the others to overrule him when I took that choice away from her. My uncle's still not talking to me. David can be laid-back and cool, but if you mess with his kids he will take you out."

It was Jacob's turn to go completely still. Nothing moved. Not even his eyes. "I fear no man."

At that moment Diego found himself unable to respond to Jacob's declaration. Again, this was another side of his friend that was totally foreign to him. He'd always found him to be no-nonsense, honest, loyal and extremely private. "I didn't tell you about your father-in-law to frighten you but to let you know what you're going to have to deal with."

Jacob blinked. "Like I said, Ana and I have a few things to work out. Whatever the outcome it will involve only the two of us."

Chapter 15

The G550 Gulfstream jet landed smoothly on a private airstrip in Miami long enough for Jacob and Ana to deplane, then they would continue on to West Palm Beach. By the time they were cleared by customs, Ana wore one of the stylish straw hats she'd purchased at the gift shop on Cannamore Cay. She doubted if anyone would recognize her with the hat and a pair of cutoffs, baggy tee and flip-flops. A redcap followed them, pushing a cart piled high with their luggage.

Henri was waiting for them along with another man who wore a lightweight black suit, white shirt and black Western-style ostrich-skin boots. With his shaved pate and dark glasses he was Henri's lighter-hued counterpart.

Diego's driver and bodyguard nodded to Jacob. "Welcome home, Mr. Jones."

Jacob shook his hand. "Thanks, Henri. It's good to be back."

Henri nodded to Ana. "Welcome back, Mrs. Jones."

She forced a plastic smile. He was the first one to call

her by her married name. "Thank you, Henri. It's good to be back."

He motioned to the man standing a short distance away. "This is Caleb. He will be your driver to Boca Raton." Henri smiled at Ana. "I have to leave now. Mr. Thomas is waiting for me."

Henri was there, then he was gone. Caleb took over when he said, "I'll bring the car curbside, then we'll be on our way."

Ana felt as if she were in suspended animation after their luggage was loaded into the cargo area of a shiny black Suburban with tinted windows. Jacob assisted her as she sat on the second row of seats, him sitting next to the driver. Knowing her life was not her own to control or dictate, she mentally resigned herself to go along with whatever the men in her family had concocted. None of that mattered because she was home. Closing her eyes, she refused to think about Jacob and their tenuous future.

Ana hadn't realized she'd dozed off until the SUV stopped. Blinking, she peered through the glass. They were parked outside Jacob's apartment building. She watched as he disappeared into the salmon-colored stucco building.

Twenty minutes later Jacob reappeared carrying a black duffel bag. He'd exchanged his T-shirt, walking shorts and sandals for one of his favorite Hawaiian shirts, jeans, low-heel boots and a black windbreaker. He motioned to Caleb to open the hatch. After securing the duffel Jacob slipped into the passenger seat and secured his seat belt. He exchanged a knowing glance with the hired bodyguard. "Let's go," he ordered softly.

Ana had fallen asleep within minutes of them leaving Miami International and during the drive from the airport to his apartment building while Jacob and Caleb had carried on a whispered conversation. Caleb was similar to Henri where they introduced themselves using only their first names, and worked for an investigative agency that utilized the unique services of former military and law enforcement personnel. Caleb had revealed to Jacob that he was a former active-duty navy SEAL during the Gulf War, and had been recruited by a man known only as Simon after he'd retired from the military.

During the drive to Boca Raton Jacob and Caleb engaged in a lively conversation about sports. The ex-SEAL who was born and raised in California favored the West Coast teams, while Jacob's loyalties were definitely East Coast. The discussion ended when Caleb, following the navigational map, turned off onto the road leading to Ana's condo. The beachfront building shimmered like a jewel along Florida's exquisite Gold Coast, a residence befitting a Cole. But then Jacob reminded himself that Ana was no longer Ana Cole, but Ana Jones. They stopped at the manned gatehouse.

Ana, rolling down the window, removed her hat. "Good afternoon, Louis. It's me, Ana Cole," she added when he gave her a puzzled look.

His jaw dropped in surprise. "Ms. Cole, I didn't recognize you. How have you been?"

"Wonderful," she half lied. Being away from home had been torture, but falling in love was indeed wonderful. "Can you please let us through?"

The security arm lifted and Caleb drove slowly along the path to where Ana told him to park. Each resident had two reserved parking spaces. "You can pull in next to the sports car with the Serenity plate."

Shifting on his seat, Jacob lifted questioning eyebrows. "You drive that?"

Caleb whistled under his breath when he maneuvered next to the two-seater. "That is some scary-fast sh…" His words trailed off when he realized what he was about to say.

Ana's dimples deepened when she flashed a grin. "Zero to sixty in three point five seconds."

Getting out and coming around to help her down, Jacob's

hands tightened around her waist. "Are you going to tell me you went that fast in three point five seconds?"

She smiled up at him frowning down at her. "Of course. I had to confirm what it said on the sticker."

Jacob knew the Ferrari to cost more than a quarter of a million dollars but he'd promised himself he would never broach the subject of money with Ana again. It was her money, not his and she could do whatever she wanted with it. If she decided to donate every penny she had to charity, then who was he to say anything?

He angled his head, pressing his mouth to her ear. "It's as sexy as its owner," he whispered.

"Once I get the keys back from Daddy you can drive it."

"Bet," he said, smiling. "Now it's time I get you inside."

"You and Caleb have to come inside with me, then you can go back for the luggage."

"Wait until I get my duffel." Punching a button on the fob, Caleb opened the hatch for Jacob to retrieve the bag. Then they made their way to the entrance.

The beauty of the spectacular lobby was jaw-dropping. No expense had been spared with the elegant furnishings. Crystal chandeliers, imported rugs, large Chinese-inspired vases filled with a profusion of fresh flowers and leather seating groupings screamed opulence. A doorman greeted Ana by name.

"I've been away and I left my keys with my parents. I need someone to open my apartment, and I'll also need assistance with my luggage."

The doorman spoke to the concierge and within seconds a valet and another uniformed young man appeared. Jacob walked half a step behind Ana as she followed the valet to a bank of elevators who inserted a card key in the slot; the doors opened silently. They stepped into the car, it rising quickly and silently after he'd punched in the floor on a remote device. Their footsteps were muffled in the deep pile of the carpet lining the hallway.

"Is there anything else you're going to need, Ms. Cole?" the valet asked when he opened the door to her apartment.

"Let the concierge know I need a duplicate key. And my driver still has to bring up my luggage."

"I will let them in."

She smiled. "Thank you, Carlos."

He back away and she closed the door. She hadn't been given enough time to adjust the thermostat and heat slapped at Ana, making it hard for her to breathe. Walking over to a wall in the foyer, she touched a switch and the sound swooshing through the vents was followed by a rush of cooling air that filled the cavernous space.

Jacob caught her arm. "Please stay here while I look around."

Still gripping the handles to the duffel, he walked into the living room that was large enough to fit his entire apartment. It held a gleaming black baby grand piano and a media area with a wall-mounted flat screen and electronic components. The wall sconces and twin chandeliers appeared to be what his interior decorator mother identified as Art Deco. He made his way through the formal dining room and into a bathroom with a free-standing shower, garden tub and a dressing area. Jacob left the bathroom and made his way along a narrow hallway to the master bedroom with a sitting area and en suite bath comparable to a spa. Ana had revealed she didn't do housework, yet everything was immaculate. Even the refrigerator was clean and free of leftover foodstuffs.

Now he knew why she'd wanted to return home. Floor-to-ceiling windows dominated every room, bringing the outdoors inside. Her residence was high up enough for ultimate privacy. The stylized furniture and accessories harkened back to a more glamorous era. Somehow he'd thought Ana would favor a more contemporary style, and he wondered just who was the woman who'd become his wife.

He returned, finding her sitting on a chair in the foyer. "Does your cleaning service come even when you're not here?"

She nodded. "Yes. Someone from management will usually let them in."

"That's not going to happen again until we take care of your problem."

Hunkering down, he leaned in close. "I don't want you to say anything until I give you the signal. I need you to trust me on this," he whispered when she opened her mouth. "Nod if you understand." She nodded. Jacob brushed a kiss over her parted lips. "That's my baby."

Opening the door, he stepped outside the apartment, and tapped his cell's speed dial for the number Caleb had given him. "Where are you?" he asked when Caleb answered.

"I just finished unloading everything. Why?"

"We may have brought back some insects. Do you have anything to get rid of the critters?"

"I think I have something. I'll bring it up."

He didn't have to wait long for Caleb. Jacob gave the bellhop a tip, closing and locking the door behind him after Caleb unloaded the cart. Shrugging out his jacket, Caleb motioned to Ana not to speak.

Ana couldn't speak even if she wanted to. The decoratively carved handle of a powerful handgun was displayed in the holster strapped to his waist. Caleb wasn't tall, but he was powerfully built. He took a wand from the jacket's breast pocket and began a slow, methodical search of every inch of her condo. No object or space was ignored. Not the pantry, refrigerator or trash compactor.

He smiled, tiny lines fanning out his light brown eyes. "It's clean."

Jacob shook his hand. "Thanks."

"No problem." Caleb's gaze shifted from Jacob to Ana. "I know you two are going to stick close to home, but if you need anything I'm only a phone call away."

"I'll walk you out," Jacob volunteered.

Ana sat in the bedroom's sitting area, staring out the window and remembering how she got up every morning to swim laps in the fitness center; she then came back to her place to shower, prepare a light breakfast, dress and leave for the office. She did the same thing five days a week with little or no deviation until that fateful day when someone decided she didn't deserve to live.

When she'd asked Diego about Tyler he told her Tyler, his wife, children, Tyler's mother and her mother were staying at his Jupiter Island estate until the madness was over. This was one time when she needed her family around her: mother, father, sister and brothers. Tears filled her eyes and Ana brushed them away before they fell. She may have come home, but she still felt estranged.

The telephone rang, startling her. It rang a second time, and she picked up the receiver. "Hello."

"Hey, baby girl. Diego told me you were home."

Her pulses were racing when she heard the familiar voice. "Yes. We just got in."

"When you say *we* I assume you're talking about your husband."

"Yes, Daddy."

"Your mama went to Jupiter Island with Parris and Dana."

"I know. Diego told me."

"When am I going to see you, baby?"

"Come over tonight. I'll order dinner—"

"Don't bother. We'll bring something."

"Daddy?"

"Yes, baby?"

"Is Jason coming?"

A soft chuckle came through the earpiece. "Do you actually think I'd come and not bring him?"

Ana felt an emotion of hope welling up inside her. "Daddy, I love you."

"I love you, too."

"I'll see you later."

Jacob walked into the bedroom before she could replace the receiver on its cradle. Her eyes were glistening with unshed tears. "That was my father. He and my brother are coming over later."

"Good."

Ana stared at her husband as if he'd grown a third eye. "Good?"

Crossing his arms over his chest, Jacob angled his head. "Of course. I'm looking forward to sitting down and talking with my father-in-law."

"When am I going to meet your mother?"

"Soon, *m'ija*," he drawled.

Pushing off her chair, she closed the space between them. "You plan to introduce me to your mother when we both know this marriage isn't going to last?"

Resting his hands on Ana's shoulders, Jacob pulled her close. "It's not going to last because you don't want it to."

"Why are you blaming me?" Ana knew she sounded defensive, but it was Jacob who had issues with her wealth.

His hands went from her shoulders to cradle her face. "Under another set of circumstances if I'd met you I would've asked you out, and hopefully dated you long enough to convince you that my intentions were honorable when I asked you to marry me."

"What about love, Jacob?"

"What about it?" he asked.

"You mention dating me, being honorable, but not once have you mentioned love. People who marry usually declare their love for each other." His expression changed, his eyes searching her face as if reaching into her thoughts.

"What have we been doing, Ana? What have we been saying to each other? When I call you *mi amor* do you think I was just mouthing the words? When I make love to you I give you all of myself—something I've never done with any other woman. And the one time we made love without a condom I selfishly prayed you would become pregnant so I would have something of you to hold on to. When Diego asked if I was enjoying my honeymoon my response was 'I love my wife.'"

"You told my cousin you love me before telling me?"

"Ana, Ana, *Ana*. You're not listening to me. How many more ways can I tell you that I love you?"

A single hot tear rolled down her cheek. *"Dígame otra vez, mi amor."*

"No, I'm not going to tell again. What I'm going to do is show you later on tonight."

"What about my money?"

The deep-set dark eyes in an equally dark face caressed her face. "What about it, *m'ija?*"

"Shouldn't we talk about it?"

"No. Talking about it will not change anything, and I'm not willing to risk losing you over something that won't change or which I have no control over."

Anchoring her arms under his shoulders, Ana pressed her face to his chest. She didn't know what made Jacob change his mind and didn't care. "You've just made me the happiest woman in the world."

Jacob buried his face in her hair. "I know we haven't had a traditional courtship or marriage but I intend to make up for it. I'm going to call you up and ask whether you'd like to go out with me. Then we'll have to establish date night where we stay home and I'll cook for you or you'll cook for me."

"I like candlelight dinners."

"Hold up, baby, I'm getting to that. We'll dance, flirt, and

if we're not too full or tipsy we can share a bath before re-
tiring for bed."

Ana swayed back and forth to the song in her head. "I'd
like for us to go down to the Keys to hang out when most of
the tourists have gone home. I want you to teach me how to
bait a hook and catch a monster fish."

"What else do you want, darling?"

"I want a baby." She felt the muscles in his arms tighten.

"When do you want to start trying?"

Leaning back, Ana met his eyes. "New Year's Eve."

A slight frown creased his forehead. "Why then?"

"I'd like for us to renew—or say our vows for the first time
on New Year's Eve. It's a tradition that Coles marry between
the week of Christmas and New Year's. Then we could say
we had a wedding night."

Jacob nuzzled her scented neck. "Now who's being traditional?"

"I never denied wanting what most women want. We want
romance, love and marriage, the house with the picket fence,
children and family pets."

"Are you allowed to have pets here?" he asked.

"No. I guess that means we'll have to look for a house."

Jacob knew he would have to compromise again. There
was no doubt he would have to do a lot of compromising in
his marriage, but he knew Ana was more than worth it. He'd
spent years holding back with women, pushing them out of
his life when they attempted to get too close. There were ones
he saw because of sex, and others he could care less about if
they did or did not sleep together.

The determining factor with Ana had been his protective
instincts. The need to take care of her was so strong it was
palpable and had nothing to do with his promise to Diego. He
also had to admit that he wasn't completely immune to Ana.
When he'd noticed her at his godson's celebration he hadn't
been able to keep his eyes off her. He'd been so enthralled by

her haughty attitude that he actually felt sorry for her hapless date. She'd admitted to liking a challenge and so did he because he never knew what to expect from her.

"How many dogs and cats do you want?"

Ana couldn't control her burst of laughter. "No more than two dogs and two cats."

"What? No birds, fish, rabbits or gerbils?"

"No!"

"Just asking," he teased. "I'm going to get those bags out of the foyer before your family comes."

"I'll help you. We can store them here and off the pantry." The words were barely off her tongue when the doorbell rang. "That's probably management with the duplicate card key."

"Stay here. I'll get it."

Ana watched him walk away. Was that the way it would always be? She having to hide out while Jacob checked and rechecked doors, the interior of buildings, and their surroundings when he helped her into and out of a vehicle? It was then she was reminded that as a U.S. deputy marshal he'd been trained for witness protection.

The intercom rang and Ana rushed over to pick up the receiver. "Yes?"

"Ms. Cole, this is the booth. Mr. David Cole is asking for you."

"Please let him through."

Her pulses racing uncontrollably, Ana smiled at Jacob. "They're here."

Wrapping his arms around her waist, he rocked her gently from side to side. "Try to relax, *m'ija.* Everything looks wonderful." They'd moved all the bags, storing them where they weren't visible. Although the master bedroom had a wall-to-wall, walk-in closet, there still wasn't enough room to store all of Ana's clothes and shoes. He'd held his tongue when he wanted to suggest she go through the closet and donate anything she hadn't worn in two years.

Dozens of lighted votive candles flickered on flat surfaces in the foyer, living and dining rooms. Even though Ana revealed her father was bringing food, she and Jacob decided to use up the perishables in the refrigerator, freezer and pantry to make deviled eggs, chilled shrimp and potato salad. They'd worked comfortably in the large kitchen, talking, stopping to dance if a selection on the satellite radio proved too infectious for them not to move.

She'd explained to Jacob her motivation for purchasing the condo and not a house was extreme security. The manned gatehouse and the semiprivate elevators served only two residences per floor, and the incomparable amenities included beach cabana service, two oceanfront pools, each with a bar, state-of-the-art fitness center with Olympic-size pool, a private café and elegant club room.

When he saw the excitement in his wife's eyes Jacob knew he didn't want Ana to have to choose where she wanted to live. Purchasing the condo had been a high point in her life not only because she'd purchased property for the first time, but also because no one knew about it until after she'd closed on the property. Owning property had become her rally cry for total independence—something she'd craved since adolescence. The excitement in her eyes told Jacob he couldn't force Ana to give up a lifestyle that afforded her the security that made her who she was.

Ana clasped the larger hands pressed to her belly. "Thank you for helping with the cooking and setting up."

"There's no need to thank me. Aren't we a team?"

"Of course we are."

"I've made a decision as to where we should live." Jacob felt Ana go completely still. "It's not what you think."

"What am I thinking?"

He smiled. "That I want you to move in with me. But,

that's not going to happen because I'm willing to move here and commute to Miami." Her body slumped slightly and he tightened his hold on her slender frame. "Once we start a family we can then decide where we'd like to buy a house. If I'm going to live here, then I'm going to need some closet space."

Turning around, Ana met his eyes. "I have too many clothes and shoes."

Jacob's eyebrows lifted. "You think?"

She smiled. "I know. I still have clothes at my parents' house. What I'm going to do is go through the closet and pack up everything I no longer wear and donate them to several charitable organizations."

Angling his head, Jacob placed a light kiss at the corners of her mouth. "That's a wonderful idea." It was what he'd hoped she would do.

"I'll call the concierge tomorrow and order cartons so I can box…" The chime of the doorbell preempted her statement. "That's Daddy."

Jacob dropped his arms. "I'll get it."

Ana stood in the middle of the living room, her heart pounding a runaway rhythm as she waited to see her father and brother. Jacob's pronouncement that he was willing to relocate from Miami had shocked her as much as his revelation that her net worth would no longer become a topic of discussion. It was apparent he wanted to save their marriage and he was willing to compromise and make the necessary sacrifices to achieve that goal. And he wasn't just mouthing the words, but that he truly loved her.

Jones men make good husbands. We support our women, protect them and remain faithful. Ana bit her lip to stop its trembling when she recalled Jacob's boast. "I love him," she whispered over and over as tears rolled down her face. She was still crying when her mother, sisters, nieces, nephews and cousins rushed into the living room, hugging and kissing her until she felt faint.

"Please stop! I can't breathe."

Jacob managed to wind his way through the throng of Coles to rescue his wife, his arms going protectively around her body as she wiped away her tears. "I know you're happy to see Ana, but right now she's a little overwhelmed because she didn't expect all of you to show up."

David, Jason, Diego and Gabriel walked in, all carrying large covered trays from which wafted the most mouthwatering aromas. "Welcome home, baby girl," David shouted loudly as he strolled in the direction of the kitchen.

"I wanted to tell you that the family was coming, but David swore me to secrecy," Diego said, as he followed his uncle into the kitchen.

Jason lingered, dipping his head and kissing Ana's cheek. "You look pretty good for an old married woman."

Ana hugged her twin. "You try marriage. It definitely has its perks." She smiled at her mother who stood motionless with the most angelic smile on her face. "Hello, Mama." She extended her arms and Ana wasn't disappointed when Serena walked into her embrace.

Serena pulled back, staring into a pair of eyes so much like her own, her gaze moving slowly over her daughter's face. "You're a little thin, but other than that you look beautiful."

A rush of joy and peace enveloped Ana like her mother's hug. She touched the graying reddish curls. "Jacob has promised to fatten me up."

Serena gave her a startled look. "Are you planning on getting pregnant?"

"Not yet. I'd like to get used to being married first."

"You're staying together?"

"Of course," Ana said glibly. "We love each other."

"Titi!"

Ana glanced down to find her goddaughter Victoria Grayslake tugging on the leg of her white slacks. Bending slightly, she picked up the four-year-old, hugging her tightly and spinning her around and around, Victoria squealing for her to go faster and faster.

She stopped abruptly, her own head spinning until she regained her balance. Pressing her forehead to the little girl's, Ana stared into a pair of hazel eyes that changed color depending upon her mood. Heavy red waves fell over the child's damp forehead. She planted a loud kiss on her cheek. "Thank you for coming to see me."

Victoria flashed a smile, and a single dimple appeared in her right cheek. "You're welcome."

The little girl never failed to surprise Ana. Vicky, as her younger cousins called her, was articulate and extremely bright. Alexandra and Merrick had enrolled her in preschool, but at three Vicky was reading on a third-grade level. Her parents subsequently enrolled her in a school for gifted children where the child blossomed like a newly opened flower.

Ana took turns hugging her older brother, his wife and their three children. Going on tiptoe, she whispered in Diego's ear that she was going to get him back for not telling her he'd arranged for the family to welcome her home.

Diego lifted her until her sandaled feet were off the floor. "If I'd told you, then it wouldn't have been a surprise."

She kissed his cheek. "*Gracias, primo.* Excuse me, but I want say hello to Vivienne, then I have to figure out where everyone's going to sit."

"Don't worry about that. Your dining-room table seats twelve, so that's enough room for the grown folks. You can spread a tablecloth on the floor for the kids so they'll think they're having a picnic. Even if they ate at a table you know that most of the food ends up on the floor anyway."

Anna nodded in agreement as her gaze swept over the assembly. "Where're Michael and Jolene? I thought they would've come down with Alex." Her cousin and his wife lived Georgetown, and Alexandra and Merrick lived in Alexandria.

"Jolene is kinda pregnant, so she decided to sit this out until she's feeling better."

Ana wanted to tell Diego there was no such thing as kinda pregnant. Either she was or she wasn't. "Where's Merrick?" It was a Saturday, and she knew he worked Monday through Friday.

Taking her arm, Diego led her away from the others. "We can't involve Merrick, Gavin or even your husband in this."

With wide eyes, she stared numbly at him. "What are you talking about?"

"Lower your voice, Ana. They're federal agents and we don't want to compromise their careers."

"Who are *we?*" she whispered harshly.

"Martin, your father, Jason, Joshua, Timothy, Matthew Sterling and myself."

Ana held up a hand. "Please don't tell me anymore." She'd heard enough. As a child she'd overheard conversations that Matthew Sterling had been a highly paid mercenary before he'd retired to become a New Mexico horse breeder.

Turning on her heels, she approached Vivienne and Jacob. The sight of her husband cradling his godson while the toddler slept on his shoulder hit her full force. Ana stared at the large hand splayed over the child's back and at that moment she tried fantasizing about him holding their son or daughter. She'd asked that he wait until after they exchanged vows to begin a family, but seeing him now had her questioning herself.

Was she being fair to him when he'd confessed to wanting to get her pregnant? Jacob had done all the compromising, while she'd remained inflexible as to what she wanted or wouldn't do. Marriage was about give and take and so far she'd done all of the taking. A satisfied smile crossed her features. It was her turn to do a little giving.

"Hi, Viv," she said, greeting Diego's gorgeous wife. Her high cheekbones, sensual mouth and tawny-colored eyes that made her appear slightly startled had most men giving her a second look whenever she entered a room.

Vivienne hugged Ana, then looping their arms steered her over to the window. "I'll have you know I gave Diego the business when he told me that he'd arranged for you to marry Jake, but when he explained why it was necessary I told him I would think about forgiving him. You know how I feel about Jake. If it hadn't been for his help in solving my ex-husband's so-called hit-and-run I wouldn't be here talking to you."

Ana stared at the woman who'd pulled her shoulder-length hair up in a ponytail. "Do you think I'm going to hurt him, Vivienne?"

"Oh, no," she said much too quickly.

"Everyone knows how controlling Diego can be," Ana said in a softer tone. "But this is one time I have to say he did the right thing. I'm in love with Jacob."

Vivienne's expression brightened. "You're kidding?"

"No, I'm not. We've decided to stay together."

"Hot damn!" Vivienne said between clenched teeth. "I know it's a little premature, but will you become godmother for my next baby."

"Your next baby? Are you telling me you're pregnant?"

Placing the finger of her left hand to her mouth Vivienne nodded. The diamond on her hand reflected off the light coming through the windows, giving off blue-white sparks. Ana was familiar with the ring her grandmother had worn for eighty-five years before she gave it to her great-grandson for his fiancée.

"It was confirmed a couple of days ago, but Diego and I decided to wait until the end of the month before we make the announcement."

"Your secret is safe with me. And I'm honored you've

asked me to be godmother." She glanced around her. "I'm not much a hostess if I'm standing around running off at the mouth." Ana hugged Vivienne again. "We'll talk later."

Chapter 16

Ana sat at the opposite end of the dining-room table from Jacob, smiling when he winked at her. Her father had ordered enough food to feed a football team. There were trays of fried chicken, *perñil*—roast pork shoulder, white rice, black beans, Southern-style oxtail, collard greens, pulled pork, *bacalaitos*—salt cod fritters, chicken and beef empanadas, *tostones* and *maduro:* twice-fried bananas and sweet plantains. Conversations in English and Spanish floated around the table, while the children, seated on the floor, chatted comfortably with one another in English.

Her gaze shifted to her father, who had been staring at her throughout the meal. Lifting her water goblet, she gave him a silent salute, then mouthed *I love you.* A network of tiny lines appeared around David's dark eyes when he smiled.

"You know you're going to have to take some of this food home, Daddy."

"Don't you and Jacob want leftovers?"

"We'll take some, but there's still too much food for two people."

Serena placed a hand on her husband's arm. "Don't worry, darling. Gabriel, Summer and the kids are going to hang out with us for a couple of weeks." She turned her attention to Alexandra. "Alex, how long do you plan to stay?"

"I told Merrick I'd call him a couple of days before we're ready to head back. You know how the kids love hanging out with their grandma and grandpa."

"What about you, Jacob?" David asked his son-in-law.

Jacob set his fork down next to his plate, then dabbed his mouth with a napkin. "What about me?"

"When are you returning to Miami?"

"Are you asking when I'll return to work?" He'd answered his wife's father's question with a question.

"No. I want to know once this *situation* is wrapped up, will you be returning to Miami to *live?*"

Jason shook his head in exasperation. "No, Dad. You tried this with Merrick and it didn't—"

David waved a hand, cutting off his son. "Stay out of this, Jason."

"I can't, Dad."

All eyes were trained on David, Jason or Jacob. "Will somebody please tell me what's going on?" Serena asked, hoping to avoid a confrontation between her husband and son.

"Jason's right," Gabriel said in defense of his brother. With liberally gray-streaked hair and pierced ears he was a younger version of his father. "I don't think Jacob's going to be as benign as Merrick when you question him about his intentions toward Ana."

Slumping back in his chair, Jacob forced himself not to glare at David. Diego had warned him about Ana's father, but he'd hoped he would confront him in private. "Before, during and after this situation is resolved Ana and I will continue to be husband and wife."

"What does my daughter say about this?" David asked, refusing to back down.

"Why don't you ask your daughter, Daddy?" Ana snapped angrily.

Serena swung her napkin at her husband. "You are impossible! When are you going to learn to butt out of your grown children's business?"

Ducking to avoid the cloth coming close to his head, David held up both hands. "I just want to make certain my princesses are happy."

"We are happy," Alexandra and Ana chorused.

A sheepish expression floated over David's features. "I'm sorry."

"Don't apologize to us," Alexandra said. "Apologize to Jacob."

David stared at his plate. "I'm sorry, Jacob."

Serena placed her hand over her husband's. "Say it like you mean it, David."

His head popped up. "I apologize for questioning your love for my daughter."

A hint of a smile touched Jacob's mouth. "Apology accepted, *Dad*."

Laughs and guffaws exploded around the table. As if on cue, all of the adults raised glasses of water, wine and sweet tea, toasting Ana, then Jacob.

Ana touched shoulders with her sister. "What are we going to do with Daddy?"

"Love and humor him. It's no different with Merrick. He babies Vicky but roughhouses it with Cordero. I have to keep reminding him that the boy is only two, but he claims he wants to toughen him up. I told him if he doesn't stop, then his son is going to become a bully."

"Let's hope not."

"When you and Jacob get some time to yourselves I want you to come to Virginia and stay with us."

"I'll talk to him about it." Ana knew Jacob still had a lot of accrued vacation, so it wasn't a question of him not being able to take off.

Vivienne entered the dining room cradling a bowl and carrying a tray with the deviled eggs. "Shame on you, Ana. I can't believe you've been holding out on us. And there's a tray of shrimp in the fridge, too."

"I forgot to put them out because there's so much food."

Diego stood up and took the bowl from his wife. "You know I'm addicted to potato salad and deviled eggs."

Pushing back his chair, Gabriel stood. "I'll get the shrimp."

The copious consumption of food continued well into the night. The children had crawled up onto the sofas and chairs to watch a G-rated movie, while the adults cleared the table, boxing up leftovers, then returned to the dining room to talk.

It was after ten when everyone prepared to take their leave. Arrangements had been made beforehand for Alex and her children to stay with her parents in Boca Raton, while the other out-of-towners would stay at the Cole family compound in West Palm Beach.

Jacob kissed S.J.'s forehead as the sleeping child clung to Diego's neck. "Thank you for making her homecoming a memorable event."

Diego nodded. "I don't think it has anything to do with me, Jake. I've seen you with Ana and it's as if she's a changed woman."

"I hope for the good."

"It is. I think David has forgiven me for meddling in his *baby's* life."

Jacob shook his head. "Don't worry about him, buddy. He'll get over it once Ana makes him a grandfather."

"On that note, I think I'll leave before Vivienne starts texting me to come down."

"Can you give me a heads-up when you think it's going to go down?"

"I'll text you," Diego promised. "Good night, friend."

"Later."

Jacob stood in the doorway, watching Diego walk to the elevator and waiting until he disappeared into the car, and then closed and locked the door. The gathering had gone well. It gave Ana the opportunity to reunite with her family and for him to become better acquainted with his new family.

He turned the lamps on the table in the foyer to the lowest setting. He repeated the action with the lamps in the living room and switched off the chandelier in the dining room. Walking into the bedroom he saw the nightgown Ana had left at the foot of the bed. Striding across the room, he entered the en suite bath to find her in the bathtub, eyes closed, chest rising and falling in a slow, even breathing. Candles in various sizes lining the vanity, low tables and the ledge along the garden tub flickered like stars in the darkened space.

"What took you so long?" she murmured, smiling.

Jacob remembered her asking him the same question before on two other occasions. "I was saying goodbye to my godson."

Ana opened her eyes. "He's gorgeous. In fact, all our nieces, nephews and cousins are gorgeous."

Leaning against the open door, Jacob angled his head, staring at the crest of her nipples peeking through the bubbles. "And don't forget bright."

"That they are."

"What about our children, *m'ija?*"

"What about them, *m'ijo?*" Her voice had dropped to a lower register, sending a chill over his body.

"Will they be gorgeous and bright?" he asked.

Ana eyelids fluttered wildly. "Why don't we make one now and find out."

Jacob pushed off the door. "Do you know what you're saying?"

"Yes, and I never say anything I don't mean. Are you going

to stand there with your mouth gaping or are you going to take off your clothes and make love to me."

Needing no further prompting, he kicked off his shoes, pulled the hem of his shirt from the waistband of his slacks and unbuttoned it. His belt, slacks and briefs followed. Resting his hands at his waist, Jacob flashed a lecherous grin. "How do you like me now?"

"I must admit I like the view. Now, get your sexy butt in here."

He got off a snappy salute before stepping into the tub filled with lavender-scented bubble bath. Pulsating jets massaged his lower body as Jacob sank lower in the large tub. "You're the one with sexy butt," he crooned, cupping her bottom. "It's not as curvy as it was a few weeks ago, but that's going to change." His hands moved up, spanning Ana's waist, he lifted her to straddle his thighs. "I've never seen you look more beautiful," he whispered reverently.

Resting her head between his neck and shoulder, Ana pressed a kiss there. "You make me feel beautiful."

Jacob caught her ear between his teeth. He wanted to tell her she'd always been beautiful. He'd thought that when he'd first caught a glimpse of her at Diego and Vivienne's wedding and even more so at his godson's celebration. Her hair was longer, framing her lovely face and the off-the-shoulder, pale pink, body-hugging dress flattered her compact figure and complexion. He'd noticed everything about her when she'd barely given him a passing glance.

Jacob gasped when Ana's tongue found its way into his ear. Cradling his lean face, she kissed him, increasing the pressure until his lips parted; their tongues dueled, thrusting, parrying, and retreating like fencers. Her tongue was a blowtorch, scorching everywhere it touched, tasted.

Tightening his hold on her slender body, he reversed their position, devouring her mouth. He pulled back, giving Ana and himself a chance to catch their breaths before taking pos-

session of her mouth again in a kiss that made her surrender
to his unyielding, relentless assault.

Ana threw back her head, baring her throat as Jacob rained
kisses along the column of her neck, shoulders and down to
her breasts. His teeth closed on her nipples and a low keening
sound caused the hair to rise on the back of her neck before
she realized it had come from her. Seconds later there was
another sound, a chorus of moans and groans when Jacob
penetrated her. Electricity arced through her body, she strain-
ing to get even closer.

He reversed their position again, pulling out, rising to
his feet and stepping out of the tub. Ana didn't have time
to react when she found herself in his arms as he took long,
determined steps, walking out of the bathroom and into the
bedroom.

Placing her body on the bed, Jacob moved over Ana and
entered her again. It was as if he'd been possessed, sucked
into an abyss of uncontrollable passion from which he
couldn't and didn't want to escape.

She wrapped her legs around his hips, and he felt the tur-
bulence of her passion sweep him up in a firestorm of the
hottest fire. He was lost, submerged, drowning in a mael-
strom of desire devouring him mind and soul. And in that
moment Jacob knew for certain that he'd never loved another
woman. He may have felt lust or even a fleeting infatuation
but never love. With Ana it just wasn't his need to protect her
or the need to procreate. It was an uncompromising love, a
true love for an eternity.

Ana didn't want it to end—not yet. However, her body refused to listen to the dictates of her brain. Raising her hips to
allow for deeper penetration, she felt the rigid hardness touch
her womb and the orgasms began, swirling uncontrollably
seeking escape. She felt Jacob's heartbeat keeping time with
her own, their bodies writhing in a rhythm as old as time as
their passions peaked.

Gripping the pillow under Ana's head in a deathlike grip, Jacob lowered his face in the pillow, smothering the groans when the explosions in his lower body rocketed him beyond any pleasure he'd ever experienced. He collapsed heavily on Ana, waiting for the lingering vestiges of ecstasy to wane.

He felt her trembling, and believing she was crying he pulled and stared at her moist face. "What's wrong, *m'ija?*"

A dreamy smile settled into her delicate features. "You should ask me what's right." Ana sighed. "Baby-making sex is incredible."

Supporting his weight on his elbows, Jacob combed his fingers through her hair, holding it off her forehead. "That's because you're incredible." His expression changed, becoming serious. "Are you sure you want to walk down the aisle with a baby bump?"

Lines of concern appeared between her eyes. "You don't want a baby?"

"Ana, please. Of course I do. I was just thinking about your family's image."

"What family image? I told you my mother was pregnant with Gabriel when she married my father. Vivienne admitted to being pregnant with S.J. before she and Diego were married. And I've lost count of some of the other Cole women with buns in the oven when it came time for them to exchange vows. But it's different with us because we're already married."

He kissed her forehead. "You're right."

They were married yet there were times when Jacob didn't feel as if they were. When he'd been assigned witness protection he usually would check into a motel with the witness, monitoring everyone coming and going. The only difference with him and Ana was they were married, and instead of living in a motel they were cloistered behind a manned gatehouse in a luxury condominium.

Rolling off her body, he pulled her bottom to his groin,

covering their bodies with a lightweight blanket. The bed was wet but that didn't matter. What mattered was Ana was safe and he would do anything in his power to keep her safe.

Earlier that evening he'd brought Jason up-to-date on his plans. Jason would drive Ana's Ferrari and he would also use her card key which would allow him direct access to the elevator and the condo. There was one stipulation: he would call beforehand to let Jacob know he was coming.

He'd also directed Ana to suspend the cleaning service until further notice and to avoid using the concierge. Jason would bring groceries, pick up and drop off laundry. His brother-in-law had become the conduit, the connection between keeping Ana alive and those planning her demise.

There was no evidence of the easygoing demeanor in Jason Ana had spoken of. The talented musician/songwriter was soft-spoken, but also direct and resolute. Perhaps it had taken the threat on his sister's life or stepping into the role as acting CEO of Serenity Records that had caused the transformation. Jacob didn't disclose any of the behind-the-scene details to bring down Irvine and Jacob didn't want to know, because it would compromise his position as a federal agent. Once it was over he wanted to be able to walk out into the sunlight with Ana at his side as wife and partner.

Ana exchanged a look with Jacob when the doorbell echoed throughout the apartment. He'd asked her to teach him to play the piano and she had found him to be a quick study. "Are you expecting anyone?" she asked him.

"No."

She slid off the piano bench. "I'd better go and see who it is."

Jacob followed her. "Don't open it until you find out who it is."

"Do you know you've said the same thing for the past two weeks."

He stared at her hips in a pair of cutoffs. "And I'll continue to say it lest you forget."

"There's no way I'd ever forget, *m'ijo.* Not every woman can say she married a superhero."

Standing off to the side of the door, Jacob watched as Ana peered through the security eye. "Yes?"

"I'm Peter from management. Your cleaning service is here."

She looked at Jacob. He shook his head. "Wait a minute." Ana knew something was wrong. She'd suspended the cleaning service two weeks ago, so why would they show up today.

Jacob moved closer, pressing his mouth to her ear. "Tell him you have to put some clothes on. The minute you open the door I want you duck behind me. Okay?"

She nodded, then whispered, "Okay."

Ana could feel her heart beating outside her chest. "Don't go away, Peter. I have to put something on."

"No problem, Ms. Cole," came the reply on the other side of the door."

The breath congealed in her lungs when Jacob opened the door to the closet in the foyer; reaching for the black duffel he unzipped it and took out a high-caliber handgun. He motioned where she should stand.

Taking a deep breath, she unlocked the door. In the time it took for her to blink the door flew open, and she wasn't given time to duck behind Jacob when he reached out and hit the man in the head with the butt of the gun. A shriek escaped her when she saw him press his knee to the man's back. Peter wore the uniform assigned to the management staff.

"Close the door, Ana!" She reacted like an automaton, closing and locking the door. "Look in the duffel and bring me a pair of cuffs and shackles." He hadn't shouted, but the authoritative tone had her following his orders without hesitation.

Hauling Peter to his feet, Jacob literally dragged the man

across the foyer and into the living room where he lay in the fetal position. He went through his pockets, smiling when he found a hypodermic. "What's in this?" Blood trickled from the cut on the man's scalp. Dark eyes and an equally dark face were filled with fear. "Peter. Is that really your name?" His captive shook his head. "Well, whatever your name is you just screwed yourself. I don't know who sent you, but I hope you're familiar with the saying about killing the messenger."

The man, who appeared to be just out of his teens panicked. "Please don't kill me."

"I'm not going to kill you, Peter. What I'm going to do is turn you over to someone who would be very interested in what you have to say. Now, tell me what's in the syringe."

Peter's lower lip trembled. "Heroin."

Jacob patted his jaw. "Thank you for your honesty." Irvine hadn't sent someone to shoot or stab Ana, but inject her with an illegal narcotic. Reaching for his cell, he tapped a number. "I have someone I'd like for you to meet. He's a little tied up at the moment, but I'm certain he will make time for you. If you decide to take him out to dinner, then I think he's going to need a change of clothes. He appears to be a forty-two long, thirty-four waist and sixteen neck. The shoes are okay. Thanks, Caleb. We'll be here."

Peter's eyes were wide with fear. "What are you going to do to me?"

"I'm not going to do anything to you. But someone I know will be quite interested in what you have to say."

Ana retreated to the balcony, collapsing on a recliner and not wanting to believe how close she'd come to mortal danger. It was if the enormity of why she'd been exiled and now in seclusion hit her like the heat from a blast furnace. Whoever had put the hit on her was relentless. He'd used up his second strike and she prayed he would be stopped before… She didn't want to think of the alternative.

Jacob found her on the balcony. "Come, baby. Don't sit

out here in the sun." Rising, she allowed him to lead her back inside where the cool air feathered over her moist face. The intercom rang. "That's Caleb. I want you to let him in, then I'd like you to go into the bedroom and stay there until I come for you."

Going on tiptoe, Ana curved her arms around his neck. "I love you."

His eyes caressed her face. "I love you, too." What Jacob didn't tell Ana was that he loved her enough to give up his life to keep her safe.

Caleb arrived and together they stripped Peter of the condo management department uniform, replacing it with a dark suit and white shirt. Jacob had cleaned the blood from his face and applied a bandage to his scalp. He'd kept his gun trained on him once the cuffs and shackles were removed.

Caleb's feral grin bordered on macabre when he picked up the heroin-filled syringe. "Let's go, buddy. You and I are going to have a little chat, and if you don't tell me what I want then you're going to beg for someone to kill you. We're going downstairs and if you make one false move or sound I'll blow your head off." As if to confirm his threat, he pulled back his jacket to display the Desert Eagle. "Ain't it purty?" The imposter's knees buckled and Caleb caught him under his shoulder to keep him from falling.

Jacob walked the two men to the door, opened and then closed it behind them. Three minutes later, after he'd regained his composure, he made his way to the bedroom. Ana lay facedown across the bed. He slipped into bed beside her, resting an arm over her waist.

"Look at me, Ana." He counted off the seconds before she turned her head and he felt his stomach muscles contract. She'd been crying. Wiping her tears with his fingertips, he forced a smile. "You're safe, baby."

"Am I really?"

"Yes. I would never lie to you."

Ana leaned closer, touching her mouth to his. "I believe you," she whispered. And she did believe he would protect her.

Los Angeles

"Mr. Irvine, Ms. Sanchez has arrived."

Basil's head popped up and he stared at his impeccably dressed houseboy. He'd tried hiring a butler, but the agency he used to staff his household had put his name on the wait list. The houseboy had come highly recommended, yet for Basil having a butler in his employ would put him above some of the other people in the toney neighborhood that still regarded him as riffraff.

"Thank you, Thomas. Please show her in."

Thomas Yang bowed politely. He turned on his heels and left the room where his boss conducted business. It was opulent and apparently no expense had been spared when it came to decorating it.

He bowed to the young woman who stood staring at the paintings lining the walls of the expansive entryway. "Ms. Sanchez. Mr. Irvine will see you." Tossing back a mane of straight raven hair, Saundra Sanchez looked at him as if she smelled something malodorous. "Please come with me."

The four-inch stilettos and pencil skirt wouldn't permit Saundra to keep up with the brisk pace the houseboy had set, so she strolled leisurely, her hips swaying seductively with each step. She'd waited a long time to meet with Basil Irvine, and now that she had the opportunity what she felt was akin to giddiness.

Smiling and exhibiting a pair of white porcelains, she extended her hand. "It's a pleasure, Mr. Irvine." Her gaze swept over his face, taking in everything about the music mogul. His complexion was what people referred to as red-bone. She found his full lips a little off-putting. They were better suited for a woman. However, his eyes were his best feature. Large, gray and mysterious.

To say Basil was larger than life was an understatement when he rose to his feet. He was tall, broad-shouldered and his massive bulk was artfully disguised under the expensive fabric of a tailor-made suit.

Basil ignored the proffered hand, dipping his head and pressing a kiss to her cheek. "It's my pleasure, Ms. Sanchez. Would you mind if I call you Saundra?"

Her smile widened. "You may, only if I can call you Basil." Throwing back his head, he laughed loudly. "What's so funny?"

"My name is pronounced Base-sill, not Bass-sill."

Saundra inclined her head. "I'm sorry. My mother was born in England, so there are times when I slip into the British vernacular."

"Please sit down, Saundra. Can I have my houseboy bring you something to drink?"

She sat on a brocade armchair. "I never drink alone."

"If that's the case, then I'll join you. What do you want?"

"An extra-dry, extra-dirty double gin martini."

Basil gave her a Cheshire cat grin. "I like a woman who knows how to drink." He walked to the decoratively carved doors to the room where he spent most of his time when at home and saw Thomas sitting on a chair at the end of the hall. He beckoned him. "I need you to tend bar. Make me my usual."

"What about Ms. Sanchez?"

Basil gave Thomas his guest's drink order. He returned to sit opposite the beautifully exotic woman whose face matched an extraordinary voice. When he'd heard the demo one of his employees had given him Basil knew he'd been redeemed. Saundra Sanchez had become his golden goose because she was the total package.

"I was blown away when I heard your demo."

"So you liked it?"

"Liked it? I loved it. That's why I asked to meet you."

Saundra's short skirt rose even higher on her trim thighs when she crossed one bare leg over the opposite knee, achieving the reaction she sought when Basil's jaw literally dropped. "Do you usually hold business meetings in your home?"

He tented his fingers. "Occasionally I do."

Combing her fingers through her long, silky hair, Saundra tucked several strands behind her left ear. "And I agreed to meet you in your home because I want a recording contract. I'm a twenty-six-year-old wannabe actress. I've gone to so many auditions that every casting director in L.A. knows my face and name." She leaned forward on the chair. "I could've gotten a few major parts, but there is one thing I refuse to do. I will not compromise my morals for anything or anyone."

"And you won't have to with me, Saundra." Basil held out his hands, palms up. "You want to become a recording artist and I'll make that possible for you. What I can't do is make you a star. But if you work with me and my people you can have any and everything you want."

Saundra smiled at the houseboy when he handed her the chilled glass and a cocktail napkin. "Thank you." She waited for Basil to accept a highball glass filled with an amber liquid. Raising her martini glass, she lowered her gaze, peering at him through her lashes. "Here's to you making me a star."

"To stardom," Basil intoned, taking a deep swallow of his drink.

Saundra took furtive sips of her drink as she stared at the large man sitting only a few feet away. "What are you willing to offer me?"

Basil drained his glass, setting it down on a round marble-topped table. "Are you always so direct?"

"Yes."

That was the last word exchanged between them as Basil's head slumped, his chin touching his chest. Saundra set her glass on the table, rose to her feet and nodded to Thomas. "Will you please show me out? It appears as if Mr. Irvine has a problem holding his liquor."

"That's all right, Ms. Sanchez. I'll help him get into bed."

The sun was just beginning to set over the Hollywood hills when she climbed into the rear of the waiting car. She waited until the driver maneuvered onto the interstate leading northward to San Francisco to pull off the wig, remove the contact lenses, methodically remove layers of professional makeup that transformed her from blonde-haired, blue-eyed Allison Turner to exotic Latina Saundra Sanchez. She completed the total makeover when, using fine-tipped tweezers, removed the transparent ovals covering her fingertips.

Allison knew Tommy would wait until the following morning to call the EMTs because he hadn't been able to wake Basil. Once he answered all the questions about his deceased employer he would return home to await his next assignment.

Chapter 17

Ana covered her mouth with both hands when she read the crawl along the bottom of the television screen: *Music mogul Basil Irvine found dead in his L.A. mansion of an apparent heart attack. He was 43.*

Springing up from the chair in the sitting room, she opened the door to the balcony. "Jacob! Come see this."

He stepped off the balcony and into the air-cooled bedroom. "What is it?" Ana pointed to the flat screen resting on the table in the alcove. "It's over, Jacob. I don't have to hide anymore."

Jacob wrapped his arms around her body, holding her close. It *was* over. Now he and Ana could live their lives without looking over their shoulders. He could take her to meet his mother, knowing Gloria would love Ana as much as he did.

His cell rang. "Excuse me, baby. I have to answer this." He returned to the balcony, closing the door behind him. "What's up, Diego?"

"Irvine's done."

"What happened?"

"I suppose he had a bad heart. His brother just issued a statement that Basil was healthy as a horse, and that he's going assume the responsibility of running Slow Wyne."

"What do you know about the brother?"

"His name is Webb Irvine. He served time for manslaughter. Reportedly he stomped a man to death when he was still a kid."

Jacob stared at the choppy waters. Meteorologists were watching a tropical depression off the coast of Jamaica that was expected to make landfall in another twenty-four hours. "Do you think we're going to trade one devil for another?"

"He bears keeping an eye on. But that's what I'm paying Simon to do. His people will make certain he won't fly under the radar. How's Ana taking the news?"

"She's shocked and relieved. I've got another two weeks before I go back to work. I'm going to take her to see her folks tomorrow, then we're going to Winter Haven so she can meet my mother. And if there is enough time we're going back to Long Key to do a little fishing."

"Ana hates fishing."

"That's not what she told me."

"Then my cousin has really changed. On a more serious note. What I can do to thank you for all you've done?"

"Stand in as my best man when we say our vows in front of the family New Year's Eve."

"Eso es una promesa, mi amigo."

"I'm going to hang up now. Ana and I have a little celebrating to do. Kiss S.J. for me and let him know I'll see him soon."

Jacob ended the call, and when he turned he saw Ana staring at him through the glass. Her dimples winked at him. Opening the door, he pulled her out into the humidity, cradled her face and covered her mouth with his.

"How would you like to go out tonight to celebrate, Mrs. Jones?"

"What are we celebrating, Mr. Jones?" she whispered.

"Our love."

Ana scrunched up her nose. "I like that."

"I love you."

"I love you more," she countered.

The banter continued as they prepared to live their lives on their own terms.

* * * * *